THE LOST ORPHAN BOY

A Gripping and Emotional Historical Fiction Novel Based on a True Story

BY BENNY EDVY

Producer & International Distributor
eBookPro Publishing
www.ebook-pro.com

The Lost Orphan Boy
Benny Edvy

Copyright © 2024 Benny Edvy

All rights reserved; No parts of this book may be reproduced or transmitted in any form or by any means, electronic or mechanical, including photocopying, recording, taping, or by any information retrieval system, without the permission, in writing, of the author.

Translation: Noelle Canin
Editing: Nancy Alroy

Contact: bennyedvy@gmail.com

ISBN 9798884478480

*The great pecan trees
are gone,
the dovecote
of noisy pigeons
has disappeared,
the old peach orchard
cut down,
and still you stand
and fight.
Father,
there are no windmills here.
Nobody to defeat.
Father,
there are
branches and trees here,
and a sturdy root.*

Chapter One

The desert sun beat down on the clay roofs of the small settlement deep in the heart of Yemen. The village, numbering about two hundred large families, most of whom were Muslim and some Jewish, was governed according to Quran Law. The only way to this place was along a dirt track across the desert, a three-day camel ride from Sanaa, the capital of Yemen. The village at the end of the road lay at the foot of a mountain range on the outskirts of the desert. Centuries old, the village was established by a Bedouin tribe that chose the place because of its surrounding springs. On the way to the village were several oases where travelers could drink water from the earth and rest in the shade of the trees growing around the springs. The road was controlled by various tribes who were equipped with arms and camels. The authorities didn't dare undermine tribal control of these areas, which the tribes exploited. Some would collect tolls from travelers passing through their area while others would rob them. It was only police and government representatives whom the tribes left unscathed. They had an informal agreement with representatives of the law – the tribes wouldn't harm them and the authorities wouldn't hinder the autonomy they enforced in their areas.

Luluah, a barefoot girl of thirteen, stood in front of her home on the outskirts of the village watching her nephews, eight-year-

old Aharon and seven-year-old Menachem. Her niece, Salma, their eighteen-month sister, was with Luluah's mother, Na'ama.
The three children of her late sister, Badreh, who had died the week before.

Luluah was trying to take in the enormity of the responsibility that had befallen her – of becoming their mother. Thoughts were rushing through her mind: how would she raise them, she herself only a child? How would she bring them up and take care of them when she was still playing in the alleys with her friends? She stood there, motionless – a beautiful child, her curly hair gathered up in a large scarf, her big black eyes open wide, her childish body enveloped in a black dress. Slowly, she approached the two children:

"Come... come to me," she said tenderly.

The two wept huskily: "Yamma... Yamma."

Hand in hand, they began to walk hesitantly toward her. Even Menachem, the younger and naughtier of the two, was sad. Luluah was their beloved aunt and, here she was – hesitant, sad, alone and lost. Her body trembling, she drew them to her and began weeping bitterly, her sobs merging with those of the two boys. They stood there in each other's arms for some time, tears streaming down their cheeks. Finally her tears stopped; she did her best to comfort the children, caressing and hugging them again, trying as hard as she could to stop theirs. Gazing down at them, she wiped their little faces with her small hand and kissed them again and again. The realization that she had a new role pierced her young mind: she was now the mother of three children.

Family members spent much of the one-week mourning period for their beloved Badreh debating about who was to take care of the children and her elderly husband, Yichyieh.

It was the matriarch of the family who resolutely decided:

"Luluah will marry Yichyieh and take care of the children!"

Nobody objected. Luluah's young age wasn't an obstacle either, for she wasn't promised to anyone, she'd already started to menstruate, and was ready to wed. Yichyieh Edvy accepted his mother-in-law's decision and said at once:

"I will treat her with compassionate and respect... I won't come to her until she turns eighteen."

He knew he couldn't take care of his beloved children on his own and was grateful they'd have a new mother in place of the one who had died. Swiftly, the wedding was arranged during the mourning period and took place when it ended. Luluah, in her Jewish-Yemeni wedding dress weighed down with traditional filigree ornaments and jewelry, stood perfumed, beautiful and innocent under the chuppah, the ceremonial canopy. All the many times she had daydreamed about her wedding, it definitely wasn't like this – standing in front of a man decades her senior. Anxiety at the unbearably heavy responsibility and fear of being Yichyieh's wife began to gnaw at her. She was afraid of disappointing her mother, the young children and, most of all, she was afraid of disappointing herself. Her family hadn't given her enough time to mourn her sister's death or prepare for becoming a wife and mother.

As she stood under the chuppah, a song began to play in her head: 'Yamma and Baba – why didn't you protect me...' Yamma and Baba, why did you leave me here alone, a little girl burdened with such great responsibility? How will I bear it? Will my elderly husband really take pity on me? How will I weep for my dear Badreh? These fears were mixed with her great love for Aharon, Menachem and Salma, her nephews and niece, and the realization that there was no alternative, her own mother had come to a definitive decision; and now, she was a mother. Her love and compassion for Badreh's children convinced her that she would take care of them, raise them well and love them. She would bear it. She would be a good mother and devoted wife.

"Behold, with this ring, you are made holy to me..." said Yichyieh and slipped a ring on her finger.

He broke the glass beside her foot, and the crowd cheered: "Holy... holy..."

She was now a married woman and the mother of her nephews and niece. The guests kissed and hugged her, but they didn't sing or dance. It all happened so fast it was as if she were dreaming. Aharon and Menachem didn't understand a thing. They held Luluah's hands and sat with her on the bridal chair. They sensed that, from then on, she was to be their mother. The inert desire for a mother, together with their love of Luluah, drew them close to her and they held her hands tightly and confidently.

At nightfall, when the brief wedding ceremony came to an end, Yichyieh took Luluah and the boys home. Na'ama decided that, for the time being, Salma would remain with her to allow Luluah some time to get used to Yichyieh's home. Luluah already knew every centimeter of the house as she'd spent hours with her older sister helping her with her chores. In the yard, to the right and in front of the entrance door, stood the tabun where Badreh had baked pita[1]. Behind the house was the toilet and a place for washing that had no roof, next to which wandered the chickens and a goat. Opposite was a creaking entrance door without a lock and on the doorpost was a golden Mezuzah. In the entrance was a little hall, a tiny table against the wall with four chairs and a stool underneath it. To the right was a kitchen with barely enough room for a woman to work in – a small window, a shelf above the window for meat and a little clay sink. To the side was a white curtain which concealed the entrance to a small room with a bed and a window; the window was covered with the same white fabric. This was where Yichyieh, Badreh and baby Salma slept. Left of Yichyieh's room was another tiny room without a curtain, nor door, nor window, and this was where the older children slept on a mattress of blankets their grandmother had spread on the floor. This was the home Luluah entered and, from that moment, she was to be mistress of the house, taking care of cleaning, preparing

---

1. Flat, Yemenite bread

food, putting the children to bed and receiving her husband when he returned from his studies or his business.

"Luluah, from now on you will sleep with the children... and I will sleep alone in my room," said Yichyieh.

"Very well, Yichyieh," murmured Luluah.

She tried to think how she and the three children would sleep together in that tiny cage of a room. She's use the blankets to pad the ground as well as to cover herself while she slept, for the nights were cold.

"I'm going to sleep, my daughter," said Yichyieh.

"Go... go to sleep. I will tidy the house and put the children to bed."

Night fell. In their homes, villagers were preparing for bed. Here and there candles shone in some of the houses and, within a few minutes, these too were extinguished and the whole village slept. Luluah washed the children with a cloth dipped in water she poured from a jar in the corner of the kitchen. They were surprisingly obedient, particularly Menachem. She glanced into the children's room and decided, at least for this first night, to sleep with them and look for an alternative for the following day. Menachem and Aharon lay on the mattress, Luluah covered them gently and went into the hall. At once she began tidying the house, checking to see there was water in the jar or whether she'd have to rise early to draw water from the well. She was already planning the following morning – she'd wake before everyone and prepare a meal for Yichyieh and the children. After her long day, she washed herself with the same wet cloth, slipped on her nightdress, and curled up between Aharon and Menachem. The children hugged her in their sleep, absorbing the safe, pleasant warmth of her body. Gradually, her eyes closed and she fell asleep.

When Luluah woke at dawn Yichyieh and the children were still asleep. Eagerly she got up from the bed of blankets and went to the kitchen. She lit the fire in the clay oven set in the wall, above which was a nook to put cooking pots and boil water. Dressing quickly and ensuring that her face was completely covered, apart from her eyes, she went out into the cool morning with a small jug in her hand. She went to the tabun and lit it; then Luluah made her way to the chicken and goat area to collected a few eggs; finally, she milked the goat – for drinking and preparing cheese. The sound of crying was coming from the house. She ran inside to the children's room and found Aharon sitting and sobbing. Menachem was still asleep. Swiftly, she gathered Aharon in her arms and left the room.

"What's wrong, Aharon? Did you have a bad dream?" she asked gently.

"No, Aunty... I want Yamma..."

"Yamma's gone, I'm your Yamma now."

"I want Yamma!" he quavered, continuing to cry quietly.

"Oh, my boy..." she whispered, "Yamma's in heaven and she asked me to be your Yamma. She told me that I'm your favorite aunt, and so she sent me to you..."

In the background they could hear Yichyieh's snores and heavy breathing.

"Come, my boy, I'll prepare you some hot milk and pita."

"All right..." he responded and stopped crying, "I also want sugar in the milk."

Hot milk was his favorite drink and, for him, the addition of a little sugar turned the drink into a delicacy.

"Sure, Aharon. I'll warm up the milk with some sugar for you."

Luluah took the fresh goat's milk, poured it into a pot and placed it on the stove above the oven. Putting the eggs into an iron pot, she added water and let it boil beside the pot of milk. Taking some flour, she poured water into another cup and quickly began to knead the dough to make pita. Within a few minutes, the dough was ready and she put it aside to rise for a while. In the meantime, she poured the boiled milk into a cup, setting the pot next to the stove to keep it warm, added a little sugar and gave it to Aharon who was already sitting on the stool at the table in the little hall.

"We'll have pita and boiled eggs soon and then we'll wake up

Menachem and Baba and sit down to eat… it's morning and the sun will be up soon."

"I want to help you, Aunty…" said Aharon. There were remnants of milk around his mouth.

"Alright… take four plates and spoons and set the table…" she told him, pointing to the tin plates next to the sink. "In the meantime, I'll go and make the pita on the tabun.

Picking up the dough in her hands, she swiftly left the house. At the tabun, she kneaded the dough again and cut it into several pieces of equal size. She repeated the action several times, rolling out each piece with her hands and waving it until the dough stretched, then immediately placed it over the sides of the tabun until the dough was finished. While the dough was baking, she entered the house, checked the eggs and moved the iron pot to the side of the stove. Aharon sat playing with something under the table in the hall. Luluah returned to the tabun and, reaching her hands inside the oven, she felt the pitas and determined that they were ready. She piled the fresh-baked pitas onto a towel and went back into the house.

It was daybreak and the desert sun was rising over the sleepy village.

"Aharon, let's go and wake Baba and Menachem."

"I won't wake Baba. I'm afraid… he'll be angry with me."

"Fine, I'll wake Baba and you wake Menachem."

Luluah glanced into the hall again and saw Aharon arranging the plates and spoons as she'd asked.

"Yichyieh, get up… breakfast is on the table…"

"I'm already awake, but I'll pray first… we'll eat afterwards," he answered and tried to rise.

Luluah held out her hand to help him sit up. Yamma, Yamma… she reflected, my husband is an old man. I'll have to take care of him as I do the children.

Aharon woke Menachem who immediately sat down at the

table and announced that he was hungry and also wanted a cup of milk with sugar.

"Yichyieh, get up. The children want to eat... I want us to eat together," she said.

"I'm coming, I'm coming... but I have to pray first."

Slowly he stumbled toward the hall. Luluah handed him a bowl of water and he washed his face. She gave him a small towel, he dried himself and announced:

"Aharon and Menachem... come on, off to morning prayers."

The boys did as they were told, took their father's hands, and the three left the house for the synagogue.

The moment they returned, the three sat down at the table. Luluah laid the pita bread on the table, poured four cups of milk, quickly peeled the hard-boiled eggs in a bowl and sat down next to Yichyieh.

"My daughter, I want coffee with Hawaj, morning coffee spice... without sugar...and you will eat when the boys and I are finished," said Yichyieh, and made the blessing over the bread.

Luluah understood that his request was actually an order which was not to be ignored. The children took pita, an egg, a cup of milk and asked for more sugar. Yichyieh began to eat with the children. Luluah got up and put a copper jug of water on the stove and, while it was coming to a boil, she added a little more sugar to the children's cups of milk.

"My daughter, we don't have much sugar... you don't have to give the children sugar in their milk..." he said with disapproval, seemingly angry with her. She put a spoonful of coffee into a cup, added some Hawaj, and said:

"Yichyieh...Yichyieh, the children need a little sweetness at the moment. They've been through a lot... and so have I..."

It was also made clear that she wouldn't be sitting with them for meals and, moreover, that Yichyieh would readily reprove her. When the water boiled, she poured him a cup of coffee and set it beside him. He quickly finished eating, and said:

"Children, eat up and we'll do the blessing after the meal."

They quickly swallowed their food and began the blessing. When they were done, he said:

"Luluah, I'll take the children to the Mori (teacher) and go and see what kind of a living I can make. We'll see what I can buy at the market… all right children, out with you…"

He didn't ask her what to buy or what she wanted to cook.

The three of them left the house and she remained alone. Eat alone, clean up after Yichyieh and the children alone, cook alone, take care of feeding the chickens and goat alone. She was enveloped in a sense of loneliness mixed with the realization that it was Yichyieh who made the decisions and she didn't have the right to object to or challenge his word.

Chapter Two

It was just before Luluah's eighteenth birthday and hotter than usual. Thoughts of intimate relations with Yichyieh began to trouble her mind. She well remembered his promise that he wouldn't come to her before she turned eighteen. She appreciated and respected him for keeping the vow he'd made and she was indeed still a virgin.

Yichyieh returned home at noon, sat down at the table and waited for Luluah to serve him his meal. Luluah was still reflecting on what would be expected of her in the marital bed and specific questions rose in her mind.

"Luluah, stop daydreaming. I want to eat..." he scolded her, adding: "You are almost eighteen and I want more children."

She served him a plate of soup, pita and Hilbeh[2].

"Ya Yichyieh, not now. Eat and take a nap... it's very hot today and you're tired," she said.

She knew that one night soon he would come to her. Just as he'd kept his promise not to touch her until she was eighteen, so he'd insist on his desire for more children and lie with her.

"Do you want more soup? There's still a little chicken...would you like some?" she asked, her mind still on thoughts of the first time she'd lie with her elderly husband.

---

2. *Hilbeh*: puree made from fenugreek seeds.

She decided to talk to her mother, ask her what to do, and how. Her mother would know all the answers, she thought.

"No, my daughter. Leave some for the children... they need more sustenance to grow big and strong. I'm old and need little..." he answered, and began to saying the blessing after the meal.

"Amen..." she said as he finished the blessing and began to rise from his chair.

She helped him up and into bed and covered him. He fell fast asleep in seconds.

Aharon and Menachem were learning Midrash[3] with the Mori and little Salma was playing with friends near the house. Luluah decided to go and see her mother. She covered her head in a full scarf that revealed only her large eyes and began to walk down the path to her parents' home. She planned to spend some time with Na'ama and return home in time to prepare the evening meal for Yichyieh and the children. She had to speak to her mother; when Yichyieh would come to her, she didn't want to make any mistakes; she wanted to be a worthy wife.

Na'ama was sitting chatting to a neighbor in the doorway of her home. It was the break between meals and all the men were napping. Her little sisters were playing in front of their mother's watchful eyes.

"Salam, ya Yamma..." said Luluah, kissing her mother three times, alternating cheeks.

"Ahalan, how are you?' responded Na'ama, "how are the children... and Yichyieh?"

"They're all fine. Yichyieh is asleep...Aharon and Menachem are studying Midrash with the Mori."

"And you, my daughter, how are you?"

"Yamma..." Luluah opened her heart to her mother without hesitation. The neighbor's presence didn't bother her. "I'll be eighteen soon and will become a wife... I'm afraid..."

---

3. An ancient commentary on part of the Hebrew scriptures, attached to the biblical text.

"Ya my daughter, come and sit beside me. I'll make you something to drink and we'll talk."

A few minutes later, Luluah's mother handed her a cup of tea. "Here you are, drink the tea... you'll feel better and calmer..."

She gazed at Luluah, caressing her head.

"You know, there was no alternative, you had to marry Yichyieh. He and the children needed to be cared for... and now he wants more children; that's a woman's role... to bring children into the world. Yichyieh is your husband, and it's natural that he wants you to fall pregnant with his child..." Na'ama sighed, "it's not so bad... you must be well prepared for the first night... you must wash thoroughly, wear perfume... you know what, I'll give you some of mine. You must wear a shift over your naked body and allow Yichyieh to show you what to do, he is experienced and he knows. Listen to him on this matter. He promised to treat you with compassion, and he will keep his promise. He was good to your sister, rest her soul. Badreh never said a bad word about him or how he behaved towards her. I'm sure he will be considerate..."

She paused, looking up at the sky.

"When you are clean and perfumed, lie on your back... and let him perform the act. Don't resist. Don't cry out. At first it won't feel natural for him to touch you in forbidden places... but he is allowed to do so, as he is your husband. Allow him to touch you and lie with you..."

"For how long?" asked Luluah.

"Until he gets off you. Until he gets up and leaves the room..."

"And then what do we do?'

"That's all. It will be over, and you are free – until the next time he wants to do it..."

"I don't understand, when will he want to do it again? Isn't once enough?"

"Ya my daughter, you must understand, your man is your man... and he may want to lie with you once a week or once a day... I don't know. He'll teach you how often and when. Remember one most important thing – you must observe the *nida*, two weeks without intimacy, you know, during menstruation. You must count four clean days after the bleeding... and then you are permitted to lie with your husband. You must explain to Yichyieh when it is permitted and when it is forbidden, understand?"

"I think so... I'm not sure."

"If you have any questions, ask me. Always ask me..."

"I will, Yamma, I will... I think I understand. But I'm still afraid..."

"Ya my daughter, that's natural. but I promise you that all women go through it. And I did too, look at me... everything's all right.

Luluah felt slightly reassured. A week later, after they children had gone to bed, Yichyieh called to her:

"Luluah... Luluah, my beautiful wife... come to my bedroom."

"A moment, Yichyieh, give me a few minutes... I need to do a few things."

"No need, come to me. Come to me now..."

Luluah realized that Yichyieh wished to lie with her at once. She remembered what her mother had said and ran quickly to the kitchen, took a towel and wet it. She swiftly washed herself as well as she could, went into the hall and retrieved the bottle of perfume her mother had given her from its hiding place and dabbed herself with the scent.

"Come to me, Luluah. Come on..." said Yichyieh impatiently.

"I'm here, I'm coming... a second, a second..."

Undressing, she put on the shift, went to Yichyieh's room and stood in the doorway to let down the curtain. Her husband was lying on the bed and smiling at her. She was beautiful, a little afraid, and standing there like a statue. He beckoned to her to approach, but she didn't move. He beckoned again and it seemed to her that his face softened, that he was showing affection, perhaps even love. He clearly desired her, and that made her feel desired, which reassured her. She approached him, somewhat hesitantly, and sat on the side of the bed. He sat up and held out his hand to stroke her hair, her face, neck, shoulders, murmuring:

"How I want you... how beautiful you are... how I desire you... you are the most beautiful of women..." He whispered in her ear, "you are my flower..."

He continued to whisper and caress her body; she responded to him and began to surrender, just as her mother had told her. He knows what he's doing, he has experience. Suddenly she blurted out:

"Don't hurt me..." and she didn't understand what brought that on or why she'd suddenly said it.

"Don't worry, my beauty... I won't hurt you... I will be gentle."

He continued to caress her and whisper words of love. She was soothed and surrendered to sensations she didn't know existed. She found herself lying on her back in bed, her husband bent over her, undressing her. He removed his nightdress and lay on top of her. Hovering over her, he penetrated her and she grimaced from the pain between her legs, almost crying out, but pressed her lips together not to make a sound. He began to move with swifter movements until suddenly he groaned, shuddered, and stopped moving. A few seconds later, he moved off her, turned over and, a few minutes later was sound asleep. Many hours passed before she managed to fall asleep.

Over the following days, Yichyieh came to her almost every day. He only left her alone for the two weeks of *nida* and didn't even touch her then, even demanding she sleep with the children and not beside him. Only after she had been clean for four days did he ask her to sleep next to him again. Every time he lay with her, he made her feel she was beloved, wanted, desired. He never did so without her consent and, when he was finished, he always turned over and instantaneously fell asleep.

About two months after the first time she'd lain with Yichyieh, she missed her period and her body felt different. She assumed she was pregnant and, as always, went to tell her mother.

"Yamma, my period hasn't come..."

"Ya my daughter, you're pregnant... congratulations, let's see your belly..."

Luluah let her mother put her hand underneath her clothing and touch her midsection. Her mother felt and stated:

"You're pregnant, congratulations, congratulations!"

Luluah was excited. She hugged her mother and left for home with cheerful steps. It was almost dark and she hurried along, deep in thought. How would she tell Yichyieh? What would she say to the children? What would giving birth be like? Where would she give birth? Would she have enough milk to feed her baby? Would it be a boy or a girl?

When she got home, she quickly prepared supper and very soon the children came in, followed by Yichyieh who said, as usual, "Ya my daughter, is my meal ready? I'm hungry and tired..."

"Come, sit down and eat," she said excitedly.

"What's happened, my daughter? Why are you dancing around like that?"

"I have something to tell you all."

"Ya my daughter, what is it?" asked Yichyieh, and the children clamored:

"Tell us, Yamma-Aunty, tell us..."

Luluah looked at the children and said:

"Soon you will have a brother or sister..." she turned toward Yichyieh: "Ya Yichyieh, you will have another child. Yamma told me that I'm with child."

Yichyieh looked at her joyfully – his prayers had been answered. The children ran to her.

"Children, slowly, slowly... your mother is with child..." They heard Yichyieh's voice and, at once, slowed down, went up to Luluah and hugged her gently.

She took Aharon's hand, put it on her abdomen, saying, "Inside this belly, a baby is growing..."

She took Menachem's hand, and then Salma's, and did the same.

"In time, my belly will grow and you will be able to put your hand on it and feel the baby move."

That night, everyone went to bed with smiles on their faces; only Luluah found it hard to fall asleep. She was deep in thought about the new baby, her first born.

Days and nights passed, turning into months. Luluah's belly swelled and she, along with Salma, rushed about preparing food for the family, feeding the chickens and the goat, collecting eggs, cleaning the house and raising the children. Yichyieh divided his time between the synagogue and his trading job. Aharon and Menachem were both growing into adolescent boys. Salma, almost six, was also becoming a more independent little girl, helping with all the chores at home like a little woman.

Nineteen years old now, Luluah was close to her due date. The hot summer was at its peak and Na'ama tried to spend as much time with her as she could, although she also had an elderly husband to tend to.

One night between Friday and Saturday, Luluah woke with strong pains. She assumed that these were contractions and immediately woke Yichyieh.

"I think the birth is starting, go to my mother and make sure the midwife arrives.

The midwife, a Muslim woman trusted by the Jewish community, helped most of the local women give birth. The contractions were becoming more frequent and more painful and Luluah was worried her mother and the midwife wouldn't arrive on time. Between contractions she woke Salma, who slept in the hall, and asked her to boil water.

"Salma, come and help me... I think your little brother will come into the world tonight..."

Salma woke at once and, with shining eyes, did what she could to help. It wasn't rare for Yemini women in those days to die in childbirth, and Luluah was afraid she'd die or become ill after the birth and would become a burden. She brushed these thoughts aside and, together with Salma, prepared their room for the birth. They changed the bedding and put on fresh sheets, laid clean towels on one side of the bed, spread out two blankets, one large and one small, and brought a stool from the hall and set it close to the bed. When they'd finished the preparations, Luluah got into bed and covered herself.

"Ya my daughter, wait in the hall for your grandmother and the midwife and I will lie here and rest… I'm in pain."

"Alright, Mamma…"

About a quarter of an hour later Na'ama and the midwife arrived and immediately entered the bedroom. Yichyieh remained in the hall. Luluah was still lying in bed, groaning occasionally.

"Ya Luluah, my daughter… we're right here with you. The midwife is here, she's here…"

Luluah gazed at them with a sigh of relief.

"Mamma, Mamma… it's so painful…"

Na'ama wet a cloth and wiped her daughter's forehead. She sat beside her and tried to reassure her:

"The midwife will examine you and take care of you… don't worry, my daughter, we're here and, with God's help, the birth will go well."

The midwife examined her, saying at last:

"I think Luluah is ready… interesting, her first birth and she's ready… she's lucky. How long have you been having contractions?"

"I'm not sure, a few hours I think. The pain woke me up…"

"We'll wait a little longer," decided the midwife, "and then examine you again."

"I'll go make you some coffee and then I'll stay with Luluah while you go wait in the kitchen," said Na'ama to the midwife.

After an hour the midwife decided it was time. The contractions had become more frequent and painful. Luluah was moaning and holding her mother's hand while Na'ama wiped her daughter's forehead and comforted her. The midwife guided Luluah, asking her to bear down and help the baby out. Though in pain, Luluah tried to follow the midwife's instructions and bore down while holding tightly to her mother's hand. She was perspiring from the effort until the midwife finally called out:

"He's coming out... here's his head... go on, don't stop now! Here he is, here he is..."

Gently the midwife pulled the baby to her, cut the umbilical cord and cleaned him.

"It's a boy, ya Luluah... it's a boy!" she announced happily. "Mazal tov, mazal tov!"

She looked at the mother to see her response – Luluah smiled with a joy she'd never felt before –she was now the mother of a son. The two older women tidied and cleaned the room and Luluah as well. The midwife placed the newborn in his mother's arms, successfully guiding him to latch onto and begin suckling at the overflowing breast. When he finished nursing he drifted softly off to sleep. Luluah was exhausted and fell asleep beside him.

They named the baby Joseph. Yichyieh had decided on the name and Luluah didn't question his decision. Her life had changed when she became a mother to her sister's three children, but now that she had given birth to a son, she was overjoyed, for this was a woman's life's purpose – to bring children into the world and take care of them. Aharon and Menachem received their new brother with love, but Salma outdid them all. At six and a half, she was devoted to him, played with him, made him laugh, caressed and soothed him. She called to their mother when she thought he was hungry and became like a second mother to him, despite her young age.

As Joseph grew, he loved Salma all the more and, when he began to chatter, he called her 'Samma.' When she heard him call her 'Samma' for the first time, she ran to Luluah and told her he'd called her 'Mamma.' Luluah laughed aloud and said:

"You're right, 'Samma' means 'Mamma.'" Joseph calls you that because you are his little Mamma and I am his big Mamma."

Menachem and Aharon continued to study Torah. Joseph grew up between the two little rooms and the hall, Salma always at his side. At first he slept with his parents then, later on, they put him to bed in the other room with his two big brothers. When he began to walk, he'd play with Salma in the chicken yard, chasing after them until his mother rebuked him:

"Leave the chickens alone! They won't lay eggs if you go on chasing them!"

She was angry with Salma, Joseph's collaborator:

"You're older and you should know better than to take Joseph to the chickens."

Laughingly, Salma would take Joseph away from the chickens and into the house.

"Joseph, say Salma," she'd coax.

And as always, he'd respond, 'Samma' and she'd laugh and smile with joy.

Chapter Three

Luluah was always the first to rise and began to wake everyone for morning Shacharit prayers.

She turned to her husband beside her: "Yichyieh... Yichyieh, it's morning... time to get up..."

Yichyieh neither answered nor responded.

She tried again: "Yichyieh... get up... time for prayers..."

Putting her hand on his arm, she shook him slightly but he didn't respond. Luluah got up to rouse the boys and Salma, who slept in the hall, was awakened.

"Where is Baba?" asked Aharon.

"Baba is asleep, maybe he doesn't feel well. I'll go check on him... in the meantime, get dressed and be ready to go," answered Luluah.

She went back into the room and shook Yichyieh again. He didn't respond. She shook him harder, but there was still no response at all. Anxiously, she put her hand on his chest and saw that there was no movement; she put her ear to his chest and heard no heartbeat. He wasn't breathing. Shaken, she left the room to be faced by four children – seventeen-year-old Aharon, sixteen-year-old Menachem, ten-and-a-half year-old Salma and four-year-old Joseph.

"What's wrong with Baba?" Aharon repeated.

"I don't know, I think he's ill." Luluah still hadn't absorbed what had happened to Yichyieh. "The three of you go to prayers, I will see what's happening with your father. Don't delay... take care of little Joseph," she said, not knowing why she'd told them to go alone.

The three boys left for prayers. Salma remained with her.

"Salma, my daughter, take care of water, eggs, the tabun and milk."

"Yes, Mamma," said Salma and went out into the yard.

Luluah went back into the room and checked Yichyieh's breathing again. He wasn't breathing, and she realized he was no longer among the living. She let out a quiet groan, but neither cried out nor screamed; she just gazed at him, caressing him:

"Yichyieh, Yichyieh, get up... what will I do now? What?'

So many thoughts were racing through her mind. After a few moments, Luluah left the room. Salma was back in the house and had started preparing breakfast for Yichyieh and the children. Luluah realized she would have to tell her mother. The children returned from the synagogue and sat at the table to eat.

"Your father isn't feeling well today and will stay in bed," said Luluah, "don't disturb him."

The boys went on their own to the Mori and Luluah took Salma with her to her parents' house. She knew the law in Yemen and that the authorities would come to their home and take the children into their custody. The law states that, if the father dies and the children are under eighteen, they would become wards of the state, to be raised in orphanages as Muslims. After some time the Jewish children would become Muslim, most of them unable or unwilling to remember their Jewish background. Feeling their family had abandoned them, their only remaining security was the orphanage – who provided them with food and clothing, where they were taught the Muslim religion and shaped by their surroundings – in a Muslim environment. The anguished Luluah was out of her mind at the thought of the children being taken from her to become Muslims. In addition to the sadness at Yichyieh's death came the thought that she'd lose her children.

When they arrived at her parents' home, Luluah told Salma:

"Play outside, I want to talk to my mother about adult things."

Luluah entered the house. Her father, Minis, was in his room and Na'ama was tidying the kitchen after breakfast.

"Ya Mamma, something bad has happened," said Luluah, choking back her sobs.

"What's happened, my daughter, what's happened?"

"Yichyieh... Yichyieh isn't breathing. I think he's dead..."

"Ya daughter, are you sure?"

"I think so... I'm sure."

"Ya daughter, let's go and see. Maybe he's just sleeping..."

"Very well Mamma, very well..."

The two went off to Yichyieh's house. They entered the room and Na'ama examined him again and again then, a few minutes later, determined that Yichyieh was indeed dead. All at once Luluah fully comprehended that her husband was dead, her children in danger, and she was overcome with fear, weeping uncontrollably. Na'ama also realized this but tried to calm her daughter. Taking Luluah's hand, they left Yichyieh's house and returned to her parents' home. Salma was still playing outside and both women went into the kitchen.

"Ya Mamma, what will become of me? What will become of the children?" said Luluah brokenly and in tears.

"God is with us, my daughter, we'll think of something," said the mother.

"Ya Mamma, if God was with us, he'd have made sure Yichyieh lived until the children were grown."

"Ya my daughter, stop that, God is not to blame. God will help us," murmured Na'ama, and began to pray to the Creator for guidance and protection for her grandchildren.

Minis came out of his room, having heard part of their conversation.

"I'm going to pray. I'm going to ask God... I'm going to ask Him to protect your children, Luluah. I'm certain He will take care of them and that they will remain Jews. I can't argue with the Muslim authorities..."

Luluah's mother finished her short prayer and said to him:

"Ya husband, don't tell anyone what has happened to Yichyieh. We need to think..."

He nodded in acquiescence. Bare-headed, he walked down the alley to the synagogue. Both women knew Minis wouldn't do anything. He was afraid of the authorities.

"Ya my daughter," said Na'ama, "Yichyieh has a relative in faraway Aden, his name is Zachariah. And there's one in the Holy Land too, his name is Abraham. The children won't be safe here, we'll have to smuggle them out of the country."

"How... how we will do that? It's against the law..."

Luluah was confused and fearful.

Ya my daughter, that's what we'll do... and no one will know. Not even your father."

"That will cost money, and we don't have much..."

"Luluah, Luluah... listen to me – the authorities don't know that Yichyieh is dead. Only we know. We will think up a story that everyone will believe; we must find a way to save the children."

Luluah was alarmed. Her world had collapsed, they would take her children from her; she was distraught with worry. In all this whirlpool she began to understand that, either way, she wouldn't see her children again – either the authorities would take them or they'd be smuggled out of the country. She was just twenty-two years old and, in just nine years, she'd lost her sister and her husband, and now she was likely to lose her four children. Helpless, she began to weep again and couldn't stop.

"Ya Mamma, ya Mamma... I can't... I can't bear it..."

Na'ama went to her and embraced her tightly.

"Ya my daughter... my daughter..."

Caressing her, she too began to weep. They sat together,

holding each other and sobbing for over an hour. When they could calm their breathing again, they decided to make a plan to hide Yichyieh's death from everyone. Apart from the two of them, only Minis knew, and he wouldn't tell a soul. They agreed to speak about the next day, and Luluah and Salma went home.

Luluah made supper for the children and, when they returned from their studies, she sat them down around the table and said:

"Sit down and eat, children. Then you will go to bed."

"How is Baba?" asked Aharon.

"Baba isn't feeling well, he's in bed," answered Luluah, "don't disturb him. He needs to rest…"

The children were disciplined and asked no questions; they finished eating and went to bed. Luluah went into their room and lay down beside her dead husband. She touched him, felt his cold skin and couldn't sleep. The thoughts about Yichyieh, the boys, Salma, and her own fate were relentless. But she relied on her mother – it was always Na'ama who resolved problems, who decided what was to be done and how to go about it. But, this time, the situation was complicated and difficult, and all night long she tried and failed to find a solution. Exhausted and worried, it was close to dawn when she finally fell asleep.

The next day, as soon as she finished her morning chores she went to her mother's house. When she saw Luluah, Na'ama said to her:

"Ya my daughter, I didn't sleep a wink. The entire night I was meditating and praying. God sent me an idea of how to take care of the children."

Luluah's eyes opened wide.

"What, Mamma?"

"We must save the boys… and then we'll see what to do with Salma."

"How, Mamma? How?"

"The police don't know that Yichyieh is dead. We'll find someone to take the boys to Aden. We'll keep Salma here with us…

and tell everyone that Yichyieh has taken the boys to relatives in Sanaa."

"How will we find someone? How will they travel that dangerous road? What about Salma?" asked Luluah, worried.

"When the boys reach Aden," continued Na'ama, "we'll make sure they board a ship, or they'll go on foot, or by camel, and they'll get to the Holy Land."

"Mamma… but how? How?"

"In Aden, Yichyieh has relatives who know us. In the Holy Land, there's a relative who knows Yichyieh…"

Na'ama paused, silencing Luluah when she again attempted to speak.

"That's it… that's how we'll do it. God is with us… and we will succeed."

Again Na'ama silenced Luluah, stating:

"It's the only way I can think of… they'll get through the journey safely and they'll reach the Holy Land. Now… we need to find someone who can take them."

Luluah didn't yet understand everything she was hearing but managed to ask, before Na'ama could again silence her:

"But what about Salma?"

Salma will stay with us… so they'll believe that Yichyieh has taken the boys. If Salma is with us and we say that the boys are with Yichyieh on their way to Sanaa, they'll believe us… if we tell them that Salma has gone with Yichyieh, they won't…"

"Mamma… in time, when nobody comes back, they'll start asking questions…"

"Ya then my daughter, we'll tell everyone that we don't know. They're on their way back and we're waiting for them. After a few months, we'll say that someone told us something terrible… that Yichyieh and the boys were caught by one of the tribes who robbed and killed them…"

Luluah listened silently. She began to absorb the situation, pondering over her mother words. They'd smuggle out the boys and not tell anyone that Yichyieh had died. Salma would remain with them. They'd say that Yichyieh had taken the boys to visit family... she started believing that this story could work. She knew there were risks and danger, but this was how the boys would remain Jewish and be raised in a Jewish environment, which was the important thing. She remembered stories from the sacred texts of ancient Jewish history, how Jews had remained Jews even when their lives were threatened, and she felt it was the right thing to do. Nevertheless, fear and worry took hold of her.

With great apprehension, the two sat there and began to plan how to swiftly smuggle the boys out, directly to the Holy Land. Aharon and Menachem were already adolescents but four-year-old Joseph would stay with Yichyieh's relatives in Aden and only later would they send him to the Holy Land. The problem was finding someone to accompany the boys out of the village. They appealed to Minis, who was in the room and listening to it all, and told him they wanted to bury Yichyieh quickly, at night, in an unmarked grave.

"Why unmarked? Why without a funeral?" the father was horrified.

"Ya husband, don't ask questions... don't ask. It's best you don't know..." said Na'ama.

She took Luluah's hand and approached her husband:

"We have a plan... you only need to know one thing... only one: Yichyieh is not dead. He isn't dead..."

"What do you mean? How can you say that?"

Na'ama and Luluah approached closely and Na'ama said forcefully:

"Yichyieh is not dead. Yichyieh has taken the children to our relatives in Sanaa. He is not dead... he's with the children on the way to Sanaa. Do you understand? That's what you need to know..." and then she added: "Husband, repeat after me... Yichyieh is not dead."

Minis was astounded, but repeated after her:

"Yichyieh is not dead..."

"Again. Yichyieh is not dead..."

And the father repeated:

"Yichyieh is not dead..."

Na'ama continued:

"Repeat after me: Yichyieh has taken the boys to visit relatives in Sanaa."

Luluah added, choked by tears:

"Yabba, Yabba... Yichyieh is not dead. He's taken the boys to relatives in Sanaa... and he'll return."

The father gazed at his wife and daughter.

"How... how will you..."

"Enough, Yabba, enough." They both stopped him in the middle of the sentence. "That's what you need to know... and it's enough. We will take care of the rest..."

Minis looked helplessly at them both, nodded and said:

"Very well... I shall ask no more. Yichyieh... Yichyieh is with the boys. In Sanaa... and he'll be back. I don't know when he'll be back..."

The two hugged the father, who could barely stand. Minis looked beseechingly up at the Creator:

"Look after them, my Father...look after them. Look after them, my King...look after my wife and my daughter. Look after my grandchildren...keep them safe...make sure they come to no harm..."

He was trembling. They hugged him and held him while he continued to pray, reciting Jonah the Prophet's prayer:

"In my distress I called to the LORD, and He answered me. From deep in the realm of the dead I called for help, and You listened to my cry... The waters compassed me about, even to the soul: And my prayer came in unto thee, into thine holy temple..." he ended brokenly, and they answered:

"Amen and amen."

Luluah was the first to let go.

"We must take care of the burial tonight, without anyone

knowing. Yichyieh is still in his bed and the children will be home soon."

"The children will sleep here tonight. Yabba, you will go and fetch them and put them to bed here. Luluah and I will take care of it tonight," said Na'ama.

The father went to wait for his grandchildren in Yichyieh's house. He fetched Salma on the way and took them to his house. They were used to staying at their grandmother's house and went with him without question. In the meantime, Luluah and Na'ama walked toward the cemetery. It wasn't unusual to see them both there as they visited their relative's graves at least once a week. They went directly to Badreh's grave and waited there. When evening fell, they began to dig a grave for Yichyieh with their hands. Quietly, they dug in the sandy soil and, after about two hours, reached the right depth for burying the body. Their hands bleeding and bruised, they left the cemetery and went to Yichyieh's house. Luluah wrapped her husband's body in a large blanket. The two removed his body from the bed and dragged it quietly along the path to the cemetery. They stopped occasionally to make sure nobody saw them, then continued to drag the body. When they arrived, they rolled the body into the pit they'd dug. Luluah climbed down into the grave and respectfully arranged her husband's body; then, weeping silently, they used their wounded hands as spades and covered it up.

"Ya Yichyieh, rest in peace. Forgive us. Your makeshift burial is the sacrifice for your children's lives. Forgive us, forgive us."

It took the women less than half an hour to complete the job, filling in the earth, sweeping away any signs of digging, and scattering underbrush on the site. From there, they went quietly to Na'ama's home. They were distressed and unnerved by what they'd done and on the way they pondered – who would take the children to Aden?

"Luluah..." Na'ama addressed her, "Yichyieh has a Muslim friend here in the village. A friend like a brother... what's his name?"

"No, Yumma, no...he's a Muslim."

"He's a Muslim, but he's like a brother."

"I don't trust him; we must find a Jew. He might regret it and call the police."

They were silent, deep in thought.

"I have an idea," said Luluah.

She was by now in command of herself and all she could see was the task of saving the boys.

"Yehuda and Shimon. They're both big and strong."

Yehuda was Luluah's younger brother and was considered the black sheep of the family. They always said that naughty Menachem was like his Uncle Yehuda who broke all the rules and wasn't interested in getting married. Shimon was Yehuda's childhood friend and they were like brothers. They were reckless, twenty-year-old bachelors who weren't afraid of anything – not of the Mori, the police, or their parents.

"I don't know," responded Na'ama, "Yehuda is irresponsible. I don't know if we can trust him... both of them gave the Mori a hard time. He'd beat them every day and they'd run away from the Midrash and the village..."

"That's true, ya Mamma, true... but I believe there's a chance they'd both take on this task and prove themselves worthy."

Na'ama hesitated.

"I'm not sure it's the right..."

"Mamma, Mamma..." said Luluah fearfully, "we have no choice, we have no other... the boys are in danger anyway. Salma too... and us."

"Ya very well, my daughter. We have to make haste. We must find Yehuda and talk to him right away.

The next day Luluah and Na'ma set out to find Yehuda. Fortunately, he was alone in a nearby field, amusing himself by growing vegetables. They greeted him:

"Ya salaam, Yehuda."

"What are you doing here in the field?" he asked in surprise.

"We have to talk to you," said Luluah.

"And you must listen, and listen hard," added Na'ama.

"I don't understand. You've come all this way on foot and..." They silenced him.

"It's urgent!" Na'ama informed him, "you must listen. Something terrible has happened and you have to help us."

He tried to say something but she hushed him again, continuing:

"Yichyieh died yesterday morning... and we..."

"What? What happened?" cried Yehuda in utter surprise.

Luluah went up to him and hugged him, putting her hand on his mouth to silence him once more.

"Listen hard to Mamma, stop talking. Just listen, it's important. Yehuda, my brother, this is a matter of life and death. You must be silent and listen."

Yehuda remained in his sister's embrace, her hand on his mouth, and listened.

"Yichyieh has died. Luluah found him dead in his bed yesterday morning. We decided to smuggle the boys out of the village to the Holy Land. We sinned... maybe a great sin, but we had no choice. We took his body and buried it beside Badreh, in an unmarked grave, in secret. We made sure to brush away all signs of the grave, so nobody would know... nobody would know someone was buried there."

She stopped speaking, glanced at Luluah and then at Yehuda. It was hard for her to continue.

"Baba is the only one aside from us that knows Yichyieh is dead," added Luluah, "and we told him not to tell anyone. He won't tell. We want someone to take the boys to Yichyieh's family in Aden... and, from there, to smuggle them out to the Holy Land."

She embraced Yehuda. He drew his mother to them as well, and the three stood embracing in the field. He was still in shock and hadn't had time to digest what they'd told him.

"Ya Luluah, ya Mamma, what have you done?"

Both wept quietly.

"Yehuda, my brother," scolded Luluah, looking into his eyes, "if we don't smuggle the boys out, you know… you know what will happen. The authorities will take them from me… from us, and turn them into Muslims. We will never see them again… is that what you want? Is that what you want?"

He wrapped his arms around them both and said, "Let's sit down now, talk this through… I have to understand everything… just a moment," he said and sat with his head in his hands.

And suddenly the realization came to him that they hadn't come to him just to announce the death of Luluah's husband.

He raised head, eyes wide, and said, "Just a moment… what do you want me to do?"

Na'ama sat down and looked deep into his eyes.

"Ya Yehuda, my boy… you will take the boys to Aden. You are the only one who can. You're strong, you'll protect them…"

He covered his face with his hands in anguish, then turned his eyes and his arms upward to the sky. "Oh God…" he blurted out, and his hands fell back to the ground.

"Ya Mamma, you're asking me to take on a heavy responsibility… a very heavy responsibility. Luluah, I will do it… may God go with me. I will take the boys to Aden… I don't know how…"

"Ya my boy, Na'ama interrupted, "there is no time to spare, you must leave today…"

At once it became clear to Yehuda that, if they wanted the plan to work, they must leave immediately; they couldn't wait and run the risk that someone would discover that Yichyieh was dead.

"Very well, Mamma, very well. What else must we do?"

"I'll get the boys ready for the journey. Mamma and I will tell everyone that Yichyieh and you are going to Sanaa to visit relatives… and you, Yehuda, will take the boys to Aden. When you return in a few months' time, you will say that something tragic happened to Yichyieh and the boys and they were killed on the journey." Luluah, continued, "Maybe Shimon will agree to go with you... it might be safer than going alone."

"I don't know... I'll think about it. I'll think about talking to Shimon but, either way, I will take them..."

They made a plan. Each knew their part, what they had to do, and each ran to their respective homes to carry out the task. Luluah prepared food and clothing for the boys; Na'ama spoke with the boys alone, without little Salma, while Yehuda prepared for the journey, debating whether to include Shimon. He went to a hiding place, took out a long sword and covered it with a blanket. In his traveling bag he packed food, clothing and other necessities. He had already made the trip several times to Sanaa and knew the way and its dangers. Although he had never traveled to Aden, he knew the route that led there. The family didn't have a camel and, when they went to Sanaa, they always joined others and would pay for the journey. This time, Yehuda didn't plan on joining anyone and had to vanish with the boys without being seen. He soon realized that it was imperative for Shimon to join him; he'd need his help with the children as they'd have to do most of the journey on foot. Yehuda hid the equipment he'd prepared and went to Shimon. He swore him to secrecy and they discussed it for over an hour. Shimon willingly agreed to join his friend, his closest friend since childhood, and journey with him to Aden.

At nightfall, after Na'ama had explained to the boys why they were leaving on a long journey and to Salma that her father, Yichyieh, was going with Yehuda and the boys to Sanaa, they all met at Yichyieh's house. Only Salma stayed behind at her grandparents' house.   The boys stood in the little hall, attentive their mother and grandmother. The women had prepared them plenty of food, particularly pita. Na'ama had kept some money in a large scarf and thrust the coins into Yehuda's pocket. While the rest of the villagers were getting ready for bed, Shimon began to recite the Travelers Prayer:

May it be Your will, G-d, our G-d and the G-d of our fathers, that You should lead us in peace and direct our steps in peace, and guide us in peace, and support us in peace, and cause us to reach our destination in life, joy, and return us in peace. Save us from every enemy and ambush, from robbers and wild beasts on the trip, and from all kinds of punishments that rage and come to the world. May You confer blessing upon the work of our hands and grant me grace, kindness, and mercy in Your eyes and in the eyes of all who see us, and bestow upon us abundant kindness and hearken to the voice of our prayer, for You hear the prayers of all. Blessed are You G-d, who hearkens to prayer."

Shimon meant each word he invoked, and everyone responded: "Amen, amen..."

The men and the boys parted from the women and quietly set out into the night, walking among the houses until they reached the end of the village and the road leading to Sanaa.

The heat was oppressive and Yehuda decided that, as much as possible, they'd walk at night and rest by day. But he understood that they would also have to journey, in part, during the day as the moon was not bright enough to illuminate their path, particularly not on the difficult and more dangerous roads. The journey was long, exhausting and discouraging. They frequently carried little Joseph on their shoulders. Aharon and Menachem's behavior was exemplary. It was hard for them, but they didn't complain and behaved like adult men. Occasionally the five had to depart from the main road to evade a passing caravan. Finally, after a week of walking, they reached the outskirts of Sanaa.

Shimon and the boys hid on the outskirts of the town while Yehuda, who had visited Sanaa before, went to see his uncle, Ya'akov. Fortunately, Ya'akov was at home and greeted him warmly.

"What are you doing in town?" he asked.

Yehuda couldn't tell his uncle the truth, so he told him he'd come alone and had to return home in a hurry. The uncle assumed Yehuda had come to buy something urgent. He fed him, let him bathe, equipped him with food and sent him on his way. Yehuda, laden with food, arrived at the hiding place. When he reached Shimon and his three nephews he discovered that little Joseph was ill. Shimon told his friend that, soon after Yehuda had set out, Joseph had begun to cough and was running a fever. Yehuda stayed back with Joseph and Shimon went off to find a better place for them to hide until Joseph recovered. When Shimon returned, he cheerfully announced that he'd found a suitable cave where they'd be able to rest, sleep and take care of Joseph.

But Joseph's fever continued to rise. It was clear to Yehuda that they couldn't linger there much longer and he decided that, if Joseph's condition worsened, he'd go to his uncle and reveal the true reason for his presence in Sanaa. They picked up their bags, Shimon carrying Joseph, and together walked to the cave.

"Aharon and Menachem, go outside and find firewood. See if there's any water around. And don't go far."

The two boys left the hideout to do as their uncle requested. Shimon sat Joseph against a rock, wet a cloth with water from a leather goatskin bag, and gently wiped Joseph's forehead. The boys returned with some firewood but found no water. Yehuda made a fire, boiled the remaining water to make soup from the produce his uncle had given him and, half an hour later, the soup was ready and they sat down to eat. Shimon poured some of the soup into a tin cup to feed Joseph. Yehuda watched Shimon as he gently and lovingly fed his young nephew, grateful for his help and the risks he was taking. Yehuda knew he'd never be able to repay Shimon. Joseph, distressed and exhausted, surrendered to Shimon's care, opening his mouth each time Shimon asked him to and drank the soup. Shimon repeated his request again and again until he felt Joseph had drunk enough. He continued to wet the cloth and wipe Joseph's forehead, but his condition didn't improve.

Night fell on the outskirts of Sanaa and they got ready for sleep.

"Yehuda, I'll sleep next to Joseph. I'll take care of him... I sleep lightly and will wake from any sounds of discomfort," said Shimon. "You sleep at the entrance of the cave and guard us."

"Very well, Shimon, thank you," said Yehuda.

"Don't forget, Yehuda, keep the sword close by. Just in case..."

Yehuda heeded Shimon's advice and took the sword out of the blanket. He made a place for himself at the opening to the cave, making sure that the sword was close to him.

"God... God, don't abandon us. Heal Joseph, make him strong..." prayed Yehuda as he slipped under the blankets he'd arranged on the ground. Menachem and Aharon said 'Amen,' and also got under their bedcovers. Shimon sat next to Joseph, both leaning against the rock. He wrapped Joseph in a blanket and continued to wipe his forehead. Within a few minutes the five were asleep, Shimon still holding the cloth to Joseph's forehead.

Shimon woke in the middle of the night to the sound of Joseph's crying. He could feel that his fever had spiked and immediately called Yehuda.

"Yehuda, wake up."

"What? What's wrong?" murmured Yehuda, still sleepy.

"Get up, come and check on Joseph. I think he's really ill."

"What? Is there something else? I know he has a fever, but what's wrong?" Yehuda continued to ask.

"Yehuda, wake up and come to Joseph. Come on." begged Shimon.

"I'm coming, I'm coming..."

Shimon helped Yehuda up and they went to Joseph, who was coughing and crying.

"Put your hand on his forehead," said Shimon, "you see, his fever..."

Yehuda stroked Joseph, then put his hand on his forehead.

"Joseph, you'll be all right. We'll take care of you, don't cry..."

He felt his soaring fever and realized his nephew's condition was serious. He turned to look at Shimon whose face revealed signs of fatigue and exhaustion in addition to the worry and concern about Joseph. Yehuda lifted his little nephew and set him on his chest, wrapping his arms around him as if to protect him.

"What do we do now?" he asked, looking at Joseph curled up in his arms. "What do we do?"

He looked at Shimon who returned his anxious gaze. They realized that the journey to Aden would have to be postponed until Joseph recovered, but they didn't know what to do or how to take care of him beyond putting damp cloths on his forehead, which they did almost the whole night, to no avail. Not only did his fever not abate, but it went up. In the meantime, it was almost daybreak and Aharon and Menachem were still asleep. They decided that they'd stay in the cave during the day and continue to take care of Joseph. The two still hadn't decided whether or not to take Joseph to Yehuda's uncle. They were considering leaving him in Sanaa with one of the men while the other would take Aharon and Menachem to Aden. Would it be better to wait until Joseph recovered and then set out to Aden with all the boys?

The sun rose over Sanaa and the city woke to another day. Yehuda continued to look after Joseph, trying to soothe him, occasionally wetting the cloth and wiping his forehead. Shimon left the cave to find more firewood and some herbs they could eat. Aharon and Menachem were awake by then. They sat next to Yehuda and tried to talk to Joseph.

"Joseph, look at me... how are you?" Menachem whispered tenderly.

Joseph looked at him with glassy eyes.

"Yes..." he answered.

"How are you?" repeated Menachem, stroking his head.

"Al... al... right..." murmured Joseph with difficulty, and closed his eyes.

"What's wrong with him?" Menachem asked Yehuda.

"He's sick... he has a high fever."

"When will he get better?"

"I don't know... we're trying to sooth him, hoping his fever drops," answered Yehuda hesitantly and with concern.

Menachem heard the hesitance in Yehuda's voice and felt his

helplessness. He turned to Aharon, who was sitting gazing at the three of them.

"What will we do if Joseph doesn't recover?"

"Hush, Menachem... hush," Yehuda silenced him, "he will recover and then we'll continue on our way. Don't forget he's your brother and we must take care of him."

"Yes, but if he doesn't recover... then..."

Yehuda silenced him again.

"That's enough, Menachem. Enough... stop talking like that."

But, inwardly, Yehuda was also having uneasy thoughts about the possibility of leaving Joseph behind and going on without him.

"Menachem, take Joseph and keep his forehead cool and wet. Try and get him to sip some water. I am going outside to see how Shimon is. I won't go far. If there's a problem, shout to me and I'll come at once."

He placed Joseph in Menachem's outstretched arms and he hugged his little brother against his chest, stroking him, wetting his forehead and trying to comfort him. Joseph's eyes were still closed; he was groaning and didn't respond to Menachem. Yehuda stayed for a few moments to make sure that Menachem was taking good care of Joseph, then he left the cave.

These were the morning hours in the Yemeni desert, hours when the heat wasn't yet oppressive. The air was clean and crisp, the wind was still blowing from the west, casting its coolness over the desert dwellers. Within a few hours, being outside in the sun would become unbearable. Yehuda didn't go far from the cave but waited for Shimon to return. After half an hour he came back with firewood and had even found water.

"Why are you outside?" he asked.

"Joseph's condition is worse... his fever is high and not coming down. Menachem and Aharon are with him."

"We'll go on taking care of him..." exclaimed Shimon on his way into the cave.

"Shimon, put the firewood and water inside and come back out here. We need to talk."

Shimon entered the cave, put the firewood near the fire they'd lit the night before, and placed the water near Menachem and Aharon.

"Children, I'm going out to talk with Yehuda. We'll be back soon. We won't be far away."

Shimon approached Yehuda and asked:

"Yehuda, what are your thoughts?"

"Let's go a bit further off so the children won't hear us."

They distanced themselves from the cave and Yehuda continued:

"Joseph doesn't look good. I think we should leave him with my uncle in Sanaa."

"No, I'm not leaving anyone behind. All of us are going to Aden."

Shimon's direct, uncompromising response silenced Yehuda. Two rascals who, only days before, had been engaged in irresponsible games now faced a tough dilemma and didn't know what path to take. The responsibility they'd taken upon themselves, the promise they'd made to Luluah and Na'ama, empowered them, guiding their way on the journey from the village to Sanaa. On the long, difficult journey, in the course of one week, the two rascals had become responsible men who understood that others were depending on them, their choices and their actions. The two close friends debated and understood that any determination they made would affect all their futures. They stood in silence for a long time.

Yehuda was the first to break the silence.

"Shimon, my friend... Joseph isn't well. I don't know when he'll recover... I'm afraid something might happen to him."

"I understand, but we promised..."

"We promised to take the boys to Aden. That's true..." answered Yehuda sadly and sighed.

"But we don't know how to take care of Joseph. If we go on like this, I'm afraid he won't survive."

Shimon digested what Yehuda had told him, but was insistent. Yehuda continued trying to persuade his friend:

"We made Luluah a promise… if we don't fulfill it and spirit Joseph away with the older boys, I don't know how I'll be able to look her in the eye. We aren't safe here… the police might ask us questions, and what will we tell them? That little Joseph is sick? They won't believe us; they'll investigate and we'll both be had up in a court of law; they'll take the children away."

Shimon realized the risks and hesitated.

"Is there no other way?" he asked, "shouldn't we perhaps wait a day or two in the cave… nobody will catch us here. And then we'll make our decision…"

"Shimon, I don't think we have any alternative. We'll leave Joseph with my Uncle Ya'akov and take Menachem and Aharon to Aden," said Yehuda decisively. "Better to set out with the two older boys. The journey won't be as hard as it would be with Joseph. Joseph will recover, God willing, at my uncle's house. When we return from Aden to Sanaa, we'll check on Joseph. If – no – when, he recovers, we'll take him to Aden as well."

This possibility seemed reasonable to Shimon – on one hand, he wasn't going back on his promise and, on the other, there was still a chance that all the children would reach Aden.

"This is not easy for me," he said, "but if you promise me that after we get to Aden we'll return to Sanaa and take Joseph as well, I will consent to leaving him here."

Heavy-hearted, Yehuda nodded, "I promise." He nodded again, as if to shake off bad thoughts.

"Shimon, we have to leave Joseph with my uncle today and set out tonight. Let's go inside and tell the children. We must tell them gently, and then I will take Joseph to my uncle."

They entered the cave. Joseph was sleeping in Menachem's arms and Aharon drowsed beside him.

"Aharon, wake up, we need to talk to you both." said Yehuda.

Aharon woke and sat up. The two young men stood there with grave faces.

"We talked outside and have come to a decision," Yehuda told them. "Joseph is ill; he's running a high fever that isn't subsiding… it's been almost two days now and his condition isn't improving. Hiding here is dangerous – we could be caught by the police be. So, we've are going to take Joseph to Uncle Ya'akov in Sanaa. We will leave him there and set out with just the two of you to Aden. Afterwards, we'll return to Sanaa and take Joseph to Aden as well."

Menachem and Aharon looked open-eyed at Yehuda. They then looked at Shimon, who nodded in confirmation. The two brothers had never parted from little Joseph since he was born and were overwhelmed with sadness. Yehuda began to question his decision. Joseph was his sister's first born son, the only child to be born to Yichyieh and Luluah. If, God forbid, something happened to the boy, how could he face his sister, explain to her that they'd left Joseph in Sanaa and gone on to Aden without him? Nonetheless, and despite Aharon and Menachem's expressions, Yehuda stayed firm in his conviction and continued:

"At nightfall, I will take Joseph and come back as soon as I can. I'm sure my uncle will take better care of him than we can. When I get back, we will leave for Aden at once. For now, Shimon will look after Joseph and you will rest."

Menachem obeyed Yehuda and passed Joseph gently to Shimon, but not before kissing his forehead. Each of the four retreated into himself, reflecting on the impending farewell from little Joseph. At nightfall, Yehuda wrapped the ailing Joseph in a blanket. Each of the three kissed Joseph goodbye and Yehuda set out for Sanaa. He walked swiftly and carefully so as to remain unseen, soothing Joseph who let out an occasional groan. When he arrived at his uncle's door, he knocked and, shortly after, the door opened and Ya'akov stood there. He looked at Yehuda in surprise, then at little Joseph, who was nestled in Yehuda's arms, and then again at Yehuda.

"I have something important to tell you," said Yehuda quietly and his uncle ushered him quickly into the house.

"What is it, my boy, what's wrong?" asked his uncle who was still stunned.

"Forgive me Uncle, I lied to you... I didn't tell you the whole truth."

"Tell me, my boy, tell me."

Yehuda told his uncle everything that had happened to them, from Yichyieh's death until their arrival in Sanaa, about Joseph's illness, and his difficult decision.

"Forgive me, Uncle, but Joseph will be safer with you. With you he will recuperate and, by then, I will be back from Aden. It's only for a short time... he's a good boy. I must, I must..."

Ya'akov interjected, "Slow down, my boy, slow down..."

Yehuda continued:

"I lied to you because I had to. I didn't want..."

Again his uncle stopped him.

"Slow down, let me digest what you have told me. Let me digest..."

Ya'akov led them into the little kitchen and sat them down at the table.

"First of all, let's see what's wrong with Joseph."

He went over to Joseph and stroked him, then put his hand on his forehead.

"My boy, he has a very high fever," he said, immediately picking up a cloth, wetting it and placing it on Joseph's forehead.

Glancing at Yehuda, he noted his exhaustion.

"Yehuda, how are Shimon and the boys? Are they healthy?"

"They're in a cave outside Sanaa. They're healthy and waiting for me to return so we can go on to Aden."

His uncle was acutely aware of what all this meant: if they left Joseph with him, he'd have to hide him and, sometime later – organize Joseph's journey to Aden and from there to the Holy Land. Every day Joseph spent with him put him at risk. Ya'akov and his wife, Reuma, were elderly people. All their children had left home, some gone to the Holy Land while others remained in Aden, waiting for an opportunity to travel to the Holy Land. Ya'akov understood he couldn't wait for Yehuda to return from Aden, as two months was a considerable length of time, a dangerous time as well. The police in Yemen were unforgiving and ruthless. The moment they caught them, they'd throw him and his wife in jail and take Joseph to a Muslim orphanage. Ya'akov wondered whether to wake Reuma and discuss it with her.

"What can I do, my boy?"

"Uncle, I have no alternative, and I have no…"

Suddenly, Reuma entered the kitchen wrapped in an enormous black gown. Still half asleep, she whispered: "What's wrong, Ya'akov? What's all this noise?"

She noticed Yehuda with Joseph in his arms, and quickly lifted her palm over her gaping mouth.

"Ay Yehuda, what are you doing her? What's wrong with Joseph? Where is everybody? Nobody told me you were coming…"

Ya'akov hushed her. "Quiet, wife, quiet."

He sat her down beside Yehuda. She immediately took Joseph from him, holding and kissing him.

"He has a fever…" she declared, touching his forehead. "Joseph, Joseph…" she tried to rouse him, but he didn't respond, his eyes too heavy to open.

Reuma stood up and went to a small cabinet at the end of the kitchen where she took out a round tin box with herbal leaves inside. She took out a few leaves, put them in a cup, added water and stirred, added a little sugar and stirred again. Then she sat down beside Yehuda and tried to get Joseph to drink.

"Joseph, open your mouth… you must drink this, all of it. It will help you get well."

After several pleas and coaxing, Joseph drank the whole potion that Reuma had concocted. She got up with Joseph in her arms and went into another room; after a few minutes she came back without him.

"I put him to bed. He needs rest and plenty of fluids. And he needs medicine, like the one I prepared for him..." She sat down. "Yehuda, my boy, what are you doing here?"

Yehuda recounted the events of the past week.

"There's no other option, I'm afraid, Aunt Reuma."

Reuma looked hard at Yehuda, considered the story he had told her and stroked his head.

"Hungry?" she asked.

"No, Aunt... no."

Again Reuma went into the other room, checked on Joseph and returned to the kitchen. She went to the small cabinet, took out a pita and samneh and handed it to Yehuda.

"Joseph will remain here," she said without hesitation, looking defiantly at her husband. "There's no alternative, Yehuda must continue his journey. We'll manage until he returns."

Ya'akov looked uncertainly at Reuma, and she looked back and said decisively:

"Joseph is staying here... until he recovers. God willing, Yehuda and the boys will reach Aden and, God willing, Joseph will recover. With the help of God we will get through it all safely... Yehuda, I'll prepare as much food for you as I can. Take it and hurry back to Shimon and the boys. Kiss them for me."

Reuma hurried to the kitchen and later returned with the parcel for Yehuda.

"There's not a moment to lose, Yehuda, not a moment to lose. Set out at once, my boy, may God go with you. Don't worry about Joseph, worry about the boys and we will take care of Joseph. Godspeed."

She urged him on and they parted quickly, Yehuda setting out in the direction of the cave.

Chapter Four

Reuma and Ya'akov lived in a tiny clay house on a street mostly inhabited by Jews. The house had a small yard for chickens and a goat, very much like Luluah's house. The little kitchen located at the front of the house had a dining table with four stools. At the end of the kitchen was the entrance to another small room where Reuma and Ya'akov slept. The only door was the entrance door to the house, made of wood and with a lock and bolt.

The Muslims in Sanaa respected the Jewish community and allowed them to live there in peace. The leaders of the community realized that, as long as they owned no property and didn't threaten the Muslim regime, there would be no reason to harm them. Nonetheless, the Jews' desire was to leave Yemen and emigrate to the Holy Land. After all, with every holiday prayer, they concluded with: '*Next year in Jerusalem, but together with the coming of the Messiah.*' The Messiah still hadn't come and so, despite their desire, they stayed where they were. Some of the younger people in Sanaa's Jewish community, among them Reuma and Ya'akov's children, intended to be among those 'to bring the Messiah,' to venture out of Sanaa and Yemen and make their way to the Holy Land. At first, very few dared to make this journey, since most of it was on foot or by camel. Later on, more and more made the arduous trek, but not in great numbers. Most of the Jewish community remained in Yemen for fear of something bad happening to them along the way or to the families who remained behind in Yemen. Members of the Yemenite Jewish community were convinced that, not only had the Muslims no interest in inflicting harm on them, but indeed guarded them from all other threats. In addition, the community was well aware of the strict Islamic laws and knew that the authorities would never allow the entire community to abandon Yemen for Jerusalem.

The day after parting from Yehuda, Ya'akov went to the synagogue to seek advice from the Chief Rabbi of the community. After listening to Ya'akov's story and concerns, the rabbi said:

"Righteous Ya'akov, all your children have gone to Jerusalem. I believe what they did was wrong, they should have waited for the coming of the Messiah."

Ya'akov sighed. "What could I have done?"

"I don't have an answer," said the rabbi, "And I don't have an answer regarding little Joseph."

"What should I do?"

"Pray, Ya'akov, pray… and the answer may come."

On his way home, Ya'akov prayed and prayed. All the way he murmured, asking and pleading with God to give him an answer and guide him. When he reached home he found Reuma in the bedroom spoon-feeding Joseph. He was still weak and barely responded.

"Wife, I've been to see the rabbi…"

"What did you do there, Ya'akov?"

"I spoke to the rabbi."

She finished feeding Joseph, covered him and said: "Rest, my boy."

She addressed Ya'akov again: "Let's go into the kitchen. What did you talk about, Ya'akov? What did you say?"

They sat down at the table.

"Wife, the rabbi doesn't have any advice for us. He rebuked me for letting our children leave Sanaa for Jerusalem…"

"Ya'akov, our rabbi knows nothing."

"How can you say that, woman?"

"Listen to me," she said firmly, "it's a good thing that our children made their way to Jerusalem. Jerusalem is where we belong. There is no other place for us... we are old already."

"Enough, woman! How can you say that?" Ya'akov tried again.

She gave him an angry, defiant look.

"I wanted to go with the children and you didn't. You're my husband, and I will go wherever you go... but it's a good thing that our children are there. I wish we were with them in Jerusalem right now."

Tears flowed from her eyes and she quickly wiped them away.

"I miss them..."

He went to Reuma and hugged her.

"Wife, I also miss them."

Reuma pushed him away.

"Now listen to me: we will take care of Joseph and do everything we can for him to recover. And then we'll find a way to smuggle him to the Holy Land. Yehuda told me Joseph has an uncle there called Abraham, and they have already sent word to him that Joseph and his brothers are on their way to him."

Reuma words didn't surprise Ya'akov; he knew her opinions, but this time she was determined and quite sure of herself, even giving him orders.

"Very well, wife," he responded, "and how will we find someone?"

"Let me think," mused Reuma, "but now we must focus on Joseph's recovery."

For the following days, Reuma devotedly nursed Joseph and he began to recover. His fever dropped but he was still weak and slept most of the day. Reuma barely left the house – it was Ya'akov who did the shopping. One morning, when Ya'akov wasn't at home and Reuma was in the kitchen, Joseph's fever broke. After two weeks in bed without seeing the light of day, he got out of bed and staggered into the kitchen. Everything was strange to him. Now that he'd he regained his strength, he could see all that was going on around him – the bed in the little bedroom, the tiny kitchen, table and stools, and an elderly woman standing with her back to him, busy preparing a meal. Reuma, wearing a large dress down to her feet and a scarf that covered her head and ran down her hunched back, was humming a song Joseph didn't know. She heard a shuffling behind her, turned around, and saw Joseph standing in the doorway. She was taken by surprise but called to him, smiling:

"Ay, my boy, come to me, I'm your Aunt Reuma…"

Joseph stood there, unmoving, not understanding who this old woman was, what he was doing there or where Aharon and Menachem were. He didn't recognize her as the woman who had nursed him back to health, a blurry figure that had been by his side for the past few days. As he didn't know the woman facing him nor the unfamiliar house, he just stood there motionless, hesitant and shy. Reuma approached him, knelt down, and put her hands on his small shoulders.

"Joseph, my boy, I'm Aunt Reuma, don't be afraid…"

He was still uncertain and stood frozen in place. She pulled him gently to her and hugged him.

"Don't be afraid, my boy, don't be afraid. We love you…"

He responded hesitantly to her warm hug, leaned his head on her breast, and his one open eye looked at his surroundings, bewildered.

"Sit down, my boy, sit down. I'll make you something to eat," Reuma said to him, seating him on a stool and turning away. She gave him food and watched him as he delicately ate the Malawach, a traditional Yemeni flatbread, and the egg. When he was finished, she cleaned up after him and sat down opposite him, saying:

"Ya my boy, do you know where you are?" she asked gently.

Joseph looked at her, still shy and embarrassed.

"No, Aunt."

"I'm your Aunt Reuma. Your Uncle Ya'akov will be here soon... he's my husband."

"Yes, Aunt," he answered quietly.

"Do you know why you are here?"

"No, Aunt."

"You're here because you were sick. You had a high fever."

"Yes, Aunt," he responded, "I want Mamma," he said, his eyes fixed on the table.

Reuma took his hand and stroked it.

"Ya my boy, try and understand what I'm going to tell you."

He looked up at her and she continued.

"Joseph, you're with us now, until we find a way to send you to the Holy Land."

Gently, she told him what had brought him to her home, what had happened to his father, and that his brothers, together with Yehuda and Shimon, were on their way to Aden. She explained why they'd left him with her, and why his mother had to send him away.

"Mamma loves you and that's why she did it."

She tried to explain to him what they'd kept hidden from him because he was so young. Reuma believed now that he had been left behind he should know the whole truth, and she believed that understanding would help him cope with what lay ahead, despite his being so very young. She didn't know how much he understood of what she told him. The entire time he kept his eyes focused on her mouth, at the table, and back at her. Again she approached him and hugged him. This time he surrendered willingly, hugging her hard in return.

"Aunt, you're looking after me..." he whispered, and she sighed in gratitude to God.

Joseph understood that she was his elderly aunt and that she was looking after him, but Reuma still wasn't sure he understood the meaning of everything she'd told him. However, she felt a certain relief and continued to explain to Joseph how he must behave while he was with them in Sanaa.

"You must never leave the house... nobody must see you or it will put us all in danger," she explained the rules to him.

He nodded his head. She emphasized to him again and again the importance of this rule, until she was sure he understood what he was forbidden to do.

The following day Reuma asked Ya'akov to find out from their neighbor when they were going to Aden. She knew they intended to send Shalom, their eldest, together with Rachel, his wife of six months, and that from there they'd go to the Holy Land. They'd decided to leave Sanaa and try and reach the Holy Land. They believed that life there would be better. According to rumor, there were more Jews in the Holy Land, they were freer, and Islamic law wasn't imposed upon them there.

Ya'akov hesitated.

"Please go to Shalom. Tell him I want to talk to him."

"And what will we do with Joseph?" asked Ya'akov.

"Don't worry, we'll hide him until we finish speaking to Shalom."

Reuma took Joseph into the other room, asking him to remain there and to not make a sound until their guest left.

Within a few minutes Ya'akov returned with Shalom and Reuma went out to greet them.

"Ahalan, Shalom. How are you?"

"Well, Aunt, well," said Shalom and they went into the kitchen.

"Coffee, Shalom?" she asked.

"Yes thank you, Aunt."

"How are you? How are your wife and parents?"

"Everyone is fine, thank God."

Reuma made the coffee and served Shalom and Ya'akov.

"Shalom, I have an important request to make."

"What is it, Aunt? Whatever you wish," he responded affectionately.

"I need your help… and I hope you'll agree."

"What is it, Aunt?" he asked again.

"It's essential that no one will know what I am about to ask of you," she said, sitting opposite him.

"What is it, Aunt? What is so important?"

"Promise me that nobody will know."

"I promise, Aunt," he said, looking at her with curiosity.

Gazing at him, she considered how to tell him.

"Shalom, if your son was in danger and you asked us for help, do you think we'd help you?" she asked.

"Who is in danger, Aunt? Who?"

"Answer me, Shalom. None of my sons are in danger," she answered truthfully.

"Yes, I'm certain you would help me," he answered, waiting intently for her to speak.

Reuma took a deep breath.

"I need your help. Will you help?'

"Yes, Aunt… yes."

She took another deep breath.

"Shalom, my boy, I'm asking you take a four year-old child with you to Aden.

"What?" Shalom was surprised and drew back, "what are you asking me to do?"

Reuma tried to reassure him and slowly explained to him. The more she told him about what Joseph had been through, the more Shalom relented, feeling compassion for the child. However, he was still shocked and hesitant. Reuma continued recounting the story, the danger he would have been in had he stayed with his mother, trying to persuade him, until Shalom finally gave in and agreed to take on the task.

"Aunt, Aunt. You have given me a huge responsibility… but I will make every effort to take Joseph to Aden," he promised her.

She smiled with satisfaction and embraced him.

"Thank you, Shalom, thank you. I wish there were more sons like you."

Reuma and he agreed that he would come the following day to meet Joseph and then she sent him on his way. It was important that she explain everything to Joseph before he met Shalom. That very evening, Reuma sat down with Joseph and gently prepared him for the meeting. She told him who Shalom was and explained that, in a week or two, he would take him with him to Aden.

"I love Shalom, he's like a son to me. You, Joseph, must listen to him and obey him."

Joseph didn't understand what she meant, but nodded his head and promised Reuma to do so.

The next day when Shalom arrived they sat down in the kitchen and Reuma called Joseph to come join them. Joseph looked at the two sitting there and hurried to Reuma, holding her hand and standing beside her.

"Joseph, this is Shalom. Now remember: from the day you leave for Aden, you must listen to him, as if he was your father. Is that clear, Joseph? It's important!"

Joseph nodded. Reuma and Shalom looked at each other with satisfaction, although they weren't at all sure that Joseph indeed understood. They agreed that Shalom would let Reuma know the day before they were to set out. During the following days Joseph was hidden inside the house. He didn't go outside, as Reuma instructed. His life revolved around the bedroom and the kitchen. It was clear to Reuma that his longing for his mother and brothers grew from day to day, so she tried not to leave the house and spent more time with him. She became like a mother to him. Every day Ya'akov would sit for hours with Joseph and together they'd read the bible and pray to the Creator of the World to protect Joseph and the family.

Three weeks went by without a word from Shalom. Reuma sent Ya'akov to find out why they hadn't yet left for Aden. The longer Joseph stayed with them, the greater the risk for the elderly couple. When Ya'akov returned, he told Reuma that there had been a delay and they still hadn't set a date to leave.

"Shalom says not to worry, they'll be leaving very soon."

But Reuma was worried, and didn't hide this from her husband.

"I hope everything really is alright. We have no choice... we'll wait."

Her worn face, which had seen a lot in the hard life in Sanaa, grimaced with skepticism. She looked up at the sky.

"Well, are You going to help us save Joseph?" Her words were intentionally reproachful.

A week later, Shalom arrived and found Reuma and Joseph sitting in the kitchen, as usual.

"Hello, Aunt," he said.

Reuma rose, looked at him and immediately realized there was a problem, there was something he wasn't telling her.

"What is going on, Shalom?" she asked with concern and he looked down.

"Aunt, my wife is afraid to take little Joseph with us. She isn't sure she can take care of him on the way. I've tried and tried to convince her... I feel I've broken my promise to you."

Reuma approached Shalom and hugged him.

"Shalom, it's a great responsibility. Go, call her to come here. Go and tell her that I want to speak to her."

They remained in the embrace a few moments more and Shalom went to call Rachel. Reuma bit her nails as she waited and, a half hour later, the two entered.

"Good morning to you both, come in... how are you?"

Reuma kissed Rachel and asked after her. Rachel looked down, and answered:

"Well..."

"Sit down here."

Reuma seated Rachel close to her.

"Ay, my daughter, Rachel, you are named for Rachel, one of our four biblical mothers, who suffered until she bore sons. Now we need to save Joseph."

"Aunt..." answered Rachel, still looking down, "we can barely take care of ourselves, and it's a great responsibility."

Reuma continued:

"Ay, my daughter, I understand... I understand. But if you don't take Joseph with you, you know what will happen to him... there isn't anyone else who can do it."

"A huge responsibility..." Rachel continued to mutter, not daring to look at Reuma.

She'd have preferred not to meet Reuma. It was harder for her to refuse her in person and Reuma knew this.

"Rachel, my daughter, you've been sent from heaven to help Joseph. You have the opportunity to do a great mitzvah. Take it... God will repay you for this."

Rachel was silent and Shalom stood aside without interfering.

Reuma resumed her plea:

"Rachel, be a mother to Joseph during the journey. I'm asking you, my daughter, be a mother to him until you get to Aden. There, his Uncle Zacharia will take him from you. Don't abandon him... don't forsake our little Joseph. You are our Rachel and he is our little Joseph, and you must take care of him."

Reuma's powers of persuasion, well known to Ya'akov, were exerted with full force on Rachel. It was impossible to withstand her and, finally, Rachel relented:

"Very well, Aunt. Very well... we will take Joseph and may God go with us. We'll take him with us..."

Shalom listened to Reuma's plea and Rachel's final assent, then went to his wife and put his hand affectionately on her shoulder.

"Thank you, my daughter, thank you..." Reuma let out a great sigh of relief, "God will repay you for your mitzvah. God will grant you health and many children."

Before they left the house, Shalom announced: "I think we'll be leaving in a week's time."

Reuma accompanied them to the door, thinking about the young couple, about the enormous responsibility she was giving them, about their hesitant agreement, and about Luluah, who apparently knew nothing of her children's fate. She thought about Yehuda and the boys on their way to Aden and about little Joseph, who had to endure an exhausting journey with people he barely knew.

In the middle of the night, two days after this conversation, Shalom came to Reuma and Ya'akov's house, where they were waiting with Joseph. The previous evening, he'd told them when they'd be setting out to Aden. They'd prepared Joseph for the long journey, equipped him with clothing and food, explaining once more about the journey to Uncle Zachariah in Aden, and then reminded him to listen to Shalom and Rachel. Little Joseph listened and understood that he had to part from his elderly aunt and go with Shalom. He hugged Reuma, who knelt down and opened her arms wide for a long hug. He refused to let go and finally she blessed him, saying:

"May God go with you, my boy."

Shalom and Joseph left the house and Reuma followed them with her eyes until they disappeared at the end of the street.

"May God go with you, my boy," she whispered again and again throughout the night.

Chapter Five

Shalom had a close relationship with his Muslim friend, Abdul. They'd known each other since they were very young and had become the best of friends. They loved each other like brothers and he knew that Abdul would never betray him. Abdul taught him Islamic customs and Shalom taught him Jewish customs. Each learned to respect the other's faith. They used to laugh together saying that, if the world depended on them, there would be no religious wars – everyone would live in complete harmony.

Abdul helped Shalom obtain a camel for the journey. He knew the journey would be nearly impossible without a camel and he paid a lot of money for it. Shalom prepared a great deal of equipment for the journey in advance – food, particularly dry food, and water – and tied everything securely to the sides of the camel. It was about four hundred kilometers from Sanaa to Aden and, at first, Shalom estimated that the journey would take about two weeks. It was clear to him that although Joseph was small, the weight of all three of them would burden the camel and he'd need more rest, which meant that the journey would take three weeks.

They left Reuma's house and walked to his parents' home where Rachel was waiting. From there, they continued into the night on their way to the gates of the city. Rachel held Joseph's hand and Shalom walked in front of them. Within half an hour, they reached the city limits and went to the meeting place where Abdul was waiting with the camel. It was important that as few neighbors as possible would see them, in order to avoid unnecessary questions that might put them at risk. When they reached the meeting place, Shalom greeted Abdul:

"Ya salam."

"Ya salam," responded Abdul, "did anyone see you?"

"I don't think so... I hope not," answered Shalom.

"You must leave at once."

"Yes, I know," responded Shalom, looking at Rachel and Joseph.

"You know the way... it will take a few weeks. Watch out for tribes... don't engage with them."

"I know, Abdul, I know."

Shalom gazed at the night horizon in the direction they were to take and wondered how the journey would pass, and how Joseph would manage. Shalom knew that Joseph had already made one hard journey in his short life but he was concerned because of his age. He lifted Rachel and Joseph onto the camel, leaving himself space in front.

"Abdul, my brother, the time has come for us to set out. I have no idea if we'll meet again..."

Abdul approached Shalom and hugged him.

"Shalom, my brother, go on your way, and may God be with you."

Shalom hugged him tightly in return and said: "I won't forget you, my brother."

"And I won't forget you, my brother, salam aleichem. May God protect you," answered Abdul.

Shalom quickly mounted the camel and steered the reins towards the road leading from Sanaa to Aden. The young couple looked back at Abdul. He stood there watching the camel walk away from him. They waved goodbye and he waved back before disappearing.

Although Shalom knew the way, he'd planned the journey well. He knew that within a two-day ride they'd reach a mountain range they'd have to cross in daylight. The path through the mountains was difficult and winding and the nights were cold. He planned to reach the foot of the range and rest there at night to gather strength for the hardest part of the journey – about thirty kilometers of ascents and descents that would entail two days of hard riding. On one side of the road was a steep mountain and, on the other, an abyss. It was a dangerous journey and they had to walk with great caution, as well as being wary of tribes and the tolls they'd demand.

Joseph feel asleep at the start of the journey. Rachel sat behind, holding onto him. The first night's journey ended after just a few hours. Shalom stopped the camel just before the town of Haris, tethering him at a tree at the side of the road, and dismounted. He didn't want to enter the city at night. He helped Rachel and Joseph off the camel and the two settled themselves next to the trunk of the nearest tree. Shalom began to unpack equipment and food from the camel's back. Joseph was still sleeping and Shalom and Rachel ate quickly and lay down to sleep on blankets they'd brought with them. Before falling asleep, Shalom contemplated the difficult and dangerous mountainous area of their travels.

Morning coolness woke Joseph. He opened his eyes and looked around him. Rachel was asleep beside him, holding him in her sleep. On his left, against the tree trunk, slept Shalom, half-lying half-sitting, a long knife in his right hand. Around them were a few more trees and the camel, some distance away, also seemed to be asleep. Joseph moved a little to free himself from Rachel's arm and she woke up and looked at him.

"Good morning, Joseph," she said, smiling at him.

She examined the area they'd slept in that night.

"Good morning," responded Joseph with a shy smile.

"Come on, let's start preparing breakfast," she said, getting up.

"I'll make a little fire here and you bring the pack of food... over there, near Shalom. Don't wake him."

Joseph went over cautiously to fetch the sack, but Shalom woke up in alarm and raised his hand with the knife. Joseph got a fright as well and froze. The moment he realized that it was Joseph standing there, Shalom smiled at him, put the knife in his belt and held out an arm to hug Joseph. Rachel saw what happened and laughed aloud.

"Joseph, it's all right. I think Shalom was having a bad dream... wish him a good morning and don't forget to bring me the sack."

Joseph didn't move. Shalom's sudden movement, together with the lifting of his hand with the knife, had stunned him.

"Everything's all right, Joseph, I got a fright. Come to me," said Shalom.

Hesitantly, Joseph approached Shalom, who hugged him with warmth and affection.

"Joseph, let's take the sack to Rachel together. We'll sit down to eat in a while... but first we'll pray," said Shalom, passing the sack to Rachel.

The two went aside and began to recite the Morning Prayer. During the prayer, every time Shalom asked God to protect them and guide them on their way, he especially raised his voice so that Rachel, Joseph, and the Creator would hear. They finished praying and Shalom put a bowl of water in front of the camel. As they were getting ready, they noticed a small caravan approaching. Shalom tensed, asked Rachel and Joseph to remain near the camel and approached the caravan, knife in hand.

It was a caravan of two camels, each carrying two people. As they came closer, Shalom continued to walk toward them. They didn't seem dangerous to Shalom, but he couldn't yet see if they were youngsters or adults. The closer the caravan came, Shalom realized that his assessment was correct – the riders were parents and two children. Shalom relaxed and smiled at them.

"Greetings to you," he said, when they reached him and stopped.

"Greetings to you," answered the man on the camel.

"Where have you come from and where are you heading?" asked Shalom.

"We're from Sanaa. Where are you from?"

"We're also from Sanaa. We're on our way to Aden. Where are you going?" Shalom repeated.

The man answered him hesitantly.

"We also want to get to Aden."

The two men were sizing each other up. During the whole conversation, Shalom didn't take his eyes off the family, although he kept smiling, just like the man in front of him. The woman and children seemed to be afraid of him, and he relaxed. He continued to smile at them, particularly at the children. They smiled back at him, glancing from Shalom to their father and back again. All this time, Rachel and Joseph sat near the camel, observing what was happening from a distance.

"We're setting off in a few minutes," said Shalom to the uninvited guests, adding: "my name is Shalom, and this is my wife, Rachel and my son, Joseph."

"My name is Abraham, this is my wife Saida, and my two sons, Issachar and Zebulon," answered the man.

He looked at Shalom's head and suddenly his face lit up and he smiled: "We're also Jews."

"How do you know that we're Jews?" Shalom was very surprised.

"A Jew can usually recognize another Jew... you should hide the signs[4] more carefully, they're peeping out from behind your ears," said Abraham with a broad smile.

Shalom turned to Rachel and Joseph, and called them over. He made the introductions and, after a brief conversation, the two

_____
4. Signs – the sidelocks characteristic of Jews in Yemen.

families decided to continue their travels together – two men could deal better with lurking dangers on the journey than one. Shalom, Joseph and Rachel mounted their camel, and the caravan set out along the road to Aden. The three camels passed through the town of Haris. The main road was crowded with people – women with covered faces wandered around the market buying food, the men were on their way to the mosque for morning prayers, and children were already playing in the streets. Camels and donkeys came and went. Joseph, Issachar and Zebulon observed the commotion around them. The aromatic scents in the air, the noise and commotion reminded the children of Sanaa. They watched what was going on in front of them while the caravan continued making its way forward and, an hour later, they reached the edge of town and went on their way. The children looked back at the town disappearing behind them.

The urban landscape was replaced by that of the desert and the sun began to beat down on their heads. They went toward the foot of the hazardous mountain range that Shalom planned to cross. They sensed their camels wanted to rest. Occasionally, they saw tiny settlements along the road and green fields worked by local people. They also met people on their way toward Sanaa, going in the opposite direction. After several hours, Shalom and Abraham noticed a narrow ravine in the distance that led to the mountain range and estimated it was time to find a safe place to rest for the night. Shalom pointed out a thicket on their right. Abraham nodded and they turned the caravan toward the wood. When they arrived, they began making preparations for the night. It was twilight and the desert evening began to fall. The men quickly said their prayers before it was dark and the women made the evening meal and prepared a place for their families to sleep. Joseph, Issachar and Zebulon, who quickly finished praying with the men, ran laughing and playing among the trees.

"Children, come and eat," the women called.

Surprisingly disciplined, they stopped playing and went to

eat. Issachar and Zebulon sat next to their mother and Joseph sat next to Rachel.

As they ate their supper, Joseph looked at Rachel and asked: "When will we go back to my mother? When will I see my grandmother?"

She was taken aback by the question, looked at him, and finally responded: "Joseph, finish eating. In a while you'll go to sleep... tomorrow I will tell you everything."

She understood that she couldn't avoid a conversation with Joseph although she knew he'd been told where he was going. She knew he wouldn't see his mother and grandmother for a long time, if ever. After they'd eaten, she put Joseph to bed beside her.

She held him, saying: "You're a good, strong, brave boy, and you must go to sleep so you'll have strength for the journey tomorrow."

While listening to her, Joseph's eyes gradually closed and he fell asleep.

The following day, the women woke first and began to prepare the morning meal. The men and the children also got up and prayed the Morning Prayer. To Rachel's relief, Joseph had forgotten his questions. They finished eating and got ready to leave for the nearby ravine. The two men knew that this was the most dangerous part of the journey and that they had to be very cautious. The caravan began to make its way slowly up the ravine toward the mountain range. The ascent took about two hours. The camels exerted themselves and, from time to time, the men dismounted and walked to make the ascent easier for them. The children didn't complain about the difficulty or about riding on the camels in the same position for so many hours, but it was clearly hard for them. When they reached the top of the ravine, they were allowed to get down and stretch their legs, quench their thirst, and rest a while.

After about half an hour, they remounted the camels and entered the ravine. From this point on, the road was straight, with mountains on both sides. They travelled right up to the edge of the mountain range. The surrounding mountains appeared threatening and the men constantly examined the road, from left to right, ahead and, occasionally, behind them. The sun was merciless, beating down powerfully on their heads. After a few hours, they passed a small farming settlement. They aroused no interest among the local inhabitants who were used to passing caravans. In the meantime, the journey passed without incident, apart from the strenuousness of the long ride.

They estimated that they had about an hour before starting the descent from the mountain range. There was still a steep, twisting ascent ahead, albeit a relatively short one. From a distance they could see the rise and decided to rest a while before the arduous climb. They were sitting in a circle, drinking and eating, when they suddenly noticed a caravan coming swiftly from the direction they'd just come from. The men tensed, making sure their swords were close by. They didn't know who the riders were, but the speed of their advance left them in no doubt – this was not a caravan on its way to Aden. Shalom and Abraham didn't know what to do – if they drew their swords, the travelers would assume they constituted a threat. If they didn't draw their swords, they might find themselves in danger. In the meantime, the caravan was approaching and Shalom and Abraham rose from their places, hid their swords in their waistbands and covered them with their shirts. They decided to welcome the caravan, but be on the alert for trouble. They told the children to stay close to the women and slowly advanced towards the riders who were waiting for the moment the two families would be unable to escape – before them was a steep incline, and five men were galloping towards them on horses. The women and children stayed behind, waiting tensely. The five riders halted very close to the two men.

"Greetings to you," said the man in the middle who appeared to be the leader. A large sword hung from his waist.

"Greetings to you," responded Shalom and Abraham.

"Where are you going?"

"To Aden, with our families," answered Shalom.

"And where have you come from?"

"From Sanaa," answered Shalom.

He spoke as briefly as possible, closely examining the movements of the man in front of him. Abraham was silent, his eyes tensely examining the five.

"Did you know that you aren't allowed to pass through our lands without permission?"

"No," answered Shalom.

The five stiffened and their eyes examined the two men facing them and the women and children who were sitting at a distance from them. The leader looked around to see if there were any more adults around that he hadn't noticed. Shalom and Abraham examined the men again and again.

"The area you are passing through belongs to us," said the leader, "and you must pay us a toll, or..."

"How much?" Shalom interrupted.

"How many people are you?"

"You can see how many we are... we're four adults and three children."

"No more?" asked the leader.

"What you see is who we are," replied Shalom.

He realized that the leader was testing them. The leader also understood Shalom's evasive answer and wondered if Shalom was answering like that because there were others hiding whom he couldn't see.

He looked at Shalom, saying again: "You must pay a toll!"

"How much?" repeated Shalom.

"Ten rials for each adult, the children don't have to pay."

"That's a great deal of money. Five rials per adult," answered Shalom.

"Eight rials."

"Six rials," said Shalom.

"Seven."

"Very well. Seven rials per adult," replied Shalom holding out his hand to the leader who was still seated on his horse. The two shook hands.

Shalom turned to Abraham and said, "Go and get twenty-eight rials."

Abraham returned at once and handed the money to Shalom who gave it to the leader. He took it, and looked around at the four people, while nodding agreement. He turned his horse around, beckoning to the other riders to return the way they'd come. The five rode quickly away and Shalom sighed with relief. Abraham approached and hugged him. What could have been a dangerous encounter had passed without incident.

"Thank you," he said, "thank you and thank God for being with us today."

They turned and rejoined the women and children and decided not to stay there any longer. They'd had enough and only wanted to put as much distance as they could between them and that place. They put the children on the camels, while the adults walked in front, holding the ropes attached to the camels' heads. The two families began to climb the steep incline. The walk was tiring and they had to rest every few hundred meters. After two hours later, they reached the summit. The sun was sinking between the mountains in the west, and they stood at the top and gazed northward and below at the way they had come. Relief and fatigue were evident. They knew the hardest part was behind them and that the road ahead was flat and easy. They got ready for a night's sleep.

The following days passed, shifting between freezing cold at night and boiling heat during the day. The caravan sometimes traveled at night and sometimes during the day, according to the type of road, and they covered great distances. Joseph liked Issachar and Zebulon and every time they stopped for a rest, if the children weren't too tired, they'd play together while the adults rested and watched them. The landscape began to change – from desert landscapes and sand dunes to more colorful, green landscapes. Occasionally, they saw green trees and lush fields.

Toward evening, they arrived at the mountain overlooking Aden and the descent towards the city. Shalom and Abraham looked at each other with a sigh of relief. The travelers stopped at a vantage point from where they could see the city and surrounding landscape. They gazed at the huge sea edging the city, and the children stood and stared, mouths agape. This was the first time they'd ever seen the sea stretching endlessly before them. The blue, together with the large city buildings and surrounding tiny towns, were impressive.

"How many are your works, O Lord," said Shalom to the children, "this is the City of Aden, our next destination."

Joseph clung to Shalom's trousers, asking: "Is that where we'll look for my uncle?"

"Yes," Shalom replied.

"And what about Issachar and Zebulon?"

Shalom put his hand on Joseph's shoulder.

"Your uncle is waiting for you. When we arrive, we'll look for him and he will take care of you."

Joseph listened without responding. He too was spellbound by the beautiful city and huge sea. Apart from the excitement at the marvel before him, he was bothered by questions to which he had no answers: What would happen to him? What would happen to Issachar and Zebulon, with whom he'd become so attached? Where would Shalom and Rachel go? What would become of him?

Chapter Six

Seated on the camel between Shalom and Rachel, Joseph gazed at his surroundings, amazed and astonished by the beautiful city of Aden. He saw the array of clay, stone and concrete houses; the arched and round casement windows that decorated the houses, and their colors – white, blue, brown, gray, and red; the minarets rising from the buildings, the huge domes of the mosques, the enormous street they were passing through; the throngs of busy people and different, strange means of transport that came and went; the stores at the sides of the street selling their food and wares, and the distant, blue sea, which he'd seen the previous day when looking down at Aden from the mountains. From there he'd seen the big ships at anchor in the harbor and smaller ships in tiny harbors along the shore. The enormous, infinite sea left Joseph in awe, even before they entered Aden. He'd never seen such sights before.

Shalom and Abraham felt safer when they entered Aden. They knew that Jews in Aden had more freedom and full, equal rights, as opposed to north Yemen, where Jews weren't allowed to ride a horse, only a donkey, and where they had to make way for any Arab riding toward them. There were different laws in the north that defined Jews as welcome guests in Yemen.

On the other hand, under British rule in Aden Jews could own property, learn general studies and engage in trade, particularly with the British authorities. Reuma told Shalom that Joseph's Uncle Zachariah, a trader, was wealthy and respected in the Jewish Quarter. She also told him that Zachariah had good connections with the British who trusted him and traded regularly with him.

Shalom and Abraham looked at one another. The hour of parting had arrived, when each family would go its own way. They stopped the caravan at the end of the busy street and dismounted from the camels. Issachar and Zebulon said their goodbyes to Joseph, and Rachel and Abraham's wife kissed each other farewell.

"May God go with you," they said to each other.

Shalom embraced Abraham and wished him safety and success on their journey.

"May God protect you," said Abraham.

Abraham's family continued on foot, the camels tied behind them, whereas Shalom's family turned in the opposite direction, on their way to find Uncle Zachariah. From time to time, Joseph turned back to look at Issachar and Zebulon, who were now further away. Shalom went in search of Jews who could help him find the street where Zachariah lived. It was easy to recognize Jews – more than anything else, their sidelocks, head coverings and beards distinguished them from others.

"Over there," he was told, "ask anyone where Zachariah lives. They'll show you where his house is. Everybody knows everybody in the Jewish Quarter."

Shalom thanked him and, an hour later, following his instructions, they reached the Jewish Quarter. As they entered the main street of the Quarter, they saw a Mezuzah on every doorpost and Star of David symbols. The street was lined with many shops, above which Jews lived. The road was crowded with people – donkeys and carts, cars, buses and bicycles. Joseph was agog at the sights around him and Shalom held his hand, keeping him close beside him. Shalom wanted to reach Zachariah before dark.

"Look around you and see if you can find the synagogue, we'll probably find someone there who knows where Zachariah lives," said Shalom.

They approached the market, which was the business center in the Quarter. He stopped a Jew coming towards him and asked for Zachariah's address. The man said he didn't know but pointed out the butcher, who knew everyone. Shalom walked cheerfully towards the butcher's store. When they arrived, he addressed a young man who was cutting meat with a huge knife.

"Greetings to you."

The young man looked at Shalom and responded: "Greetings to you."

"Do you know where Zachariah the trader lives?"

"Of course."

"Can you direct me to him?"

"Who are you?"

"I'm Shalom from Sanaa. I arrived in Aden today, and I have need of him."

"Why do you have need of him?"

"This boy, Joseph, is a relative of his. I need to find Zachariah."

The young man looked at Joseph, who looked down, then looked back at Shalom as if sizing him up.

"Why do you have need of him?" he asked again.

"Zachariah knows I am bringing Joseph to him," replied Shalom, adding hesitantly: "he is expecting him."

It wasn't a rare occurrence for Jews to arrive in Aden from the Yemen interior, wanting to live in the city where the liberal British government made sure they were safe and enjoyed equal status. Although Arabs would occasionally harass, and even attack Jews, the British usually protected them.

The young man gazed at them, then finally turned to Joseph, asking him: "Joseph, who is Zachariah?"

Joseph looked from the young man to Shalom, who nodded as if permitting him to answer the man. Joseph looked up at the young man, looked down, then up at him again, his eyes shining with excitement, and said: "Zachariah is my uncle and, with God's help, I must find him."

The young man relented, smiled at Joseph and said: "Don't worry, I'll direct you to your Uncle Zachariah," and then he turned and called out: "Amnon, my boy, come here a minute."

A boy slightly older than Joseph emerged from the store.

"Yes, Father?"

"Take these Jews to Zachariah and tell him his order is ready, he can come and pick it up."

"Thank you," said Shalom.

"You're welcome, my son will show you where Zachariah lives."

Amnon began walking quickly, followed by Shalom, Rachel, Joseph and the camel. They passed through narrow alleys and between buildings, their doors opening directly onto the street. Some of the houses had courtyard entrances. Joseph ran beside Amnon, quite excited by the approaching meeting with Uncle Zachariah, about whom he'd heard all the way from Sanaa. After a few minutes, Amnon slowed down and pointed out a nearby house.

"There you are, that's Zachariah's house."

They approached an impressive entrance gate.

"Wait here" said Amnon, "I'll go in to Zachariah."

Opening the gate, he strode inside. He was followed by Joseph, Shalom and Rachel with the camel in tow. The path leading to the house was covered in mosaic and on either side were lemon trees, beyond which were other trees and bushes that weren't familiar to Joseph. A few meters onward they came to a huge entrance door. Joseph stood in front of the door and looked up at its furthest point, then to the right at the wall of the long house, and at the large windows that were wide open.

What a big house, he mused, listening to Amnon call out: "Zachariah, Zachariah."

From inside the house came a muffled reply and the sound of

steps approaching the front door. The huge door slowly opened and a man appeared with sidelocks tucked behind his ears, dressed in black pants, a white shirt and black shoes.

"Hello Zachariah," said Amnon, "I've brought some guests who are looking for you."

Zachariah looked at Shalom and Rachel and then at Joseph. As he looked at Joseph, his eyes shone with great excitement.

"Joseph, my boy, is it you?"

Joseph had never met his uncle and turned to look at Shalom, who nodded in confirmation.

"Yes, Uncle Zachariah, it's me," replied Joseph, overcome with mixed feelings.

He'd been told many times that he had to get to Uncle Zachariah and here he was, standing in front of him. The man before him didn't look anything like he'd imagined him. But he was glad he'd finally arrived. He'd learned to love Shalom and Rachel during the long journey and knew they'd soon be taking their leave. His joy at meeting Uncle Zachariah conflicted with the sadness of parting from Shalom and Rachel.

"Joseph, my boy" repeated Zachariah, looking at Joseph, "we've been waiting for you."

He bent down to Joseph, both arms opened wide. Joseph didn't move; he was shy and hesitant. Large eyes gazed up at Uncle Zachariah and he seemed choked with tears. He'd waited for this moment for so long, and here he was, standing before his uncle, whose arms were opened wide to embrace him. For so long, he'd lived with people who'd been strangers to him, passing from one family to another on his way to Aden.

"Joseph, my boy, don't be afraid. I'm your uncle. Your father, Yichyieh, may he rest in peace, and I are cousins. He was my favorite cousin," said Zachariah tenderly, "you are Yichyieh's son and now you will be like a son to me. I will take care of you, come, come to me."

Zachariah bent forward and Joseph looked at him. In his mind echoed the words: "You will be like a son to me," and his eyes filled with tears. Again he looked at Zachariah, into the kind eyes looking down at him, into his gentle, welcoming face. With faltering steps, he approached his uncle, who gathered him into a tight, loving hug.

"I know you've had a very hard time," said Zachariah as he hugged him.

Joseph didn't respond, trying as hard as he could to stop the tears streaming down his cheeks. Zachariah's large hand stroked his head and, very slowly, Joseph's arms rose to embrace his uncle's large frame. Resting his head on Zachariah's chest, the tears continued to fall.

"Weep, my boy, weep. It's alright to weep," said Zachariah, continuing to caress him.

"Zachariah, Babba said to come and fetch the order he's prepared for you," said Amnon. He'd observed scene without daring to say a word. "I'm going back to the store, Babba is waiting for me."

"Tell Babba, I'm coming. Thank you for bringing my dear guests, Amnon."

Amnon looked at everyone then, waving goodbye, he turned and ran quickly back to the store.

Zachariah, still hugging the sobbing Joseph, now picked him up.

"Come in, come in," he said to Shalom and Rachel. "Shimei will be home soon. Please sit down, you must be thirsty, I'll bring you water."

Carrying Joseph, who was still weeping with his head on Zachariah's shoulder, he went into the kitchen and returned with glasses and a jug of water. He poured water for Shalom and Rachel before pouring a glass of water for Joseph and putting it in his hand. Joseph began to look around at the glorious home.

"How are you? How was the journey?" Zachariah asked Shalom.

Shalom told him about the hardships on the road and how grown-up Joseph had been. He added that they were on their way to the Holy Land and that they couldn't take little Joseph with them. Zachariah nodded understandingly and said: "From now on, I am responsible for Joseph and will treat him like my own son."

The front door opened; Zachariah's wife, Shimei, had arrived. She put her basket down in the entrance hallway and, hearing her husband's call, she entered the living room. Zachariah introduced her to their guests and she greeted everyone. Shimei turned to Joseph and swiftly gathered him into her arms.

Before going into the kitchen, she said: "We'll sit down to eat soon."

In the kitchen, Shimei asked: "How are you, my boy? Joseph, I'm your aunt and I will take care of you. Tell me about the journey here. How is your mother? Brothers? Salma?

Joseph listened to Shimei and was silent. She pressed him to her breast with one arm and, with the other, took out plates and ladled hot soup from a large pot on the portable paraffin cooking stove until five plates of soup were arranged on the table next to the wall. She took out saloof[5], a plate of fenugreek and cut up several tomatoes and onions, and put it all on a tray in the middle of the table.

"Come and eat," called Shimei.

Zachariah and the guests came into the kitchen, crowded around the table, made the blessing over the food, and began to eat. Joseph looked around, observing Shimei as she was running around serving her guests; he looked at the large pot, the kitchen cupboards hanging on the wall above the sink and at the taps under the window. It was the first time Joseph had ever seen water coming out of a tap in the wall. Shimei sat Joseph next to her, pulled his chair closer to the table and cut him a piece of saloof.

"Eat, my boy, eat. You must be hungry."

---

5. *Saloof,* large thick pita.

Joseph saw that everyone was eating and began to eat too, though slowly and hesitantly at first. He looked at Shimei, as if to make sure that everything was alright, and she nodded for him to go ahead and enjoy the meal. Her kitchen was larger than the one in Sanaa and, to Joseph's astonished eyes, it seemed that the kitchen alone was the size of his uncle and aunt's house in Sanaa. The window was bigger, there were cupboards, more space for the stove, a larger table; five people could sit around it and eat while Shimei could still get up and walk around the kitchen.

"Stay and sleep here tonight," Shimei invited her guests, "it's already late."

Shalom and Rachel looked at each other and nodded.

"Thank you, Shimei," said Shalom. "Thank you, Zachariah. In the morning we'll be on our way."

When they finished their supper, Shimei left Joseph in the kitchen with Zachariah and took Shalom and Rachel to one of the guest rooms, made up the bed, showed them where they could wash, gave them towels, and asked: "Will you let me know when you're finished? I want to bathe Joseph as well."

Shalom and Rachel got ready for bed. When Shimei returned to the kitchen, she found Zachariah sitting with Joseph on his lap, eyes closed.

Zachariah stroked his head, whispering: "Joseph's asleep. He must be very tired. When he finished eating, I called to me and sat him on my lap. I began to ask him questions, but after a few minutes I saw his eyes were closing and he fell asleep."

"Hush, stop talking," Shimei silenced him, "I'll make up his bed and come and get him."

"Very well, Shimei, very well."

When Shimei went off to make Joseph's bed, Zachariah didn't wait for her. He got up, lifted Joseph, taking care not to wake him. He walked slowly toward the bedroom and waited for her to finish. The moment the bed was made, Shimei picked up the blanket and waited for Zachariah to lay Joseph on the bed so she could cover him. Joseph tucked in, they made sure he was still asleep and then quietly left the room. Outside, Shimei noticed Zachariah's eyes were moist. She kissed him on the forehead and went to clean up the kitchen.

When she entered the bedroom, she said to her husband: "Zachariah, we need to think about what to do with Joseph."

"Shimei, my good woman, Zachariah stopped her, "we're going to sleep now. Tomorrow, after we send Shalom and Rachel on their way, we'll see what to do with Joseph."

Shortly after, all occupants of the house were sound asleep.

Joseph was wakened by the first rays of sunlight and didn't know where he was. He opened his eyes and looked around at the enormous ceiling, the elegant lamp hanging from its center, and at the two large windows. The sun was shining through one of them. He looked at the big wooden shutters and at a large picture standing on an old wooden table in the corner. Three small children and two adults were gazing out from the picture. Joseph got out of bed, went over to it and examined each of the figures, one by one. They weren't familiar to him. Beyond the closed door he could hear the voices of a man and a woman and thought he heard his name mentioned in the fragmented conversation. He didn't understand what they were discussing, but the sound of the voice was familiar, and then he remembered.

Shimei slowly and quietly opened Joseph's bedroom door and peeped inside. Joseph turned and looked at her.

"Joseph, my boy, you're awake."

"Yes, Aunt," replied Joseph.

"Come and wash, I'll get you some clean clothes," she said gently, adding: "Zachariah is back from prayers and we'll sit down to eat soon. You must be hungry."

"Yes, Aunt," replied Joseph, approaching her.

Putting her hand on his head, she led him to the kitchen table and sat him down.

"Joseph, how is your mother? How are Aharon and Menachem? And Salma?"

"Where are Shalom and Rachel?" asked Joseph.

"They left early this morning."

"Where did they go?" asked Joseph.

"They went to find out about something."

"Will they come back here?"

"I don't know, maybe. Depends on who they meet... well, tell me... how is Mamma?"

"Mamma is fine, a bit sad. Salma is also sad."

"And what about Aharon and Menachem?"

"They went with Uncle Yehuda."

"Where did they go?"

"To the Holy Land."

"Oh, my boy, what a journey you've had!"

Joseph looked up at her, then at once looked down again.

"We left Mamma, and Uncle Yehuda and his friend Shimon took me and Menachem and Aharon. We walked for a long time, a very long time... I miss Mamma. And Salma... and Menachem and Aharon."

"Hello," called Zachariah as he entered the house.

"Hello," answered Shimei and called him into the kitchen.

Zachariah came into the kitchen and immediately addressed Joseph:

"Good morning."

"Good morning," chorused Shimei and Joseph.

"Shall we sit down to eat? Shimei, my good woman, can we eat?" asked Zachariah and turned to Joseph: "I didn't wake you for prayers this morning but, from now on, you will come with me to the synagogue."

"Very well," nodded Joseph.

Shimei placed zalabiyeh[6], a jug of mint tea, and three glasses

---

6. Zalabiyeha – a fried bun.

on the table. The smell of the zalabiyeh was new to Joseph and he looked at Zachariah as if waiting for permission to start eating. Zachariah looked back at him, waited for Shimei to be seated, and then he made the blessing: *"Blessed are You, Lord our God, King of the universe, Who brings forth bread from the earth."*

He began to eat, and nodded to Joseph. The taste of the zalabiyeh was new to Joseph, reminding him of the pita he used to eat at home.

"Joseph, we have to see what to do about sending you to your uncle in the Holy Land. You're still young and the journey isn't easy... it's very long," said Zachariah after they'd finished eating and said the blessing after the meal.

"Gently, my man... gently... the Holy Land is far away. We have time, there's no rush," Shimei interrupted him, "first of all, we'll see what will be with Shalom and Rachel. But..." she paused, looking at Joseph, "you cannot leave the house alone, only with me or Zachariah. Is that clear?"

Joseph nodded, looking down at the plate in front of him.

"Very well, very well," Zachariah relented, "we won't make any plans about the Holy Land just yet. However, until we know what will be, I want Joseph to study. I want him to attend the Midrash[7]."

"He can't go on his own," Shimei said firmly.

"There's a Midrash not far from here. I know the Mori, Sa'adiya, and he will take care of his education. Agreed, my good wife?"

"Agreed... and there's something else that's important..." again Shimei looked at Joseph, "from now on, you must call me 'Yamma' and Zachariah 'Yabba'... it's very important."

Joseph nodded again.

"I'm going out and I'll be back this evening," said Zachariah.

Joseph and Shimei stayed home. She was busy with various tasks and he wandered about the large house, going from one room to another. There were four large bedrooms in the house, each with

---

7. A school for the study of the Bible.

a large bed, a closet, and a table and chair; in the large kitchen were two sinks, taps with cupboards above them and, in the corner, was a dining table and chairs; there was also an enormous living room with a long table and large wooden chairs, cabinets with glass doors that were filled with books, elegant, silver chandeliers hanging from the tall ceiling, and decorative colorful tiled flooring. Joseph was enchanted. He walked again and again through the house until he came to the room where he'd slept the previous night. There, he found Shimei. She was removing clothes from the closet and laying them out on the bed. Shimei sat Joseph down beside her and began to fit him out with clothes. She occasionally asked him to try on a garment in order to make sure that it fit him. She arranged the clothes that fitted him in the closet and showed Joseph where they were. She also showed him the tzitzit (ritual fringes attached to the four corners of the tallit, the Jewish prayer shawl, and explained that it was important he change the tallit and his clothing regularly.

The next morning, Zachariah took Joseph to the Midrash. On the way, he explained about the Mori.

"The Mori Sa'adiya is a good teacher, but you must listen to him and never misbehave… understood?"

Holding Zachariah's hand, Joseph nodded.

"If there are any problems, the Mori will tell me. You should know that you are among the youngest children there… will you promise me to behave and study properly?"

"Yes."

After a few minutes' walk, the two reached the Midrash. Going down three steps, they reached the entrance door and could hear children's voices. Zachariah opened the door and, standing on the threshold of the Midrash, they looked inside – it was a small room with three tables. Students were sitting around them and on each table was one book. Joseph saw small children sitting around a table; older children were sitting at a middle table and, around the furthest table, sat the eldest children. The Mori Sa'adiya was covered with a tallit and his sidelocks reached his chin. He was standing at the eldest children's table holding a thin cane and reading a sentence aloud, which the eldest children repeated after him. After them, the other children repeated the sentence. The Mori again read out the sentence and, again, the older children repeated it, followed by the others. When the Mori Sa'adiya noticed the visitors, his face lit up. He told the children to continue reading and turned to Zachariah and Joseph. While reciting the sentences, the students gazed at the two standing in the doorway. One look from the Mori made them lower their eyes to the book before them and go on reading and repeating.

"Hello, HaMori Sa'adiya. This is Joseph, I spoke to you about him."

"Hello, Zachariah, hello Joseph," responded HaMori.

He looked at Joseph, who merely kept his eyes on his shoes and held onto Zachariah's hand.

"Hello," Joseph answered faintly.

"Hello, HaMori," he corrected. "You must say 'HaMori.' And a bit louder, so I'll hear you."

"Hello, HaMori," replied Joseph more loudly.

"I understand that you know Amnon."

"A little."

"Then sit next to him and he will look after you."

Amnon smiled at him and made room for him on the carpet. Joseph looked at him and then at Zachariah, who nodded. Joseph let go of his hand and walked hesitantly to the space Amnon had made for him and sat down with other students, all of whom were older than him.

"I'll come and fetch you at noon. Don't go home with anyone," said Zachariah.

He took leave of the Mori, turned, and left the Midrash.

It was the first time that Joseph had attended Midrash, but he vaguely remembered his two elder brothers going to study every day. The Mori Sa'adiya again read a sentence, which everyone repeated. Joseph felt awed by the Mori Sa'adiya, as did all the children, and joined the others in repeating the sentences. Joseph turned his attention to the book in the middle of the table and at the index finger with which one of the students was following each word, but he wasn't able to read. It was the first time an open bible had been set in front of him. In the course of the day, the students were divided into two groups – those who knew how to read and those who weren't yet able to read. Amnon was among those who knew how to read – but never out loud. Joseph and the others sat in front of the Mori Sa'adiya as he taught the little ones the letters of the bible and how to pronounce them properly, correcting them several times until each could accurately articulate the sound. The Mori would point to a symbol on a small board and all the little ones chorused the sound of that letter again and again while gazing at the board.

Everything was so new to Joseph, but he felt comforted by the warm atmosphere and being in the company of children of his own age, who were like him. Time passed quickly and it was already noontime. Zachariah came to take him home for lunch. At the end of the meal, they rested for a while. Towards sundown, the two went to the synagogue next to the Midrash for the evening Arvit prayer. During the prayer, Joseph noticed that children a little older than him were reading the prayer aloud and the adults would correct them whenever they pronounced a word inaccurately. Zachariah held the prayer book in his hand and showed Joseph the part they were reading. Joseph, who had just started learning to read and how to pronounce the words, began to recognize some of the letters, and even read aloud whenever he managed to catch on. Zachariah encouraged him, occasionally correcting him. At the end of the evening prayer, they sat together and Zachariah read the weekly portion to Joseph and explained what the chapter meant. When he arrived at the part that said, *'and you taught your sons to speak,'* he added, "you see, Joseph, you need to know the bible, understand what is written, know the Mitzvoth (commandments) and learn what is forbidden and what is allowed. It's important that you know and understand."

Joseph's weekly routine was the same – in the morning he went with Zachariah to the synagogue for Morning Prayer; afterwards, they ate breakfast, Zachariah went to work and Joseph attended Midrash with the students. He studied from morning until noon when Zachariah came to fetch him for lunch, rest, and then back to the synagogue for the evening Arvit Prayer.

And every evening after Arvit, Zachariah would sit with Joseph for about an hour and teach him the meaning of what they'd read that day in Midrash. From there, they'd go home and to bed. During lessons there were also short breaks when the children would run around and play in the little yard between the Midrash and the synagogue. Amnon took Joseph under his wing, taking care of him like an older brother and, when necessary, protecting him from the other children. He already knew how to read and pray and would occasionally even go up to the podium to read the bible in the synagogue.

On the Sabbath, between prayers, Joseph and Amnon would play together in Zachariah and Shimei's yard. They knew that Shimei forbade Joseph to leave the yard but, occasionally, they'd go out and wander about nearby, sometimes playing together in Amnon's father's closed store. Passersby knew who Amnon was, but not Joseph.

"He's like my brother, and he belongs to Zachariah and Shimei," he would say to his Muslim acquaintances.

Occasionally they'd encounter a British policeman, murmur in English and fool around with him until he'd growl at them, "Where are your parents? Go home," and send them off.

When they were caught, they were punished.

Months went by and Joseph grew into a Jewish Yemenite boy with curly sidelocks. By the time he turned seven, he could read fluently with nearly precise pronunciation. Zachariah was proud that he was a quick learner. From time to time he'd take him up to the podium in the synagogue to read from the Torah. It was a great honor for Joseph to go up and read from the weekly portion in front of the congregation. At first he was a little nervous and, as he read aloud, could hear he was being corrected. Soon his confidence grew and the correcting grew less.

Joseph remained with Shimei and Zachariah for about two and a half years and learned to love them like parents in every way. His memories of his mother, brothers and sister became vaguer and he rarely missed them.

One day Zachariah sat Joseph down and told him:

"You must start preparing for the journey to the Holy Land. Joseph my boy, I promised I'd send you… and I must keep my promise."

Joseph had gotten used to living with Shimei and Zachariah and felt completely at home with them. He felt a familiar dread in his belly and became silent.

"I love you. You know that," continued Zachariah.

"I love you, too."

"Promises must be kept."

"Yes."

"Your brothers have reached the Holy Land. And Uncle Abraham will take care of you."

"Yes."

"I do love you… but you must be in the Holy Land, not here in Yemen. Shimei and I are too old to make the journey, and you are still so young…"

"Yes," replied Joseph, overwhelmed with sadness.

"I've started making enquiries about how to send you there. It will take time… but I wanted you to know…"

"I understand."

"In the meantime, you must go on studying and behaving as usual, alright?"

"Very well," replied Joseph.

He did remember being told that he'd be sent to the Holy Land, just like his brothers, but the years he'd spent with Zachariah had made him forget. Zachariah pulled Joseph into his arms and hugged him.

"Don't tell anyone about this conversation, alright, my boy?"

"Alright."

"You can talk to Shimei about it… but no one else, not even Amnon."

"Alright."

The dread that had filled him earlier only increased. Joseph was familiar with this feeling – it was the sense of parting. The trepidation that any minute now, in a day, a month, without much warning, he would have to leave the people closest to him, the adults who raised him, his friends whom he studied with every day, leave a place where he knew every corner. He would be separated from Zachariah, whom he loved and respected, and from Shimei, who had taken care of him like a mother; from Amnon, who had become his closest friend and watched over him like a brother, and from the Mori Sa'adiya, his mentor and teacher.

Chapter Seven

Zacharia estimated that the ship would arrive at the port on time, but he wasn't sure they'd allow him access to it. He paid a great deal of money in advance to Mahmoud for arranging a place for Joseph on the boat sailing to the Holy Land. They agreed that the rest of the money would be paid once Joseph was on board the ship. Mahmoud told Zacharia that it was a Dutch ship – the sailors were Dutch and the captain, Johann, would be responsible for Joseph until they reached their destination. Johann always insisted on being paid fully in advance, which is what they planned to do. Once Joseph was on board, he would be under Johann's care. Mahmoud promised Zachariah that Joseph would definitely reach the Holy Land.

"Don't worry," he told him, "I've worked with Johann for many years, and he has faithfully honored every business arrangement I've made with him. I trust him."

"And I trust in God and the money I have to pay him once Joseph is on the ship," replied Zachariah.

"Yes, I know..." responded Mahmoud, adding: "the moment the ship enters the port, I will meet Johann at his usual spot and I'll come to an agreement with him regarding the details of the deal. Then we'll know when Joseph will board the ship. Afterwards, I will let you know when the ship leaves. Everything has to be precise."

On Tuesday morning, Johann and Mahmoud came to see Zachariah and informed him that the ship would set sail from the Port of Aden for the Holy Land on Friday night. Zachariah didn't think twice and told them he would be there with Joseph.

"Friday at 23:00, Zachariah, not during the day..." said Johann.

"I know, Joseph will be ready," answered Zachariah, "when will he reach Tel Aviv?"

"According to plan, twenty-five days later, on a Tuesday at noon."

"Johann, when you get to Tel Aviv, you'll know where to take Joseph?"

Johann took a piece of paper out of his pocket and read it:

"Yes, I'm to take him to 12 HaCarmel Street in Tel Aviv, where someone will be waiting for him.

Zachariah nodded and Johann added: "Tell me, Zachariah, you Jews don't travel at night on a Friday. Why is it that you're allowing Joseph to travel on your Sabbath?"

"It's true, we don't travel on the Sabbath," replied Zachariah, "but this is a special case. The boy must be on that ship..." He added: "Remember, Johann, you promised me that Joseph will get to the Holy Land, and that you will make sure he reaches the address I gave you."

"You Jews... you say that, according to your customs, you are forbidden from travelling on Friday night and Saturday but, when it suits you, you make an exception," Johann chuckled, "don't worry about Joseph, Zachariah, I will take care of him. He will reach his destination."

Johann and Mahmoud went on their way, leaving a worried Zachariah. He went to tell Shimei about the voyage. By then, Joseph had been with them for almost five years. They had managed to hide him from the Muslims, preventing his conversion to Islam. They'd raised him according to the Yemenite Jewish tradition; they had been like parents to him, and now the moment they had waited for had come. Their joy was mixed with sadness, letting go of Joseph, whom they'd loved as if he were their own throughout the long period he'd been with them.

"We have to prepare the boy for a long journey," said Zachariah to Shimei, but his eyes were upon Joseph.

"I know, Zachariah. It will be hard for me... to send him off alone, to say goodbye to him... so hard for me."

"The moment we knew in our hearts would eventually come has arrived, Shimei, and we should be glad. Joseph is going to the Holy Land, to his Uncle Abraham and, don't forget, his brothers are already there. We must send a message to Abraham letting him know that Joseph will reach Tel Aviv in twenty five days."

Zachariah and Uncle Abraham had long ago agreed on the meeting place; all they needed to do now was tell him the date of arrival.

"We have to prepare clothing and food for Joseph," said Shimei, still contemplating the coming separation.

Friday, just before sunset, Shimei finished preparing the Sabbath meal and went to rest. She was waiting for Zachariah and Joseph to return from the synagogue for the evening meal. The house was clean and the Sabbath candles lit. On the table she'd placed a bottle of Kiddush wine, for the blessing recited over wine or grape juice to sanctify the Shabbat, and the special glasses, as well as two loaves of challah, the traditional Jewish leavened bread, covered with a cloth.

Zachariah and Joseph arrived home and came to the dinner table scrubbed clean and dressed in white. Zachariah, as on every Sabbath night, burst into the song: "Where will you find such a woman of valor," and, together with Joseph, they sang a song of praise for his wife. Zachariah sat at the head of the table, Joseph on his left and Shimei on his right. At the end of the song Zachariah rose, followed by the other two. He raised a glass of wine and blessed the Sabbath, took a sip, and passed the glass to Joseph to drink from and then to Shimei. He raised the two challahs with his two hands, holding them back-to-back and said the blessing. He then broke off a piece, sprinkled it with a little salt, and put it in his mouth; he broke off another piece for Shimei and another for Joseph. As soon as Zachariah and Joseph sat down, Shimei began serving them all soup. They ate in silence. Joseph gazed wide-eyed at the silence around him and at Zachariah and Shimei. This evening was different from any other Friday night. He sensed the tension around the table but had no idea that, just a few minutes later, Zachariah would tell him that this was the night he would be leaving them.

They finished supper and Zachariah and Joseph said the blessing after the meal. Afterwards, Shimei sat down at the table, which she didn't normally do, and looked at Zachariah. Holding out her hands to Joseph, she asked him to put his hands in hers. Zachariah looked at Shimei and then at Joseph.

"Joseph my boy, it is time for you to go to the Holy Land..."

Joseph stared at him in disbelief. From the day he had arrived at their door, they had always been clear with him that they would care for him until the day came when he would make the voyage to the Holy Land.

"I understand," he replied, looking at Shimei.

He saw that her eyes shone with tears and, although she put on a pleasant smile, she looked sad. He lowered his gaze.

"Joseph, my boy," said Zachariah, choked up, "look at me... I've been trying to find a way to send you to your Uncle Abraham... I promised to take care of you until you were old enough to travel... and promised to make sure you would reach the Holy Land..."

Throughout most of his emotional speech, Joseph eyes were upon Zachariah, as he'd requested. Occasionally, he took a glance at Shimei.

"Joseph, my boy... the day has come. I've taken care of everything."

Shimei took her hand from Joseph's and covered her mouth, trying valiantly to suppress a sob. Joseph continued listening to Zachariah.

"You will set sail on a ship with Captain Johann. He promised me you'd reach Tel Aviv... and..."

Zachariah looked from Joseph to Shimei and back at Joseph, then said in a trembling voice:

"You will leave tonight... board the ship tonight."

"No!" blurted out Joseph, looking down, "I... I want to stay with you."

He felt very uncomfortable saying 'no' to Zachariah. He had been taught to obey Zachariah and Shimei, to respect them as he would a father and mother and not argue with them. Zachariah put his hands on his little head and Shimei rose to embrace Joseph. They both explained that there was no choice, they had to get him out of Yemen, and as quickly as possible. They had to honor the promise they'd made: to keep him out of danger and make sure that he would safely reach the Holy Land.

"There is no danger there of your being converted to Islam," they explained, "everything is ready, the ship sets sail tonight from Aden to Tel Aviv. The Captain is waiting for you and will watch over you until you reach Tel Aviv. It will be an exciting voyage."

Joseph neither responded nor interrupted. He listened helplessly. What else could he do? Vague pictures arose in his mind – his mother whom he'd left behind, his brothers who had already reached the Holy Land and his sister, Salma, who'd stayed Mamma. These memories made him homesick.

"When will I see you again?"

"We don't know. First and foremost, you must leave Yemen and get to the Holy Land... after that, we'll see what happens..." responded Zachariah.

Shimei caressed Joseph's arm and then went to his room to pack for him. Zachariah remained with him for a long time, stroking his head and comforting him. When night fell, Zachariah urged them all to hurry; he didn't want to be late. At the door, Shimei hugged Joseph. Tears choked her, she hugged him tightly and couldn't let go.

"Joseph, my boy, you are a good and wise child... you will prosper. Take care of yourself...may God be with you, all the way to the Holy Land and thereafter."

Joseph kissed her and then, holding Zachariah's hand, the two began to walk up the road and to the port and Johann. Once at the port, they met the captain. Zachariah handed over Joseph's large suitcase and, bending down, he placed his hands on the boy's head and blessed him, reciting the Traveler's Prayer:

"May it be Your will, Lord, our God and the God of our ancestors, that You lead us toward peace, guide our footsteps toward peace, and make us reach our desired destination for life, gladness, and peace. May You rescue us from the hand of every foe, ambush along the way, and from all manner of punishments that assemble to come to earth. May You send blessing in our handiwork, and grant us grace, kindness, and mercy in Your eyes and in the eyes of all who see us. May You hear the sound of our humble request because You are God Who hears prayer requests. Blessed are You, Lord, Who hears our prayer... Amen."

Joseph repeated after him: "Amen."

"Johann... Joseph is now in your care. Look after him and get him safely to the Holy Land."

"Don't worry," replied Johann, taking Joseph to the gangway.

The two went up the gangway, leaving Zachariah on the dock. From time to time, Joseph turned to look at him. When they reached a large door, Joseph looked back once again and could still see Zachariah standing there. He waved until he saw Zachariah's hand waving back. Then he turned and entered the ship together with Johann. Johann led Joseph through long passages in the belly of the ship until they reached the living quarters. Lifting Joseph's suitcase onto one of the bunks, he told him:

"Joseph, this is where you'll be sleeping until we reach Tel Aviv."

Pointing at the door next to Joseph's bunk, he said:

"My cabin is through there, that's where I sleep. If there's a problem, you call me. And now, come with me and I'll show you the ship."

Although Johann spoke only English, Joseph understood, although not every word. His long stay in Aden and his relations with the British there enabled him to understand and speak a basic, broken English.

Johann began to walk away from the living quarters and Joseph followed him. Along the way, he showed Joseph the toilets and showers. On they went, turning right and left, going up narrow stairs, opening doors; as they walked, Johann gave instructions to several sailors they encountered on the way. After a few minutes, they went out on deck where they could see the lights of the port and the sea, which was black at that late hour. Johann pulled Joseph forward and explained what they could see from the ship.

He pointed up at the bridge and said: "Most of the time, I'll be up there, it's where I navigate the ship."

He turned to look out at the harbor and explained to Joseph how the boats are anchored and how they leave port. He continued and pointed at the exit from the port to the sea. Because it was night, Joseph could barely see the opening.

"You see, Joseph, that's where we'll go out to the huge and wonderful sea. I promise you will enjoy the voyage. Don't worry, I will take care of you. Come on, let's go up to the bridge and make sure that everything is ready to set sail. We are due to leave in half an hour."

Together they went towards the nearest steps and up to the bridge. There, they found several busy sailors. When the two came up, all the sailors turned around to them, and saluted Johann. He returned a quick salute. Joseph also stood still and saluted everybody. The sailors smiled.

Johann also laughed, saying: "You don't have to salute, you're my guest. Everyone, this is Joseph. He will be our guest for the voyage and I'm asking you to help him get comfortable and settled. This is his first voyage."

The sailors nodded understandingly. It was clear to Joseph that they all had great respect for Johann.

"Feel at home, Joseph. You can wander around here, just don't touch anything... understood?"

Joseph nodded. Johann walked among the sailors, checking, noting, and giving orders, before finally taking his seat in a large wooden armchair in the center, huge windows in front of him. Joseph gazed out through the tall windows that were even taller than him. Through the windows, all he could see were the stars in the sky. One of the sailors lifted Joseph so he could see the surrounding landscape. Now, all he could see were the lights of the port.

"Are you hungry?" Johann asked Joseph, still perched high in the sailor's arms.

"Yes," replied Joseph.

"And tired?" added Johann.

"No! I'm not tired."

"I think you are also tired... the sailor will take you to the kitchen, where they'll make you something to eat. Then you will go to bed... it's still nighttime. When you awake, the sailor will bring you to me. Off you go with him. Don't worry, Joseph," said Johann firmly, and continued giving instructions to the rest of the sailors.

The sailor took Joseph to the kitchen and took out cheese, two slices of sausage, two slices of bread, a tomato and a glass of water. Joseph looked at the food in front of him, turned to the sailor and said:

"I can't eat that."

"Why not? Eat, it tastes good."

"I can't... it's forbidden."

"Why?"

"It's forbidden to eat milk and meat together."

"Why?'

"It says so in the bible."

"But we eat it... it tastes good and it's healthy."

"I'm not allowed to."

The sailor looked at Joseph, picked up the cheese and put it away.

"And now?" he asked.

"Thank you," replied Joseph, and quickly ate the food in front of him.

When he'd eaten it all, the sailor took him to the tiny cabin, to the bunk Johann had shown him. Joseph got ready for bed and the sailor left him alone after saying:

"If you need me, call me, I'll be around."

Joseph sat on the bed and read the Shema Yisrael[8]. He prayed, asking to reach Uncle Abraham in the Holy Land, as Johann had promised, and for the ship to arrive safely. He prayed for the safety of Zachariah and Shimei, whom he was already missing. He prayed he would see his brothers and his unknown Uncle Abraham in the Holy Land. He prayed that his mother and Salma would also be in the Holy Land, and that he'd see them again. He could barely remember their faces.

He looked up at the cabin ceiling and whispered: "Help me, Lord... help me." Joseph got into bed and covered up. Tears filled his eyes and he brushed them away with his hand. He imagined his reunion with his mother, his sister and brothers and, within minutes, he was asleep.

When he woke the next morning, he could feel the motion of the ship. His cabin seemed to rock from side to side and he realized that the ship had left the port and was now on the open sea. He knocked on the door to Johann's cabin and opened it when he heard him say, "Enter." Johann was sitting at a desk in his large cabin. He looked up and saw a hesitant Joseph.

"Good morning, Joseph," he said.

---

8. Shema Yisrael, or the Shema, is the central affirmation of Judaism. The prayer expresses belief in the singularity of God, that is, in God's oneness and incomparability. It is traditionally recited twice a day, as part of the morning (Shacharit) and evening (Arvit or Ma'ariv) services.

"Good morning," replied Joseph.

"Come in, sit down here opposite me."

Joseph went in and sat down on the other side of the desk facing Johann. He examined the pictures and maps hanging on the walls behind Johann's back, and the big bed in the corner. Then, he looked back at Johann, at the desk in front of him and at the papers scattered on it.

"How did you sleep?" asked Johann.

"Fine," replied Joseph.

"Did you feel the motion of the ship?"

"Only this morning."

"Some people have trouble sailing, did you know that?"

"Yes," nodded Joseph.

Johann examined the slight boy who didn't directly return his gaze but looked down at the table in front of him. He looked at the small person before him with compassion mixed with admiration. The boy wasn't yet ten years old and he was alone, but showed no signs of fear. A boy who was trying to be mature, trying to be a man who didn't shed a tear, who was acclimatizing quickly, uncomplainingly, to a new environment.

Johann began to explain to Joseph: "The motion of the ship makes some people vomit. I've noticed that you don't feel sick and that you seem to be a strong young man. We'll be at sea for a long time before we reach Tel Aviv, and I'm sure you will manage easily. Time will pass quickly for you and, don't worry, Joseph, we'll get there, I promised I would get you there and I will."

Days on board ship turned into weeks and the ship continued on its way towards Tel Aviv. Joseph's daily routine was consistent. He'd wake early, pray and then have breakfast with the sailors. He quickly learned the intricacies of the ship's corridors, the way from his cabin to the narrow toilet, the shower, the dining room, the command bridge and the deck. During the day, he wandered among the sailors. Occasionally they would scold him, telling him not to bother them while they were working and, when they sent him away, he would move to another area of the ship until the sailors there would ask him not to bother them. He'd go up to the bridge and play there until Johann admonished him and told him to leave. When he went up to the bridge and Johann wasn't there, he'd ask one of the sailors to lift him up so he could see the expansive sea. He would gaze right and left at the waves churned by the ship as it forged ahead. Sometimes the sea was stormy and the waves would beat against the side of the ship, rocking it from side to side. Every now and again the sailors who had finished their shift would play children's games with him, especially hide and seek. In time, once he'd learned the labyrinths of the ship and its hiding places, they had a hard time finding him. There were even times when the sailors would take bets among themselves on who would find Joseph first, and whoever did would take the entire sum. And then there were times when not one sailor could find him and then they'd give Joseph some of the money, keeping the rest for the next bet. Joseph kept the money in his cabin. He quickly became popular with the sailors. They'd playfully tug at his tallit fringes, affectionately pinch his cheek, give him candies and chat with him.

In the evenings, he'd pray the Arvit prayer, eat, and go to his cabin. There he'd read the Shema Yisrael again, get into bed, and his eyes would fill with tears. He longed for his family and, from night to night, the longing intensified. He tried as hard as he could to remember the faces of his brothers, his sister and his mother, but their images gradually blurred and disappeared. Every night he'd fall asleep imagining his arrival in the Holy Land and his meeting with his family.

Johann was like an older brother for Joseph. He treated him gently and with understanding. Joseph felt Johann's affection for him, his concern, and knew he would not abandon him. Every evening before going to bed, Joseph would go into Johann's cabin to say good night. Very soon Johann began to hug Joseph and wish him 'good night and sweet dreams.' Then Joseph would happily go to his cabin to sleep. If he couldn't find Johann in his cabin, he'd go up to the command bridge. If he didn't find him there, he'd search the ship until he found him. He couldn't sleep without seeing Johann before going to bed, without his wishes for a good night.

The days of the week became so jumbled together that Joseph found it hard to differentiate between the Sabbath and an ordinary weekday. Aboard the ship, all the days were the same and all the nights were the same. The ship moved at a consistent speed through the sea and her sailors worked, ate and slept in shifts. There were no formal breaks or weekly rest, no collective prayers or festive Friday night dinners. No synagogue or bible. There were even Fridays when Joseph forgot the Sabbath. If he remembered during the Sabbath, he'd at once change his prayers and keep the commandments of the Sabbath. If he forgot, and the Sabbath passed, he'd ask forgiveness from the Creator when he went to bed that evening.

One evening Johann called for him, sat him down and said: "Joseph, we will reach Tel Aviv next Tuesday at noon."

His wide-open eyes and shining face showed his joy, although he didn't make a sound. He didn't cry out with happiness like most children would, expressing his exuberance to all those around him. His joy was subdued. Johann examined Joseph, again admiring his maturity. That night, Joseph found it hard to fall asleep. Thoughts raced through his mind, but his eyes didn't fill with tears; strong emotions overwhelmed him, emotions he didn't know how to deal with. The day he'd dreamed of for so long was now close – within a week, he'd see his brothers, his uncle and, perhaps, his mother and Salma. Within a week, he'd be with his family.

The week passed agonizingly slowly for Joseph until Tuesday finally came. Dawn broke and the ship sailed on calm waters. Johann called Joseph to stand with him on the command bridge.

"Joseph, in a few hours we'll reach Tel Aviv."

"Captain... when?"

"We'll see Tel Aviv in three hours' time."

"And then what will we do?"

"When we arrive in Tel Aviv, we'll anchor, and you will go into the little room next to the engines… if anyone comes on board to inspect the ship, they won't find you. This is important, Joseph – do not come out until I come to you."

"Yes, Captain. Where is Tel Aviv?"

"Look ahead towards the horizon, where the sea touches the sky. In a few hours, that's where we'll see Tel Aviv."

"I can't see anything…"

"Be patient, boy."

Joseph remained standing beside Johann until the shores of Tel Aviv and Jaffa appeared on the horizon. The first moment they saw distant land, Joseph jumped up and declared: "Captain, I can see Tel Aviv!"

"Yes, Joseph, we'll slowly start to see Jaffa and Tel Aviv, the shore and the buildings."

The ship approached Jaffa Port and Johann navigated her through the port opening to the anchoring harbor. Within a few moments, the ship came to a stop. Joseph had time to part from the sailors who had become big brothers to him and to pack his few belongings. Johann sent him to the room next to the engines, reminding him not to come out until he came to get him.

In those days, the Holy Land was ruled by Britain who'd received the Mandate from the United Nations. The population of the Holy Land consisted primarily of Muslims and Jews. Johann waited until dark before fetching Joseph from his hiding place in the belly of the ship.

"Now we must find a way out of the port without being seen. I don't want to waste money bribing officials. I will personally take you to the address I was given we will wait there for your Uncle Abraham…"

"Aye aye, Captain," said Joseph, saluting him.

This was one of the few times he was happy and mischievous in front of Johann.

"Joseph, this is no time for jokes... we need to be serious now," Johann rebuked him.

Johann and Joseph disembarked and began to make their way out of the port. Johann tried to avoid port guards and the staff. It was crucial that he not to be caught with a small boy and have to give explanations or bribes. Joseph held Johann's hand the entire time, sensing his anxiety and tension during the prolonged wait for people to pass by and then Johann's fast walk, forcing Joseph to run beside him. A few minutes later, they exited the port and arrived at a large street in Jaffa.

"Taxi," called Johann, holding out a hand to a passing car. The car didn't stop. Again Johann called 'taxi' until, at last, a car stopped. The two got in, and Johann said: "To HaCarmel Street."

The driver nodded and the taxi sped away from the port. Joseph held tightly onto Johann's hand while looking out of the window at the changing street lights and quickly passing buildings. Some of the structures looked like those in Aden. Soon I'll meet my family, thought Joseph, in a few minutes, I will meet Uncle Abraham, and maybe Mamma and Samma, maybe Aharon and Menachem. His heart was filled with joy and he smiled as he continued to look out at the passing landscape.

Chapter Eight

Johann and Joseph arrived at No. 12 HaCarmel Street in Tel Aviv, where they waited for Uncle Abraham. The two stood there and waited – Johann in his captain's uniform and Joseph, a boy of nine-and-a-half, long curls on his cheeks, a large black yarmulke on his head, and four fringes sticking out from under his shirt.

On his shirt was pinned a tag, written in Hebrew:

'My name is Joseph Edvy and I have to reach Abraham Edvy at No. 12 HaCarmel Street, Tel Aviv.'

Johann had grown attached to Joseph during the voyage and felt obliged to stay with him until his Uncle Abraham arrived. He couldn't just leave Joseph there alone, although this was the agreement with Zachariah. He decided that until he spoke to Uncle Abraham and made sure he was indeed Joseph's uncle, he wouldn't leave the boy. Johann sensed the anxiety of the approaching parting. He took Joseph's hand in his and held it firmly.

Finally, a man on a bicycle arrived and asked: "Are you Joseph who has to go to Abraham?"

Joseph replied that he was, and tried to translate to Johann what the man on the bicycle had said to him.

Johann told Joseph that he understood and looked at the cyclist, asking in English: "And who are you?"

"I am Ephraim, Abraham's friend. He sent me to bring Joseph to him," Ephraim replied in sloppy English.

"Where is Abraham?" asked Johann.

"A few streets away... I'll take Joseph to his uncle on the bicycle."

"Absolutely not!" declared Johann. "I will accompany Joseph to Abraham."

Ephraim looked from Captain Johann to Joseph, nodded uncomprehendingly, but said: "If you wish, we can all go together. I'll show you where Abraham is."

Johann heaved a sigh of relief. He felt responsible for Joseph and the task he'd undertaken – to safely bring the boy to his Uncle Abraham. The two got into the front of the bicycle, the place intended for cargo, and Ephraim pedaled his way through the illuminated streets under Johann's watchful eye.

Joseph put his hand on Johann's knee and gazed ahead, tense with expectation. A few minutes later, Ephraim stopped and informed them that they'd arrived at their destination.

"Here we are, that's the door to the house, let's go inside."

Johann looked at the door Ephraim had pointed to, looked around and, when his doubts were allayed, he got off the bicycle. The three stood in front of the entrance door and he addressed Ephraim: "Go inside and call Abraham, I want to talk to him."

"Very well," he answered and knocked at the door, calling to Abraham to come out.

A few seconds later, the door opened and a tall, thin, brown-skinned man stood on the threshold. Johann thought he saw a resemblance between the man and Joseph.

"Hello," said Johann, "are you Uncle Abraham?"

"Yes, I'm Abraham Edvy," replied the man.

He glanced from Johann to Joseph and from Joseph to Ephraim.

"Ephraim," said Abraham, "thank you, you may go back to work, thank you."

Abraham looked at Joseph, bent down and examined him thoroughly.

"Joseph?" he asked.

Joseph nodded, then looked to Johann.

Johann felt his hesitation and addressed Abraham: "How can I know for sure that you are Abraham Edvy, Joseph's uncle?"

Abraham felt Johann's question was impertinent and, standing up, he responded reprovingly: "How did I know that you would arrive at 12 HaCarmel Street today?"

Joseph moved closer to Johann. Johann got the message and straightened up, gazed directly at Abraham and said:
"Abraham, I don't know you, and neither does Joseph. I promised Zachariah in Aden that I would bring Joseph to his uncle, Abraham Edvy, and I want to know that you are indeed Abraham Edvy. I hope you understand the situation."

Abraham looked at Joseph, who was clinging to Johann, sighed and muttered confused sentences to himself: "May God help me, and at midnight too... they don't believe me and it's such a big responsibility. Very well, very well, okay. I'll go in and bring a certificate... to calm you down."

He turned and went into the house. Although Abraham hadn't invited them in, Johann pulled Joseph in with him and, together, they followed Abraham into the small, dim house. On the right was a living room, more a tiny room where several small children were sleeping, probably Abraham's children. When Abraham saw that Johann and Joseph had followed him, he directed them to a very small kitchen on the left, turned on the light, and asked them to wait there. He walked to the end of the corridor and entered a room between the living room and the bathroom, which was adjacent to the kitchen, and returned at once, waving a document.

"Here you are, Captain... here is your proof that I'm not deceiving you."

Johann examined the document, read it, looked at the picture and then at Abraham, who was starting to lose patience. Johann relaxed and stated to Joseph, with a smile:

"Joseph, we have reached Uncle Abraham."

"I'm tired," announced Abraham.

Johann was uneasy. He tried to question Abraham about his plans for Joseph, but the man wasn't cooperative and held him off with laconic responses, all the while sitting there and muttering about the responsibility imposed upon him, about his hard life, that Joseph was a little boy and he had no option but to take him in, about how it was difficult enough feeding his own children and now he'd have another child to take care of. Throughout the conversation, Abraham didn't look at Joseph or express any gladness or affection for the small child standing at Johann's side. Johann didn't like what he heard. He was fond of Joseph and it was important to him to know that Joseph would be well-looked after, that someone would care for him after they parted. However, he understood that he had no choice, he had to hand Joseph over to his uncle as he'd been asked to do. He felt Joseph's hand tightening onto his own.

"Joseph," Johann addressed him, "my boy, from now on Uncle Abraham is in charge of you. My role here is over... you have to understand, Uncle Abraham will be like your father."

It was hard for Johann to look into Joseph's wide eyes. This time, Joseph looked directly into Johann's.

"Alright," he responded softly.

Johann continued to stroke Joseph's head, adding: "Joseph, I promise to come and visit you here. Don't worry... you know I keep my promises. You will be fine here, I promise you. You'll see, it will be alright... I have to go back to the ship now, Joseph... I'm the captain, you know, and I have to do my job... goodbye, Joseph, my boy."

While bending over Joseph and hugging him, he addressed Abraham, looking him straight in the eye: "Abraham, I'm leaving

Joseph in your care, and he is now your responsibility... promise me you will treat him as if he were your own... promise me."

Abraham nodded as if in assent. Johann straightened up. It was hard for him to part from Joseph, but knew he had to do it quickly, no matter how difficult it was. He bent over the child again, hugged him hard and kissed his head. Then he straightened up, saluted Joseph, said "goodbye," turned, and left the house.

Joseph moved to the kitchen door to look out at the entrance door that had closed. He didn't show the feelings that overwhelmed him – he loved Johann. He returned to the kitchen where he'd stood between the adults throughout the long conversation. Now Abraham and Joseph were alone.

They stood there quietly for another long minute, then Abraham explained to Joseph: "We'll go to bed now and tomorrow we will take care of all the necessary arrangements."

He showed Joseph where he'd sleep, said, 'good night,' and went to his room. The bed Uncle Abraham had indicated was a narrow mattress with a blanket on it. A child slept on either side of it. Two other children slept next to the far wall. Joseph, who was tired and emotional, removed his shoes, lay down on the mattress, covered himself and closed his eyes. Thoughts rushed through his mind, making him restless, and he couldn't fall asleep. He hadn't seen his mother, his brothers and his sister as he'd expected, deep in his heart, and he felt profound disappointment. He was alone again, but the tears no longer filled his eyes. It was an hour before he finally fell asleep.

Morning came and Joseph woke to the noise of children's voices around him. He saw the children were older than him, two boys and two girls. They noticed that Joseph was awake and began to ask what he was doing in their house. They didn't wait for answers or remain long beside him. One by one, they went into the kitchen, stayed there for a while and then left the house. Joseph stayed in bed. Nobody told him what he should do. As he wondered, Uncle Abraham came into the living room.

"Get up," he said, "get up, get dressed and eat something. Then I will tell you what's happening."

Joseph got up and went into the kitchen, where he found a woman. She put a plate on the table with a hard-boiled egg, a tomato and slice of bread, and said: "Sit down and eat, I don't have time to waste."

Joseph sat down at the table. He sensed the woman's hostility towards him, said, 'thank you,' and began to eat without praying or blessing the food as he usually did. The woman didn't rebuke him, but left the kitchen. As he ate, he heard the conversation between Uncle Abraham and his wife.

"I can't take care of him, I'm overburdened as it is and, anyway, there's no room," said the woman.

"I had no choice, Joseph is family," said Uncle Abraham, "I don't know what to do with him."

Then the door of the room opened and closed at once and Joseph no longer heard them. A few minutes later, Uncle Abraham entered the kitchen and sat down opposite Joseph.

"Joseph, I have no choice, we will have to find a solution for you."

Joseph looked uncomprehendingly at his uncle. He noticed the woman standing in the doorway watching them.

"I have no alternative, Joseph, we can't take care of you," said Uncle Abraham, looking at his wife.

"What?" asked Joseph.

"We'll have to find a place for you to sleep, study and eat."

Joseph didn't understand a word of what Uncle Abraham was saying to him, but sensed he wasn't wanted. He noticed that the woman wasn't looking at him but at Uncle Abraham, while he was looking at her. The glances between them lasted a while. Suddenly Uncle Abraham got up and announced:

"Joseph get your suitcase and come with me."

Joseph got up, fetched his suitcase from the living room and followed Uncle Abraham to the door. The two left the house and Joseph heard the door close behind him. Abraham took his suitcase from him, put it on his shoulder, held Joseph's hand and began to walk quickly up the street. Joseph trailed behind him, looking at the passersby, at their dress, which was unfamiliar to him. Occasionally, he saw policemen like those he'd seen in Aden.

Abraham slowed his pace and asked: "Joseph, do you understand that we have no room for you in our small home?"

"Yes."

"There's no choice... we've thought about what to do with you," Uncle Abraham wondered aloud. "Do you know that your two brothers are here?"

"Where are they?"

"They don't live near us... they'll come and visit you."

"When?" asked Joseph.

"Aharon has a wife and two daughters younger than you... they live far away. Are you tired? Thirsty?"

"A little."

"We'll be there soon," said Abraham and continued: "do you want something to drink?"

Joseph nodded. Abraham asked Joseph to wait and a few seconds later he returned with a bottle in his hand, took a sip and handed it to the child. Joseph drank what remained in the bottle. Uncle Abraham sat down again next to Joseph.

"We'll be there soon... soon. We'll rest and go on... you know, we don't see your brother Menachem and know nothing about him. Aharon works in construction and can barely buy food for his daughters. He knew you were coming, but we didn't know when... Ephraim wandered about the street where we arranged to meet you many times this past month... finally, he found you..."

Joseph listened intently.

Uncle Abraham stopped talking for a while, then continued: "The last time we saw Aharon was more than three months ago... he wanted you to go and live with him."

Joseph's eyes lit up.

"But... his wife has health problems and he doesn't know what to do... he can barely take care of his own girls and his wife. I told him I'd try and keep you with me... but it is impossible... there is a place you can go to... they'll take better care of you there than Aharon or I can. There you can study, eat, sleep... and I will visit you there."

He stopped with a sigh, and Joseph didn't understand where his uncle was sending him. A relative he didn't know?

Uncle Abraham sighed again, and went on: "You'll manage there. You'll be fine there... I promise you. You'll be better off there than with me and my wife..."

With another sigh, he got up from the bench and took Joseph's hand.

"Get up, come, let's go on. This is hard enough for me... I promised you'd be with me, and I'm not keeping my promise... I can't, I just can't... come on."

He pulled Joseph after him and they continued on their way. After walking for half an hour, Uncle Abraham stopped at a large door on the right side of the street. On the door were the words: 'Golda Orphanage.' Joseph looked at his uncle, at the wide steps leading to the large door, and at the big walls above and alongside the door. The walls stretched from one end of the street to the other and had tall, narrow windows. Uncle Abraham knocked on the door with the knocker hanging there. They waited for a few minutes until the large door opened and a woman stood in the doorway.

"Can I help you?" she asked.

Abraham answered: "Yes, can I speak to the director?"

She took them into an entrance hall and asked them to wait until she called them. A few minutes later, a man came in. He was dressed in black and had a long, black beard, large spectacles on his nose, and a black hat on his head. He immediately addressed Abraham, while noticing the child sitting beside him.

"How can I help you?"

Abraham gave the man in black a lengthy explanation about Joseph and everything he knew of what he'd been through, and asked him to board Joseph at the orphanage. The director took Abraham to his office, leaving Joseph to wait in the entrance hall and examine the place. He heard the sound of children praying, or reading something together, but couldn't see them. After some time, the two returned from the director's office. Uncle Abraham sat down beside Joseph and the director sat opposite them.

"Joseph," began his uncle, "Rabbi Eliyahu is the director of this place. It will be your home, for the time being... if everything goes well and you behave well, then maybe it will be your home until you grow up. They will educate you here... Rabbi Eliyahu told me that if you behave well, you can stay, and if not – then he'll ask me to take you away."

Uncle Abraham got up, looked at Joseph and added: " I ' m leaving you here, and I'm sure you'll be fine... Rabbi Eliyahu is like your Mori."

He looked at Rabbi Eliyahu who nodded in agreement. Then Abraham began to walk alone toward the door, leaving Joseph behind. Rabbi Eliyahu took Joseph to the House Mother, the woman who had opened the door for them.

Rabbi Eliyahu gave her a sheet of paper, which she read aloud and asked: "Is your name Joseph Edvy? Son of Yichyieh and Leah?"

"Yes," replied Joseph.

"I am House Mother, so you must always add 'House Mother' when you answer me."

"Yes, House Mother."

"Good, and now we will get you settled and into a framework."

House Mother pulled Joseph into a bathroom with a chair in the middle of the room. She asked him to strip and sit down on the chair. Joseph didn't move. He didn't understand what she intended to do, or why he had to strip in front of a woman.

"Joseph, no nonsense... undress at once. I want to bathe you."

Joseph didn't move.

"Honestly, you smell bad... if you don't undress, I will bathe you in your clothes, and then you will have to undress... and if you don't undress then, I will call for help, and we will undress and bathe you by force," she said sternly.

Joseph remembered his uncle's words, he had to behave politely and listen to Rabbi Eliyahu. He undresses and sat on the chair in utter shame. The House Mother took a hose and began to spray him with cold water. It splashed his body and face. He shook with cold, but didn't say a word. She stopped hosing him and gave him some soap. He soaped his whole body and she hosed him down again. Finally, she handed him a towel. Joseph was shivering, but still kept silence. He didn't want them to say he wasn't a good child and didn't listen to Rabbi Eliyahu or to the House Mother. When he finished drying himself and sat down, she cut off his sidelocks. Joseph was astounded but didn't react. She continued to shorn his curls, which fell on the ground together with his sidelocks. When she was done, she sprayed him again and asked him to dry himself and put on other clothes, which were placed in a corner of the room – underpants, an undershirt, pants, a white shirt, a pair of socks, a pair of shoes and a hat. She took his clothes away with her when she left the bathroom. Joseph was on the verge of tears but managed to hold them back. In an instant, the House Mother had cut away what had been a part of him all his life – his sidelocks. How could he go about without his fringes or signs? In a single moment, the House Mother had left him alone, without family and without his Jewish identity.

When she returned and entered the bathroom, Joseph was already dressed in clothes that were a little too big for him.

She ordered: "Joseph, come with me," opened the door, and went out.

Joseph followed her. They turned right into a narrow corridor, toward a staircase. At the top of the stairs, they again turned right, passing several doors on their right and left, until they reached the last door in the corridor. There, the House Mother stopped, opened the door and instructed Joseph to enter the room with her. Inside were four double bunk beds, eight beds in all.

She put her hand on the top bunk in the far corner of the room and announced: "This is your bed."

She pointed at the top half of a closet between the two beds and told him that this section was his.

She gave him a small packet and said: "From now on, these are yours. Get ready and, in five minutes, come to my office. It's next to the bathroom."

Joseph was left rooted to the spot, trying to digest what was happening to him. He opened the packet, took out what was inside and laid some of them on the bed, putting some in the closet. Almost everything of his had disappeared the moment he'd arrived at the orphanage. He left the room and went to the House Mother, as she'd asked. On his way, he encountered several children and asked them where the House Mother's office was. They directed him. When he reached the office, he saw a number of children sitting on a bench outside her room. He approached the door and they chorused:

"No, don't open the door."

Joseph looked questioningly at them.

"It's not allowed," they explained, "only if the House Mother calls to enter."

From inside the room came the sound of crying and the children outside told him: "She's punishing two children who were fighting and not behaving well. Our turn will come next and we'll also be punished."

"What is the House Mother doing?" asked Joseph, "how is she punishing them?"

"She hits with a belt or strikes the palm with a ruler, and sometimes on the back of the hand."

Joseph was horrified. He remembered the cane used by the Mori to beat children who didn't study or who disturbed the class. He hated the beatings but the Mori seldom punished him. The children entered the House Mother's office, one after the other, for their punishment and came out crying. At last, she called Joseph's name. He entered the office and stood in front of the House Mother's desk. She sat on a chair in front of him. She explained why the children had been punished and that he'd be punished if he didn't behave nicely and politely, if he didn't learn, or other misdeeds deserving of punishment. She went on to explain how he'd be punished and when this would happen, with a strap or a ruler, and so on and so forth.

"And you are never allowed to leave the orphanage," she continued.

Joseph stopped listening. The events of that day were too much for him. A lot had happened, a lot had been said, he'd met a lot of new people. His eyes became glassy. The House Mother continued to speak but his thoughts wandered to other places. When she noticed that Joseph wasn't listening to her, she said furiously, 'Joseph' and threw a pencil at him. The pencil missed his head by a few centimeters. He was alarmed by the fury in her voice and surprised by the pencil she'd thrown at him. At that moment, he decided to run away. He had no intention of staying in that frightening place. He didn't know how he'd escape or where he'd go, after all, he didn't know Tel Aviv or the Holy Land, but he knew he wouldn't be staying there. Maybe he'd talk to Uncle Abraham when he came to visit, and tell him they'd cut off his sidelocks, that the House Mother beat the children, and he wanted to leave the orphanage.

In the following days, Joseph tried to listen and do as he was told, without questioning and without being rude. He learned to know the orphanage corridors, doors and various rooms, and eagerly awaited his uncle's promised visit. Days passed and Uncle Abraham didn't come. Joseph tried in vain to remember the way to his uncle's house.

Every morning, the children gathered for prayers and, from there, they went to breakfast. Joseph barely ate. Afterwards they went to class, mainly bible studies, and then there were social activities. In the evenings, they prayed Arvit and then went to the dining room, after which they gathered in the hall to listen to Rabbi Eliahu's lesson. After the lesson, they went to bed. The House Mother continued to treat the children harshly, and Rabbi Eliyahu supported her. Joseph's acute senses taught him to avoid any participation in events that could lead to an undesirable encounter with her. All this time, Joseph thought about how to escape from the orphanage, since Uncle Abraham hadn't come to visit as he'd promised. What preoccupied him was what he'd do and where he'd go when he escaped.

After a few weeks, he noticed a back door that opened only when goods were delivered to the kitchen. The truck driver and his assistant would meet the House Mother there. While the products were being transferred from the truck to the kitchen, the House Mother would wait in the kitchen, receive the products and check their contents and quantity. Afterwards, she'd accompany the two workers to the door and lock it again. Joseph also discovered that, every Sunday, the truck arrived in the afternoon. He made up his mind that Sunday would be the day of his escape. About a month after he'd arrived in the orphanage, on a Saturday night, he prepared a little bag with a few things he thought he'd need, and got into bed. In the morning, he took the bag and hid it in the toilet stall nearest the back door. At around noon, he asked the teacher if he could use the toilet. He made his way swiftly, afraid of being caught and harshly punished. He was determined to escape.

Joseph waited in the stall until he heard the sound of the truck's engine, the steps of the House Mother and the creak of the back door as it opened. He waited for a long time, fearing they'd come looking for him. He heard the House Mother's steps, which made him jump, but her voice continued to sound in the direction of the back door. He heard her and the driver talking and peeped out through a crack in the bathroom door, where he saw the two in conversation. When they finished their conversation, they parted –

the driver went outside to the truck and the House Mother walked into the kitchen. Joseph prepared to run outside. He saw the two workers carrying boxes into the kitchen. When they vanished from sight, he opened the door to the toilet and, bag in hand, began to run towards the opening. His heart was beating fiercely and powerfully; he was overcome with fear, but he didn't stop running. He got into the yard and, from there, he ran into the street. As he ran, he looked back to make sure no one was in pursuit.

The street he'd reached was crowded with people. He continued toward the wide street he remembered walking along to the orphanage with his uncle. When he got there he remembered the drink his uncle had bought him and very quickly found the kiosk. There he sat down to rest on a bench, looking back towards the way he'd come. He saw nobody familiar, no one looking for him. Joseph was swallowed up in the busy crowd and, very gradually, he calmed down and tried to work out how to reach his uncle's home. More than anything, he was afraid of the encounter with Abraham, afraid he would force him to go back to the orphanage. After resting for a few minutes, he got up and began to walk in what seemed to him to be the right direction. He walked along streets, some of which he remembered, though not all. He turned right and left and after a few hours he still hadn't found the house. It would be evening soon, he thought, and he didn't know what to do. He was hungry and thirsty but didn't stop his search. Joseph looked in all directions, trying hard to find a familiar landmark or building. He sometimes thought he'd found the house, but realized he was wrong and doubts began to gnaw at him. Evening began to fall over Tel Aviv and dim street lights turned on. Joseph was very tired.

He prayed: "I need help... have you abandoned me? I know I have no fringes or sidelocks, they took them away from me, cut them right off my head."

Not waiting for an answer, he began to ask passersby if they knew his uncle, Abraham Edvy, but wasn't able to receive any help from them. Suddenly, as he was looking around, out of nowhere, Ephraim appeared on his three-wheeled bicycle and stopped in front of him.

"Boy, is that you?" he asked, looking intently at Joseph.

The sidelocks were gone and the fringes weren't peeping out from under his shirt, which confused him at first, but Joseph's huge eyes convinced him that it was indeed Joseph, his friend Abraham's relative. Joseph was momentarily alarmed, thinking that someone from the orphanage had found him. He was getting ready to flee when he glanced at Ephraim and his bicycle and recognized him.

"Boy, what are you doing here?" asked Ephraim.

"I want to get to Uncle Abraham," replied Joseph.

"Alright, Joseph," responded Ephraim. He noticed Joseph's sad eyes. "Come on, get in and we'll go to Uncle Abraham... has something happened?"

"I want to go to Uncle Abraham, please... I'm thirsty."

"Ephraim took out a bottle of water he had with him.

"Here you are, we're on our way... I'll take you to him. In the meantime, drink this."

All the way to Uncle Abraham's, Joseph was silent, despite Ephraim's pleas to tell him what had happened and the many questions he rained down on him. A few minutes later, they reached Abraham's house. Joseph recognized the street and the door. They got down from the bicycle and knocked on the door. When it opened, Uncle Abraham stood in the doorway.

He looked at Ephraim and Joseph and asked: "What's wrong?"

There was no answer. Ephraim gestured and Abraham took them both inside. All the occupants of the house were asleep, except for Uncle Abraham.

Abraham sat Joseph down in the kitchen and asked: "Are you hungry?"

"Yes."

While Joseph ate, Abraham and Ephraim whispered at the side of the kitchen. In the course of the conversation, Uncle Abraham glanced at Joseph several times and examined him. He wasn't the same child who had arrived at his house; something had happened. Where were his signs and fringes? A few minutes later, Ephraim approached Joseph, kissed his forehead, said 'goodbye' and left the house.

Uncle Abraham made up a place for Joseph to sleep in the living room, stroked his head and, when he'd finished eating, said: "We'll talk tomorrow."

Joseph got into bed and fell asleep at once. The next day, he woke late; the children had already left the house. He heard voices from the street and also heard his uncle and his wife talking in the kitchen. He remembered they didn't want him there, but they were the only family he knew here. Getting up, he went to the toilet. When the couple noticed him, they stopped talking.

"Joseph, after you've washed, come into the kitchen, please," said his uncle.

Hesitantly, Joseph entered the kitchen and Abraham sat him down. The woman served him food and left the room. Uncle Abraham watched Joseph eat his breakfast and wondered: what had happened to the child?

"What's wrong?" he asked Joseph after he finished his meal.

Joseph began to tell him what had happened to him at the orphanage. Abraham listened, occasionally encouraging Joseph to go on. Joseph didn't leave anything out. He didn't cry or sob as he spoke. From time to time, he looked into his uncle's eyes, but immediately looked down.

Uncle Abraham listened compassionately, stroked Joseph's head and said: "Joseph, my boy, forgive me... forgive me for not coming to visit you. I should have enquired about you... it won't happen again, I promise you."

They sat there in silence for a long time. Abraham racked his brain about where to go from there.

"Joseph, there's a place in Jerusalem that might suit you. I've heard only good things about this place... I don't know if they'll be able to take you in, it's far from here and so, at first, I didn't want you to be there. That's why I took you to the orphanage in Tel Aviv, closer to me... what do you say?"

"Will they hit me there?" he asked.

"No, I don't think so but, if it does happen, I will take you away. I promise I will visit and find out."

"It's in Jerusalem?" asked Joseph with increasing curiosity.

"Yes."

"Jerusalem? The Holy City?" Joseph asked again.

"Yes, yes, Holy Jerusalem, where the Temple was," replied Uncle Abraham.

"All right, Uncle Abraham," assented Joseph, "if they don't hit me, then it's all right... I'll be in Jerusalem."

Joseph's thoughts wandered to prayers, longing 'next year in Jerusalem...' and joy filled his heart. I'll be in Holy Jerusalem, he thought.

The next morning, Uncle Abraham and Joseph said goodbye to the family and set out. They arrived at a large bus station and, after a journey of an hour and a half, they reached Jerusalem. As soon as he entered the city, Joseph began to feel excited. Uncle Abraham answered all his questions and told him about the city, which he'd visited many times. He told him about the Western Wall, which was very difficult to reach, about the various neighborhoods in the city, and about the fact that Joseph was able to see Jerusalem and live in it.

"I promise I'll take you to the Western Wall at my first opportunity to come and visit."

From the Jerusalem bus station, they took another bus and, half an hour later they arrived at their destination – 'The Diskin Orphanage.' They entered the building and were directed to the administrator's office. From the conversation between the administrator and Abraham, Joseph understood that there was no room at the orphanage.

Abraham took some banknotes out of his pocket and gave

them to the administrator who, after considering the matter, announced: "There is room for Joseph. I promise to treat him well."

Uncle Abraham took Joseph out of the administrator's office and told him: "There is room for you here, from now on you will be at this orphanage. Joseph, I will come and visit... I'm in a hurry now to catch the bus and get back to Tel Aviv. Don't worry."

Uncle Abraham turned and left the orphanage without waiting for a response.

The first day at the orphanage in Jerusalem was similar to that in Tel Aviv. This time a man dressed in green washed him with a hose, handed him soap and rinsed him. Joseph had a bad feeling; he sensed that this place was like the previous one, that again they'd treat him harshly and punish him. The man examined his hair and announced that he didn't need a haircut. He scolded him for not having a head covering and immediately went to fetch a large, black yarmulke for him, which he put on his head. From there, he led Joseph to a small room where three other Yemenite children slept. They didn't have sidelocks or fringes either. A conversation immediately started among the children. They all told the same story, each in his own way – when they reached the first orphanage, their sidelocks were cut off, they were sprayed with water and some substance they couldn't identify, they were given other clothes, similar to those Joseph had been given.

"Do they punish you here?" asked Joseph.

"Yes," chorused the children.

"How do they punish? With a belt?"

One of the children lifted his shirt and showed Joseph his back.

"You see?" D'you see the welts?" he asked.

Joseph was horrified. The welts on the child's back were red and distinct.

"That must have hurt," said Joseph, remembering the Golda Orphanage.

"It hurt a lot," replied the child, "but it's not so scary. It passes quickly... you mustn't make mistakes. You must do as they tell you, don't fight with other children, go to bed on time and get where you need to go on time... that's it! And then you don't get punished."

"So, why did they hit you with a belt?" asked Joseph.

"I was late three times for morning prayers... it wasn't the first time I was punished. It doesn't hurt that much."

The casual way in which the child recounted the punishment surprised Joseph. The children continued to tell him about the customs there, the location of the showers and toilets, and the dining room. They showed him the little closet for his clothes and helped him get settled. They were friendly and tried to help him as best they could. Joseph absorbed the events of that exhausting day and, when he was told to go to bed, he at once got into bed and fell into a deep sleep.

In the morning, Joseph was woken by the children's voices. He opened his eyes and looked around.

"Get up, there's no time," his roommates told him.

He got out of bed and, within minutes, there was nobody in the room. Joseph dressed quickly and ran out of the room. He saw the last child hurrying to morning prayers and increased his speed to catch up, in time to see him open a door and enter a room. Joseph didn't know the location of the synagogue or where they prayed, but assumed that this was the synagogue. It took him a few seconds to get to the door, he opened it and found an adult before him.

"You're late," he said, "What is your name, boy?"

Joseph told him. The adult wrote Joseph's name in a notebook and took him into a large room that served as the synagogue. Joseph found a place and sat down. They finished the Morning Prayer and then went to the dining room for breakfast. In the dining room were other adults, who directed the children to seats and watched over them. From time to time, one of the adults scolded a child. Joseph asked one of the children next to him what they were supposed to do, and the boy explained the times, the places to get to, and what happened there. He told him about the prayers, the food, the studies and sleep times.

At the end of the meal, the first adult to approach Joseph stood at the doorway and announced: "I will read out the names of children who must remain in the dining room and not go to their classrooms."

He read out Joseph's name. When the children left the dining room, the adult told the four remaining children to go with him to the administrator's office. They got up and followed him, sitting down on a bench outside the office. Joseph didn't understand why he was there, and asked the other three who were there with him.

"We're all here because we were late and so we'll be punished."

Joseph remembered the back of the boy from the previous day and was fear-stricken. He'd be beaten again, humiliated again, and he'd run away again, but to where? He was now in Jerusalem, far away from Tel Aviv.

"Joseph," called the adult.

"Yes," replied Joseph.

"Go inside to the administrator."

Joseph went inside with great trepidation. On the other side of a large desk sat the administrator who had received him at the orphanage, the same administrator who had promised Uncle Abraham that he'd treat him well. Joseph calmed down a bit, for the administrator had given his word.

The adult who had taken him into the room stood beside him without moving.

"I'm told you were late for Morning Prayers," said the administrator to Joseph.

"Yes," replied Joseph."

"Why?"

"Because I didn't know."

"What didn't you know?"

"I didn't know when or where we pray."

"Do you think that'll let you off?"

"No," said Joseph.

"What's to be done with you? On your first day here and you're already making trouble!"

"I'm not making trouble," whispered Joseph.

"What?" the administrator raised his voice, "you aren't making trouble? You are! On your very first morning you're late. There are schedules everywhere and you didn't read or ask. I assure you, this will not happen again."

Joseph didn't say a word.

"Joseph, sit down here in front of me!" ordered the administrator.

Joseph sat down and looked at the administrator. Behind him stood the other adult.

"Joseph, hold out both hands and place them on the desk!" ordered the administrator.

Joseph held out his hands to the administrator who turned his hands palm up. He held out his right hand that held a ruler, raised it, and Joseph realized he was about to strike him on his palms. He pulled his hands away from the desk in alarm. The administrator got angry and instructed Joseph to place his hands on the desk until he told him he could remove them. Joseph didn't move. The administrator gestured to the adult standing behind Joseph and he placed Joseph's hands on the table, holding them by force. Joseph tried to resist, but didn't have enough strength.

"You will now learn to listen!" shouted the administrator and Joseph felt the ruler land on his small palms.

It was very painful. Joseph gasped with pain, but no tears reached his eyes. He didn't cry. The administrator counted the number of blows and, when he got to five, he stopped. The adult released his hold on Joseph, who didn't move. He didn't pull his hands away until the administrator ordered him to do so:

"You may go, wait outside!"

In pain and humiliated, Joseph left the room. The other three children, one by one, entered the room; each of them was beaten and cried; each of them came out of the room in pain, sobbing, and sat down on the bench beside Joseph. It was clear to Joseph that he would run away from this orphanage too. He would run away from the administrator of the orphanage, who had promised Uncle Abraham to treat him well, but who had beaten and humiliated him.

In the following days, Joseph behaved as he had at the Golda Orphanage in Tel Aviv. He made sure to carry out all his tasks, arrive on time and give no reason to be beaten or punished. He learned to know the orphanage rooms and exit doors, but didn't know what he'd do after managing to escape, so he put it off. He tried to find out from other children what happened outside the orphanage.

"Do they take the children out on a trip in Jerusalem, to the Western Wall?"

"We don't leave the orphanage unless relatives come to visit us," they replied.

Despite taking care not to get into trouble, he found himself punished more than once in the administrator's office. Two weeks after his arrival at Diskin Orphanage, he was called again to the administrator's office. What have I done now? He thought to himself, I'm not in trouble and I haven't been late. He was practiced by then. He got to the bench outside the administrator's office, sat down and waited to be called in. Finally, the door opened and someone called him in. He entered hesitantly; the administrator was sitting at his large desk as usual. Opposite him sat a woman.

She rose at once when he entered and addressed him: "Joseph?" she asked.

She was dressed like the women in Yemen – a large, long dress with pants peeping out from underneath. On her head was a hat-like covering.

"Yes," Joseph replied.

"Joseph," she repeated and he sensed the warmth in her voice. He looked at her, and answered: "Yes, ma'am."

Putting her hand on his head, she said: "I'm related to you."

Joseph's large eyes opened wide and he stepped a little closer to her.

"How are you, Joseph?" she asked.

"Fine," he replied.

"The boy feels fine here," interrupted the administrator, and Joseph stepped back at once.

He was still afraid of the administrator's reaction if he did something the man didn't like. The woman looked into Joseph's eyes, looked at the administrator and back at Joseph. She noticed the boy's uneasiness, his step back and fearful expression.

She addressed the administrator: "I'd like to take Joseph out for a walk, I'll take him to see the Western Wall. I promised his Uncle Abraham that I'd take Joseph there. May I, with your permission, take Joseph with me?"

"Of course you may," replied the administrator, adding: "he must be back by evening."

"Thank you very much," said the woman, and she took Joseph's hand and led him out of the administrator's office and from there to the door exiting the orphanage.

After a short walk, when they were a considerable distance from the orphanage, she asked: "How are you?" and immediately recalled, "Oh, I haven't told you who I am... I'm Rachel Azani. You may call me Aunt Rachel. I'm a relative... my maiden name was Edvy. I'm the daughter of your father's brother."

Stopping, she breathed heavily. Joseph looked at her, still sensing the warmth in her voice and in the way she looked at him.

"I know you've been through a lot... Uncle Abraham came to see me. He came to me after he left the orphanage... and asked me to come and visit you as soon as I could, because it's very hard for him... and for an old woman like me, it isn't easy either, but here I am, I've come to visit you. Let's sit down a while on this bench."

She went over to a bench under a tree and sat down, drawing Joseph down beside her.

"How are you? Tell me how you're getting on here. How are your studies going? she asked.

"Alright," he responded.

"Look at me, Joseph… don't be afraid. I'm your Aunt Rachel."

"It's hard," said Joseph.

"What is hard? Is it hard because you're here alone without family?"

"That too."

"You know… I live in a neighborhood that's far from here, but it is in Jerusalem… tell me what's hard for you."

"They punish me."

"Well, didn't the Mori punish you?" she asked with a smile.

"The Mori did punish us… but it's different here."

"What's different? They smack you to wake you up and learn?"

"No, Aunt, no."

"What then, tell me."

"They hit me with a ruler and a belt," he said, seeing the concern in her face.

"Go on, don't stop… tell me everything," she said.

Joseph felt comfortable and safe, and told her everything, from the moment he'd arrived at the first orphanage. Rachel couldn't believe her ears.

"That's no way to treat orphaned children," she said in amazement.

For a moment, Joseph sensed that maybe Aunt Rachel didn't believe him. He got up, turned around, lifted his shirt and showed his Aunt the welts on his back from a belt.

"Good heavens, child, good heavens, Joseph… that's what they did to you?" She was shocked, "you can't stay there. You can't. Impossible! Impossible…"

She hugged him to her and stroked his head.

"I'm taking you away from there…this very day. I'm taking you away today… good heavens," she continued to murmur.

"Children shouldn't be treated like that, they shouldn't, it's simply abuse. They're only children..."

They sat in silence for a long time. The whole time, Rachel hugged Joseph and caressed his head. That very day she removed him from the orphanage.

She informed the administrator: "I will inform the police of what you are doing to the children!"

Joseph was very glad that Aunt Rachel had taken him away from that place, and glad he had another aunt he hadn't known about. That very evening, they went to Aunt Rachel's home – a small one-room apartment on the outskirts of Jerusalem. The little apartment had a tiny kitchen, toilet and shower. She asked Joseph to wash and gave him a nightshirt that was too big. She sat him down at the little kitchen table and put a bowl of soup in front of him. The smell of the soup with the lahuhua[9] and fenugreek she served reminded Joseph of home and his mother. As he ate, Aunt Rachel told him that she had no children and that her husband had died many years ago. The two sat in the kitchen, Joseph listening to his aunt – she told him stories about her childhood in Yemen, about her late husband and life in the Holy Land. Very late that night she put him to bed on a blanket next to her bed and she, too, went to sleep.

A week later, Uncle Abraham arrived at Aunt Rachel's apartment. She'd managed to get word to him that Joseph was staying with her. The three sat down to eat in Aunt Rachel's little kitchen. Uncle Abraham had heard from her what had happened when she went to Diskin Orphanage, about her conversation with Joseph and her decision to remove him from the orphanage. At her request, Joseph lifted his shirt and showed Uncle Abraham his bare back and the welts received from the administrator of the orphanage. Uncle Abraham was also shocked.

---

9. Lahuhua: Yemenite Flat-bread.

"You did well," he told Rachel, "I'll take Joseph with me… and this time I will make more careful enquiries before I leave Joseph alone."

"And visit him more regularly," added Rachel.

"Yes… yes…"

Chapter Nine

At Uncle Abraham's house, the days passed in inactivity for Joseph as he waited for them to find him a suitable place. Abraham would go to work and to look for an orphanage for Joseph, a place where they treated the children as orphans should be treated. One evening, Abraham returned and called Joseph to him.

"I may have found an orphanage in Tel Aviv. People say that it's a good place for children, but it isn't religious. I looked for a place where you could maintain your religious customs, but I haven't found one. At this orphanage, there are religious and secular children, but very few Yemenites, most of the children are from Europe and they also speak Yiddish.

Abraham looked at Joseph for a response, but he said nothing, merely listened.

"This time," Uncle Abraham said to Joseph, "this time, I will make sure they treat you well... I think this place treats orphans with respect... I will take you there tomorrow, and will come and visit a week later... I hope everything will be all right."

Joseph nodded assent.

A few days later, Uncle Abraham told Joseph that he'd visited the Bluvstein Orphanage, where he'd spoken with the children, the administrator and the counselors.

"I got the impression that it would be a good place for you.

They'll treat you well. We'll go tomorrow afternoon and you'll probably remain there."

The next day, they set out for the orphanage. They walked for about an hour, and Joseph tried to remember the way. He recalled what had happened the previous time and thought it would be a good idea to remember the route, in case he had to run away again. When they arrived, they went in through an open entrance gate into a large yard with play areas. A paved path led from the gate to the large entrance door of a two-story building. To the right of the path was a large area with play facilities at the far end where children were playing. To the left of the path was a lawn surrounded by flowers. A group of children were sitting on the lawn listening to an older woman who was talking to them. The two continued up the path to the door and Uncle Abraham didn't knock but opened it wide and stepped inside. Hesitantly, Joseph followed him. He examined the door, which wasn't locked, and looked around the entrance hall where children of all ages were running about. From the entrance hall, they passed a counter where an older man sat.

"Where are you going?" he asked.

He directed them to the administration office. They knocked on the door and, upon receiving a response, went inside. In front of them was a large desk where the director was sitting, just like at the other orphanages.

"Welcome, come in... sit down," he said kindly.

Getting up, he pointed to two chairs on the other side of the desk. They sat down and looked around, at the book cases behind his back, at the walls decorated with brightly colored children's drawings, and then at the director again, who gave them a welcoming smile.

"Abraham, is this the Joseph whom you told me about?" he asked.

"Yes, one and the same."

"Joseph, my name is Abraham Scheinzon and I'm the director

of the orphanage. Everyone here calls me Scheinzon and you can too. How are you?"

"Alright," answered Joseph fearfully.

"Don't worry Joseph, we'll look after you. You'll see… you'll be fine here."

"Yes, Director," responded Joseph cautiously.

He still remembered the promises the others had made him, the strict discipline demanded of the orphaned children and the punishments he'd received.

"No," said Scheinzon gently, "no… call me Scheinzon. Not 'director' and not 'director Scheinzon.' It's alright, Joseph. Uncle Abraham has told me what happened to you at the other places. That won't happen here. Do you understand? Do you understand that here we don't give punishments like the ones you got there?"

"Yes, Director," answered Joseph apprehensively.

"Joseph… please say 'yes, Scheinzon.'"

"Yes… Scheinzon," replied Joseph, looking hesitantly at him to see the expression on his face. Scheinzon smiled at him.

"Well, Abraham, let's take Joseph on a tour of the orphanage together and we'll show him his room," announced Scheinzon, getting up.

He approached Joseph, who also rose, and took his hand. Joseph recoiled slightly at the touch of Scheinzon's hand but let him hold it as Uncle Abraham was beside him. The group left the director's room and began a tour of the orphanage. They went in the direction of the counter. In the entrance hall opposite, there were still children running around.

"This is Nathan," Scheinzon introduced the man sitting behind the counter, "he's the House Father and responsible for the whole orphanage. If there's any problem, you turn to him first. If there's anything you need, or something happens, you go to him. I promise you, Joseph, he will help you."

Nathan gave Joseph a fatherly smile. From there, they continued the tour. Scheinzon explained to both of them, particularly Joseph, where everything was. They reached the dining room and kitchen, where Scheinzon introduced Zelda, the cook. From there they continued to a small store room for cleaning materials and utensils where Joseph was introduced to Esther, who was in charge of cleaning. From there they went to another room where the teachers, Sasha and Alick, were sitting. Children's drawings hung on these walls too. Going upstairs, they reached two large class rooms. The corridor led to the other side of the building, where they came to a number of children's rooms. Each room had four beds, four closets, four chairs and four small desks. The walls of these rooms were also covered in drawings. Going down another staircase on that side of the building, they passed through another, wide, corridor leading off to other children's rooms and, on the inside of the building was a large, closed hall filled with chairs. When they reached the end of that corridor, they were back in the entrance hall. Joseph was amazed, and still a little fearful. He looked at the children who were running about and noticed that there were no Yemenite children among them. They were all light-skinned and dressed in a uniform – khaki pants with matching shirts. They stepped out into the orphanage yard and Scheinzon explained about the playground, the times they were allowed to be there, and about the synagogue, which was adjacent to the orphanage. They stayed in the yard for a while, watching the children – some played on the equipment, others with a ball, and some sat on the lawn.

Scheinzon looked at Joseph and asked: "How do you feel now?"

"Alright, Director... alright Scheinzon."

"Good, Joseph, and now let's show you your room," he said, taking Joseph with him.

When they entered the room on the first floor, three children were waiting there. To Joseph's surprise, one was a Yemenite boy. The others were light-skinned.

"You see, Joseph, this is your room. This is your bed, closet, table and chair. And these are your roommates," explained Scheinzon.

He introduced the children by name – Chaim'keh and Ara'leh, brothers who'd been smuggled out of Poland to the Holy Land, and Amnon, who was an orphan from Yemen, just like Joseph.

"Let's go and finish the paperwork," said Scheinzon, and walked towards the door.

Uncle Abraham put Joseph's backpack on the bed and the three left the room and went to the administrator's office. When they'd completed the registration, Scheinzon accompanied Uncle Abraham to the front door of the orphanage, where he and Joseph stood gazing at each other.

"Don't worry, Joseph, I will come to visit, I promise."

"Alright," replied Joseph.

He met Uncle Abraham's eyes with his large eyes, then looked down. He didn't know whether or not to believe his uncle.

"I promise you, things will be good here," Uncle Abraham repeated, bending down to caress Joseph's head, "and, this time, I will visit you to see how you are feeling," he repeated. He felt Joseph's lack of confidence and his hesitation. He pulled Joseph into a hug. "This orphanage is near my home and I will visit you, I will visit you every two days."

Joseph looked up at his uncle, sadly remembering Johann's promise; Johann, who still hadn't visited him.

He asked: "Promise?"

"Yes, I promise," he said, looking at Scheinzon.

He nodded assent. Joseph accompanied his uncle to the gated entrance outside the orphanage. They parted and Joseph followed his uncle with his eyes, wondering if he'd keep his promise, and continued to watch him until he vanished around a corner at the end of the street. Would he really be happy at Scheinzon's orphanage?

That very evening, Joseph went to arrange his few things in the closet allotted to him and discovered that there were already khaki clothing, white undergarments, a sheet, a blanket and a pillow inside. Chaim'keh, Ara'leh and Amnon turned out to be kind children, helping and guiding him about how to get along at the orphanage. They seemed to be happy. Chaim'keh, the elder of the two brothers, was taller and more responsible.

Ara'leh, the younger, noisier and more mischievous brother, was the one who needed looking after. The slim Amnon sat on his bed, which was adjacent to Joseph's. He was the quiet one of the three. Joseph noticed that Amnon didn't wear signs either, neither fringes nor a head covering. None of the three wore a head covering.

"Amnon," Joseph addressed him, "I see you don't wear signs."

"None," replied Amnon.

"Why not?"

"I took them off… don't need them."

"Why not?"

"Don't need them."

Joseph didn't ask any more, he sensed that Amnon didn't want to talk. Joseph remembered very well how they'd forcefully cut off his signs and taken away his fringes. He never understood why; he hadn't worn fringes again and his sidelocks hadn't grown in yet, but he made sure to wear a head covering. Chaim'keh turned over in bed, facing the center of the room.

He looked at Amnon and Joseph and said: "Look… we don't have yarmulkes, hats and fringes. We're in the Holy Land now, in Tel Aviv, and we don't need them here."

"Why not?" asked Joseph, "we're Jews."

"Yes, we're Jews," sighed Chaim'keh, "we're Jews who are being persecuted… we've heard that Jews are being killed in Poland… and we've been here alone without parents for a long time. We don't need a head covering… it doesn't help."

"It helps," whispered Joseph, and asked: "Where is Poland?"

"In Europe… and it doesn't help. It just makes things worse… look at Ara'leh and me, we wore head coverings and prayed… and what happened? What happened? We're alone, like orphans. We haven't seen our mother in ages… and since we've been without sidelocks and a head covering, we're happy. We have Scheinzon, he's like a father to us. Look at Amnon, he came here alone... he escaped from Yemen and he's also alone, without a mother or a father. He no longer wears the signs of a Jew... not one. And he's happy here too. He also has Scheinzon to take of him... we all do." Chaim'keh stopped talking, and added: "You'll see... you'll take off your head covering... it won't make any difference."

Joseph listened to Chaim'keh, as he was older, and gazed at Ara'leh and Amnon. They didn't say a word. He recalled that he'd stopped saying daily prayers lately, sometimes forgetting to pray altogether. Thoughts raced through his mind: maybe there was something in what Chaim'keh was saying, maybe it didn't really help.

It was obligatory to pray, keep the Sabbath, wear a head covering; he was, after all, a Jew. All Jews were the same in Yemen. They all wore the signs of a Jew. It was only here, in the Holy Land, that not everyone wore the signs, not everyone kept the Sabbath, not everyone prayed. Hesitation and doubts continued to plague him. Maybe Chaim'keh was right. He too was without his family. He was alone. Until now, he'd been badly treated at the orphanages. He might be happier from now on, even if he occasionally forgot to pray and didn't wear his fringes and signs.

"Joseph," Chaim'keh addressed him, interrupting his thoughts, "do you know how many prayed and nothing happened? Do you know that every night Ara'leh and I would sit and pray we'd see our mother again, and it didn't happen? We were told they were killing Jews there... and we don't know what happened to our parents. Prayers didn't help us... so why should we pray?"

Joseph didn't respond, but was turning over Chaim'keh's words in his mind. They continued talking for a long time until it grew dark.

A call over the loudspeaker – "Good morning everyone" – woke Joseph from his sleep.

The voice over the loudspeaker continued: "Please be in the yard at seven o'clock for morning exercises; breakfast is at seven-thirty; and at eight-thirty, everyone must be in class. Good morning, everyone."

Joseph hurriedly got dressed. He noticed that Chaim'keh helped his brother and Amnon to dress.

"Do we go and pray first?" he asked.

The three looked at him in surprise.

"We don't pray anymore," replied Chaim'keh, "we're going to the yard for morning exercises."

Joseph remembered their conversation of the previous evening and nodded. He left the room and headed for the synagogue. On the way he met Nathan, the House Father, and they went to pray Morning Prayers together. The synagogue was unlike any prayer house he'd ever been in. The hall was large, its windows were ornate, and chairs were arranged at counters, in complete contrast to what he'd known in Yemen, where everything was small and narrow with long benches. Ten Yemenite synagogues could fit into this hall, thought Joseph.

Nathan handed him a Sidur[10] prayer book, sat him down on one of the chairs and said: "Later, I'll find you an empty place that will be your own comfortable spot."

Only then did Joseph notice that some of the spots were allocated, with names. Opening the Sidur, he saw that it was different. Joseph paged through, immediately finding the 'Shacharit,' the Morning Prayer. Although he knew all the prayers by heart, he began to read the prayer aloud with the Yemenite trill. The children around him stopped praying and looked at him. He didn't notice, continuing to pray aloud.

One of the children nearest him touched him and said: "Read the prayer in a whisper or in silence."

Joseph fell silent and raised his head to look around. Then he heard the cantor reading the prayer aloud, and all those present repeated certain parts after him, responding with 'amen' to others.

---
10. Sidur, meaning 'order' in Hebrew, is a time-based order of daily prayers and contains the Sabbath liturgy for the whole year.

He had difficulty understanding what was read – this version of the prayer was foreign to him. The words were in Hebrew, but not the Yemenite Hebrew he knew.

Occasionally there were words in a strange language, which he later understood were Yiddish; however, he fully understood some of the words, since the pronunciation was somewhat similar to Yemenite prayers. He read the prayer quietly in Yemenite Hebrew while listening to the Cantor and trying to keep up with the pace of the prayer, so he could pray with everyone.

When prayers were over, Joseph ran to the exercise yard and got there on time. He found Chaim'keh with Ara'leh and Amnon. They waved him over to stand with them. All the children were standing in lines facing Scheinzon, who stood on a little stage at the front of the yard.

"Hands up, to the sides, forwards," instructed Scheinzon through the loudspeaker, and everyone obeyed.

They exercised for some time, until Scheinzon announced: "Morning exercises are over. Good morning and good appetite. No running..."

The children quickly went to the dining room. Joseph sat down to eat with his roommates. Unlike the previous orphanages he'd been in, Joseph enjoyed his breakfast. From the dining room, the children went to their classrooms. Ara'leh and Amnon went to one classroom and Chaim'keh took Joseph to his classroom, explaining to him that they would be studying together. Chaim'keh acted as elder brother to both Ara'leh and Amnon, and took Joseph under his wing as well. Being seated next to him, and having his guidance and protection, gave Joseph a good feeling, one he hadn't had for a long time.

Days followed days, weeks followed weeks, and months went by. Uncle Abraham's visits diminished. The more he saw that Joseph was managing at the orphanage, making friends, and that Scheinzon and the staff treated the children with love and respect, the less frequently he checked on him. Joseph was adapting well to the orphanage. He tried to pray regularly, but occasionally skipped prayers. He tried to keep the Sabbath, although his roommates didn't. There were times when Joseph didn't keep the Sabbath either, but he always wore his yarmulke. He no longer wore fringes, nor did he grow his sidelocks. He quickly learned to pray like the others – a little in Yiddish, and the rest in local Hebrew. He excelled at all his studies and, in his free time, he played in the yard with his friends. He felt this orphanage had become his home and his family.

As Joseph's thirteenth birthday approached, Scheinzon asked to meet with him. Several other children his age, from his class, were already seated outside his office. Joseph knew that he would be included in this year's Bar Mitzvah[11] ceremony. The children were invited to enter Scheinzon's office, where he began to explain the meaning of being a 'bar mitzvah' and the coming ceremony:

"Until today, you have been children. From the day of your Bar Mitzvah, you will be grownups, and responsible for your actions. Remember that. From the day of the ceremony, you will be adults, and I expect you to behave accordingly. If any of you have relatives you wish to invite, see Nathan and he will take care of the invitation to the ceremony."

He paused for a moment, took a sip of water and continued: "Every year, I choose a Bar Mitzvah boy to read the Haftarah[12]. This year, I have chosen Joseph, on condition he reads the Yemenite version of the portion. It's time we all hear how the Yemenite Hebrew sounds..."

The astounded Joseph blurted out: "I can't."

"You can, Joseph, I promise you that you can," responded Scheinzon, looking affectionately at him.

"I've forgotten..."

---

11. Bar Mitzvah – the Jewish coming-of-age ceremony. For boys, this is at the age of 13, for girls at 12.
12. Haftarah or portion – Selected reading from Old Testament prophets recited in Jewish synagogues during the morning service on the Sabbath and on festivals.

"Believe me, you haven't forgotten."

"I... I've prayed in Hebrew and read Torah in Hebrew... for... for many years now, but I haven't prayed in Yemenite Hebrew in ages..." stammered Joseph.

"Joseph, this is a privilege, not an obligation. You've received this privilege... I'll sit with you and, if you don't succeed, I'll call on your Uncle Abraham to help us. I'm certain you'll remember and read the portion correctly and beautifully."

"I'm not sure..."

"We'll try, and I believe we'll succeed. If not, we'll do something else. Alright, Joseph?" Joseph nodded. He trusted Scheinzon and believed his promise – he wouldn't have to read the portion if he didn't want to.

"And now, children, go to the closed hall. I've invited all the children to the hall... there's an issue I need to tell you about."

The Bar Mitzvah group left the director's office and joined the other children. The hall quickly filled up with children and staff, who were standing together in a corner. Joseph looked around at everyone chattering and he remembered Scheinzon's announcements in the past. This wasn't the first time Scheinzon had summoned them – if he was gathering all the children and staff together, it meant something had happened.

There was that time when Scheinzon had told them that the Arabs in the Holy Land were fighting the British and the Jews and harming them, and that they must be careful not to wander outside the orphanage or away from the compound.

Scheinzon entered the hall and Nathan asked everyone to sit down.

"I've called you here so I can tell you something important," said Scheinzon gravely. "You know there's a war going on in distant Europe... You know that they are harming Jews. We've told you in class about the Nazis and the other countries who are helping them, including some Islamic countries. Britain is fighting the Nazis, together with the Allies, and the Jews in the Holy Land are helping them as much as they can. I want you to know that the Nazis are also located in Africa. Although they are far away from us, we need to think about what we will do if we ever find ourselves in danger..."

Not one child, not one adult, spoke or even moved. Scheinzon surveyed the full hall, and continued:

"We've received instructions from the British Government about how to act and what to do, and there are also Jewish guards who will keep us safe. The government has promised to protect us and the Holy Land... we have tasks to carry out, and know what actions to take to prepare. I've instructed the teachers regarding which tasks each class will carry out, and they will explain it to you later. Now, if anyone has questions, please ask."

There were no questions and the silence in the hall went undisturbed. Scheinzon instructed the children to go to their classrooms. He gathered the teachers around him and gave them last instructions. The children hurried obediently and silently to their classrooms, sat down and waited for their teachers. When the teachers entered, they began to divide the children into groups, each of which had a task. Joseph was allocated to the group that was to fill sacks with sand. Another group took the sacks to designated places. Fortunately for Joseph, Chaim'keh was in his group. The younger children, guided by Nathan, taped dark paper on all the windows. All that day and the following days, Joseph and Chaim'keh filled sacks with sand until their backs ached from the hard physical work. Despite the pain, they didn't stop until they'd completed their task.

One week later, the children and staff had completed all the tasks allocated by Scheinzon. Then the older children were told that they and the teachers were in charge of the younger ones. Joseph was almost thirteen and Chaim'keh was fifteen. They were responsible for Ara'leh and Amnon, who were both ten. Scheinzon insisted they practice a drill in case they had to get to a safe place and, every morning after exercises, he reminded the older children of their roles, the locations of the safe places, and that they had to pay close attention to the announcements over the loudspeakers.

The anticipated Bar Mitzvah celebration grew near. Even with all their drills and preparations in case of danger, Joseph learned to read the Yemenite version of his portion. Initially he didn't remember the sounds and pronunciations but, within a short time, he was reading his portion as if he was in a synagogue in Yemen. The intensive studies at the Midrash in Yemen quickly came back to him, which made him happy. Every time he read the portion, vague memories of his home in Yemen came to mind: his mother, whose face he'd forgotten, his two brothers who lived in the Holy Land and whom he hadn't seen – he didn't even know what had happened to them. He remembered nothing more.

On the Saturday of the Bar Mitzvah, Joseph awoke with anticipation. He put on his white shirt and went to the synagogue. This time, Chaim'keh, Ara'leh and Amnon joined him. They wanted to be there for his celebration, to rejoice in his happiness. The closer the Sabbath Shacharit prayer came, the more nervous Joseph grew. The Torah reading began, the older boys read the verses with the cantor, and Joseph knew that, in a moment, Scheinzon would call him up to read his portion.

"And now I have the honor of inviting Bar Mitzvah celebrant, Joseph, to come up and read his portion – in the Yemenite version. "Joseph, come up to the stage," called Scheinzon, continuing: "I asked Joseph to learn to read the portion with the Yemenite pronunciation, because I thought we should hear another version, that of Yemenite Jews. Everyone here comes from different places, and it's important to know there are Jews all over the world who have prayed the same prayers and read the same bible for thousands of years... each community in its own way, each community with its own pronunciation... but everyone prays the same prayers."

Joseph made his way through the benches, through the congregation, and heard from all sides, 'may your strength persist' and 'all the honor.' He was nervous and his heart was pounding fast. Uncle Abraham didn't come to the event and neither did his brothers. He went up the two steps to the cantor's stage where Scheinzon received him with an encouraging smile, and placed him in front of the Torah and his portion.

"*Praise to You, Adonai our God, Sovereign of the Universe, who has chosen faithful prophets to speak words of truth.*" Joseph made the blessing in a slightly trembling voice, and the whole congregation said 'Amen.'

"*Praise to You Adonai for the revelation of Torah, for Your servant Moses, for Your people Israel and for prophets of truth and righteousness.*" And again the congregation said 'Amen.'

Joseph began to read the portion with the Yemenite pronunciation:

"*Sing, barren woman who has never had a child! Burst into song, shout for joy, you who have never been in labor! For the deserted wife will have more children than the woman who is living with her husband,*" says ADONAI (Isaiah 54:1-6. The Complete Jewish Bible).

He began to gain control of his trembling voice. He remembered every word, every pronunciation, every verse and intonation, and he read on. After he finished his portion and said the blessing at the end, all the Bar Mitzvah children gathered around him on the stage. The congregation responded 'Amen' and began to rain down candies on the Bar Mitzvah group. Joseph stood there beside Scheinzon, proud of the honor bestowed upon him and relieved he'd managed to read without any mistakes.

One by one, they came up to congratulate him. Chaim'keh was the first to hug him, followed by Ara'leh and Amnon. They smiled happily, grabbed his hands and called out: 'Mazal Tov, Mazal Tov'… Congratulations… Congratulations. Cheerful and joyous, the congregation continued praying until the end, then all ran to the dining room where a festive meal was being served. Joseph was euphoric that entire day. The honor Scheinzon had bestowed upon him, in addition to the acknowledgment of his ability and maturity, gave him satisfaction and joy. He was no longer a little boy who needed to be taken care of, he was a grownup bearing responsibility; and, when his studies ended, he would be going out on his own – to work, make a living and find his place. He'd met others who'd completed their studies at the orphanage and would come to visit from time to time.

The festivities continued throughout the week. During meals, the Bar Mitzvah class sat with Scheinzon at a special table in the dining room and he explained to them the meaning of responsibility and maturity.

"Today you are men, adults. In a few months' time, you will finish your schooling here and go out to an independent life. It won't be easy, but it will be interesting and challenging. Today, in the Holy Land, life is complicated – the British rule here, the Arabs don't want the Jews, the Germans and other countries are harming Jews everywhere, and there are ongoing attempts to bring Jews to this country and establish a state for them, for us... this is the chaos you will meet. We will arrange guidance and explanations for you until the end of the year, before you go out into independent life."

The graduates listened attentively to Scheinzon, taking in every word he spoke. They greatly loved and respected him.

The following Monday, sirens started wailing; at first in the distance but, within minutes – nearer and nearer, and then at the orphanage. Joseph was in his room with Chaim'keh and both quickly realized they had to run to take shelter. They'd practiced many times, this time it was real.

"Where are Amnon and Ara'leh?" Joseph asked Chaim'keh, as they ran towards the stairs and out of the orphanage.

"In the playground," replied Chaim'keh as he ran, "Ara'leh he told me he'd be there with Amnon."

"We have to find them, fast."

There were many children out in the playground at the time. Within seconds, Joseph and Chaim'keh arrived in the yard. Jospeh was the first to spot Ara'leh, who was standing motionless against the wall.

"Chaim'keh, Ara'leh is over there against the wall," shouted Joseph, pointing in his direction, "where is Amnon? Amnon! Amnon!" he shouted loudly.

The noise of the approaching airplanes grew closer. Joseph rushed around the playground looking for Amnon, but couldn't find him.

He continued to call out: "Amnon! Has anyone seen Amnon?"

Chaim'keh reached Ara'leh, took both his hands and dragged him quickly towards the nearest shelter.

"Amnon went outside the orphanage... Joseph, run outside," he shouted in Joseph's direction,

Joseph rushed out of the front gate, looked on either side, and found Amnon standing alone, shocked by the chaos around him and the terrifying noise of the sirens and planes, which were now actually above them. Joseph ran fast.

"Amnon, Amnon..." he shouted as he ran, but Amnon didn't move.

As he got closer, deafening explosions could be heard nearby. Passersby were rushing around aimlessly, shouting and crying and looking for shelter. Joseph finally reached Amnon and grabbed him, pulling his hands.

"Run Amnon, run."

Looking around him, he saw a wall and a small, muddy ditch near the right of the wall. He lifted Amnon and jumped with him into the ditch. At that moment, there was a deafening blast; Joseph didn't know how close it was. He lay on top of Amnon, protecting him, just as Scheinzon had instructed him. Amnon was crying and shaking. Shrapnel, metal parts, cement and asphalt were flying around, and the two shrank helplessly into the ditch. The bombing didn't stop, but the sound of the planes was further away now; and suddenly, there was quiet. Silence. At once, the nearby sound of weeping grow louder.

"It hurts," a voice was heard not far from them. "He's dead," another voice said. And then came shouts and cries for help, screaming and wailing, complete chaos. Joseph raised his head and saw the horror around him. People were running everywhere in shock, while others lay motionless, some covered in blood.

Confusion reigned, and all Joseph could think about was getting Amnon back to the orphanage. He ignored what was happening around him and checked Amnon.

"Amnon, Amnon, are you alright?"

At first, Amnon didn't reply, he was still crying.

"Amnon, everything is alright, get up. We must go quickly and take shelter in the orphanage, it's dangerous out here."

When he understood that Amnon was in shock and wasn't able to respond, Joseph picked him up and ran with him to the orphanage. He went back into the yard and to the nearest shelter, where he found Chaim'keh and Ara'leh, both safe and sound. Excited and afraid, they hugged each other.

"Are you alright?" Chaim'keh asked.

"Yes, I'm fine, and so is Amnon," replied Joseph, examining Amnon again.

He was still holding and hugging him.

"And you two?"

"We're fine... we were worried about you..."

"And the others?"

"The bombs didn't hit the orphanage. I think everyone is safe... I hope no one was outside the compound. What happened there? I heard bombs falling quite nearby."

"It was very close... we were lucky," replied Joseph, looking at Amnon again, who was still shaking.

"It was very close to us, too."

"Yes, in the street outside the entrance gate. A lot of people were injured... what happened here?"

"No, no, nothing happened here. Everyone is still behind the sacks and they haven't come out yet... scary. Remember, nobody comes out until it's safe, those were Scheinzon's instructions."

"Yes, I remember," murmured Joseph, beginning to stroke Amnon's head in an attempt to calm him.

He felt Amnon hugging him hard.

"I think we should wait until Scheinzon tells us over the loudspeaker that we can come out."

"We'll wait," replied Chaim'keh, laying his head on one of the sacks.

After an hour of tense anticipation, Scheinzon's voice came over the loudspeaker. He called everyone to come out of their hiding places and go into the large hall. Gradually, the children came inside and began talking excitedly among themselves about what had happened. Scheinzon stepped up onto the stage and everyone was silent.

"I've just heard over the radio that those planes coming from Italy who has joined the Nazis and that bombed Tel Aviv. Many have been injured and the authorities are trying to reach everyone to give them medical assistance. As I've explained to you, the world is at war, and so, we too are at war. Fortunately, things are relatively quiet here. I urge you to be alert and disciplined and to listen for sirens and our loudspeakers, it's very important. Since the situation still isn't clear, I ask all of you to go to your class rooms, to listen to your teachers and stay alert."

That entire week, Joseph, like all the children, was tense and afraid, every noise making him jump in alarm. Scheinzon continued to sit with the Bar Mitzvah group at their designated table. In his conversations with them, over and above responsibility and maturity, he spoke about the importance of graduates joining one of the Jewish organizations in the country.

The end of the school year was approaching and Joseph was called to Scheinzon's office, along with the other graduates. One by one, they went in and came out, until it was Joseph's turn.

"Joseph, sit down in front of me," requested Scheinzon.

Joseph sat down on the chair facing Scheinzon, who looked at him and cleared his throat:

"Well Joseph, where do you want to go from here?"

"I'm not sure, but..." replied Joseph rather hesitantly.

"Look, Joseph, you're a fast learner and can continue your education in other places that are suitable for your age."

"I'm not sure," murmured Joseph again.

He knew that Scheinzon had his best interests at heart.

"Joseph, Joseph, you must continue your schooling. Education will help you later on, it's important you study."

"I don't know, I think I want to go out to work and make a living."

"I want to explain a few things to you," interrupted Scheinzon, "look, there are several possibilities, one of which is going out to work but, it is my opinion that you should continue your education. You have great ability and easily absorb things. Listen to me, there are two possibilities for you to continue your studies – one, at the Kfar HaRoeh Yeshiva, where you can continue your Torah learning, and I'm sure you will succeed there; and the second is to study at the Mikveh Israel Agricultural School, where you can study agriculture as well as other subjects.

Personally, I recommend you study at the Kfar HaRoeh Yeshiva. You read and understand the bible very well, and you come from a place and a family that preserved the Torah and the Mitzvoth, the commandments, for hundreds of years."

All this time, Joseph gazed at Scheinzon and listened. He debated between studying at the Yeshiva and going out to work and make a living on his own.

"You know what?" Scheinzon interrupted Joseph's thoughts, "let's try. From here you will go to the Kfar HaRoeh Yeshiva, remain there for a few weeks and see how you do there. If you don't want to continue, come back to me, and we'll consider the alternatives. Alright, Joseph?"

"Alright," replied Joseph, hesitant and uncertain.

The confidence he'd gained from his stay at the orphanage was undermined. Maybe this was because, once again, he had to part from those close to him, from people he'd learned to cherish and respect, and from his friends who had become family. Or perhaps it was because he hadn't fully given his consent and didn't really want to continue his studies; he preferred to make a living and become independent – he was a graduate, after all.

Chapter Ten

The bus stopped at the intersection near Kfar HaRoeh Village. Joseph knew he had to get off the bus here and walk some distance to get to the Yeshiva. Scheinzon had given him a letter for the Head of the Yeshiva, Rabbi Goldberg. Two light-skinned Yeshiva students also got off at that stop. They were dressed in all black, with long sidelocks and a hat on their heads.

Assuming they were Yeshiva students, he asked them: "Are you going to the Kfar HaRoeh Yeshiva?"

They nodded and began walking. He heard them murmuring to each other in Yiddish, and began to follow them. They passed a village of houses and continued.

After about half an hour, they reached the Yeshiva buildings and Joseph asked: "Where can I find Rabbi Goldberg?"

Again they murmured in Yiddish, didn't answer him and went on their way. Joseph wandered around the buildings, trying to find Rabbi Goldberg. Fortunately, he met an older man, also light-skinned with sidelocks, and dressed in black. The adult looked intently at Joseph and directed him to one of the rooms.

"That's where you'll find Rabbi Goldberg," he said.

Joseph reached a door with a sign that read *The Rabbi's Office*. He knocked on the door but there was no reply. He knocked again and again, but still no reply. He tried to open the door and found that it was locked. Joseph looked around, looking for someone who could help him find the rabbi, but he couldn't see anyone. He decided to wait, and sat down on a wood bench near the door. Minutes and hours passed. Occasionally he got up and wandered around the office area, but there wasn't a soul there. He sometimes heard students' voices in the distance. The square, the open area in front of him, was enormous – it had several tall trees with paths running between them, and only at the other end were buildings with asbestos roofs. Joseph sat watching the paths and distant buildings. Finally he saw several men exiting the buildings and walking toward him. He got up, noticing that they too were dressed in black. He waited for them to reach him.

"How can I help you?" one of them addressed him.

"Scheinzon, director of the orphanage, sent me here to meet Rabbi Goldberg," replied Joseph hesitantly.

One of the men came forward.

"I'm Rabbi Goldberg, why are you here?"

"Scheinzon sent me to you," replied Joseph, handing Rabbi Goldberg the letter.

"Aha… Scheinzon sent you… he wants you to study here," murmured Rabbi Goldberg as he read the letter. "Come on, let's go to the office and see what we can do for you."

As they entered the office, the rabbi said, "You know, if Scheinzon sent you to study Torah here, I think that's enough. How is your Hebrew?"

"Very good."

"I think you'll get on well here, there are students from all over the country and from all ethnic backgrounds. Students learn Torah, Mishnah, Gemara, and other holy books. They study Torah all day and, at the end of the day, they also study some agriculture," the rabbi shared his thoughts with Joseph, continuing, "each new student goes through a trial period until he is either accepted or not. It depends on his behavior. Is it your wish to start studying here?"

"Don't they learn a profession?"

"They learn Torah, not a profession. A little agriculture, so when they finish here they can go to a religious kibbutz or moshav[13], and can also make a living in agriculture, but primarily, you will be trained to offer religious services to the community you live in."

Joseph knew how to read the bible, understand what was written, and how to pray but, in recent years, he'd grown away from the religious experience. He hesitated. He wasn't sure he wanted to study only Torah and become religious. Why would he go back to being religious? His parents weren't with him, his brothers weren't with him; he'd encountered too many people who were supposed to support him but who had caused him suffering. Ever since he could remember, he had to part, again and again, from the people he loved and ended up alone. He learned to rely only on himself, to decide what worked for him and what didn't. The first thing he needed to do was become independent. He knew he couldn't be dependent on others and no longer agreed to allow anyone else to decide for him. He was a graduate, after all.

"So... that means... only Torah is taught here?" asked Joseph hesitantly

"Yes."

"I'm not sure that's what I want."

"It's your decision. In order to study here, you must want exactly that."

"I don't want to study here," said Joseph decisively.

The rabbi looked at him in surprise.

"I don't understand why not. But, if that's your decision, I won't stand in your way. I will only say that it's a pity," replied the rabbi.

Joseph looked at him, hesitated, and said: "Thank you for agreeing to meet with me and for your help."

"How have I helped?"

---

13. Moshav – collective farm.

"You've helped me figure out what I want to do; now I know."

A few hours later, Joseph stood in front of the orphanage wondering whether or not to go in to Scheinzon to tell him he didn't want to study. He wanted to work. He knew that the moment he told Scheinzon about his conversation with Rabbi Goldberg, it would disappoint him. Essentially, Scheinzon had strongly recommended he continue his studies, and he chosen not to. Finally, Joseph decided to go to his Uncle Abraham, hoping that he would help him find work. He also planned to try his luck with his brother, Aharon. Turning around, he set out for Uncle Abraham's house.

Joseph didn't have Aharon's address and he didn't know where Menachem lived. He understood that *nobody* knew where Menachem lived. When he reached Abraham's house, he greeted him.

"Hello, Joseph, how are you?"

"Fine, thank you... I've finished my schooling and am now independent, you know," replied Joseph.

He said nothing about Scheinzon's recommendation to continue his schooling.

"Come inside and we'll have a meal together."

The two sat down to eat in the little kitchen.

"You know..." began Uncle Abraham, "I know you're asking for help, but I can't, I can barely manage on what I have."

"I understand."

"I have a family, wife and children... I'm barely making a living."

"I understand."

"You should go and see your brother Aharon, he should help you."

"I understand, but Aharon has never come to visit me... I don't remember him. You helped me."

"I can't, my boy... I can't... you must go and see Aharon."

Joseph sensed his uncle's distress.

"I'll manage, but perhaps you could help me find a job? That would really help me."

"I'm barely managing... if you had some money, I'd ask you... I can barely feed my family. Things are bad, and there isn't any work," Uncle Abraham explained again. "I can't help you, and you can't stay here."

"I understand," replied Joseph.

He thought about Aharon – how could he go to him and ask for his help? He no longer remembered him. Aharon knew he was at the orphanage and had never come to visit him. Having no other choice, Joseph made the decision to go see his brother.

"I understand, Uncle... I understand. I'll go to Aharon.

"Good, my boy, good... I'm sorry."

Uncle Abraham packed him some food and gave him Aharon's address. They hugged and kissed goodbye. With his modest backpack on his back, Joseph walked to the nearest bus stop. As he walked, he decided he would go back to the orphanage and talk to Scheinzon, who might help him find a job. He didn't know Aharon, didn't know if his brother would recognize him or how he'd treat him. He'd spent his last years at the orphanage, which had become a home to him, and learned to trust Scheinzon and his close friends. He knew he'd disappoint Scheinzon but, despite the butterflies in his belly, he found himself once again in front of the gate to the orphanage, still hesitating. Finally, he went to Scheinzon's office. He knocked at the door and went in without waiting for an answer. Scheinzon was sitting in his chair, as usual, and looked at Joseph in surprise.

"Joseph, how are you? Is something wrong?" he asked.

"No. Everything's fine... I want to ask your help."

Joseph briefly told him of his decision. To his surprise, Scheinzon showed no disappointment and asked no further questions. He was used to the difficulty some graduates experienced when it was time for them to assimilate into the outside world.

"How can I help you?" asked Scheinzon.

"Help me to find work and, perhaps, a place to sleep."

"What's happening with Uncle Abraham?"

"Uncle Abraham can't help me... he told me he can barely manage, that there isn't any work, and that I have to go to my brother, Aharon, who might be able to help me. I barely know my brother, he's never come to visit me here..."

"He's your brother! I think you should try and meet with him."

"I thought of that all the way here... and I decided not to go to him. I want to get a job and make a living."

Scheinzon looked into Joseph's eyes and saw determination there. He also noticed that Joseph was talking freely and not in his usual brief fashion.

"All right, Joseph, all right. I will see what I can do... in the meantime, find a place to sleep. You know our ways here... come to my office tomorrow and I'll let you know if I've found something suitable for you."

"Thank you, Scheinzon," said Joseph, turning and leaving the room.

The next morning, Joseph reported to Scheinzon's office and he welcomed him with a broad smile.

"How did you sleep?" he asked.

"Same as always."

"Listen, Joseph, I've made inquiries and there might be a place I can send you to. It's mainly agricultural work, would that suit you?"

"Any work suits me."

"I also understood that you can sleep there, so it really might be a good solution for you."

"Thank you."

That very day, Joseph set out again for Kfar HaRoeh. On his previous journey, he slept most of the way and hadn't noticed a thing. This time, he sat next to the window, alert to his surroundings. The bus from Tel Aviv to Petach Tikvah was full and it was a long journey. Leaving the bustling city, Joseph gazed out of the window at the passing landscape, looked at the few trees, at the road with its potholes, and he thought about the orphanage, about his home, the brother he didn't know, and about what was waiting for him at Kfar HaRoeh.

Scheinzon had instructed him to find the farmer, Abraham Kishler. How would Kishler treat him? What work would he be assigned and how would he get along there? Occasionally, the bus stopped to let people get on and off.

After an hour or so, the bus stopped and the driver announced: "Petach Tikvah Bus Station, last stop. Everyone out."

Joseph collected his belongings, stepped off the bus and looked around. He walked into the busy bus station. Just a little while later he was on the bus from Petach Tikvah to Kfar HaRoeh. He arrived at his destination and, just like his previous journey, he got off the bus on the main road at the entrance to the village. The village itself wasn't far and Joseph began to walk along the sandy path. As he walked, he noticed birdsong, the smell of earth and surrounding agricultural fields, some of which were cultivated. As he got closer, there were tall trees on either side of the track and, in the distance, he noticed houses at the edge of the village. Upon entering the village, he met a farmer with a horse and cart who stopped beside him and directed him to Kishler's house. A few moments later, he arrived at the house and knocked on the door.

An older man wearing a yarmulke opened the door and asked: "Hello, how can I help you?"

"Hello, my name is Joseph. Scheinzon sent me to you. Are you Kishler?"

"Yes, I'm Kishler," he replied, examining Joseph from head to toe.

"Scheinzon told me I could work for you and make a living. He also told me I could eat and sleep here."

Again Kishler examined Joseph.

"You're too young and too thin. Have you ever worked in agriculture?"

"No, but I'm hardworking and a fast learner."

Kishler debated. He needed more workhands and his only son wasn't enough to take care of the farm.

"Listen here, if Scheinzon sent you to me, he probably sees in you a few things that I don't," he said, examining Joseph again. "You know what, we'll give you a week's trial here and see how you do and, if you don't work properly, I'll send you away. I need workers who know how to work, and we work hard.

"All right," nodded Joseph.

"Wait here, let me check with my old lady."

A few minutes later, Kishler returned to the doorway holding a bag. He called Joseph to follow him outside and around to the back of the house.

"You see, here on the right is the chicken house where they lay their eggs. Every morning, we collect the eggs and a large truck comes to pick them up at exactly seven o'clock in the morning." They continued walking, and he explained: "On the left here is the barn for milking cows and, next to that, is the barn for pregnant cows who are nearing birth. We have to milk them, clean out the manure, and always make sure the cows are well. Beyond the cow sheds are the orchards. There we grow grapefruit and oranges."

Kishler stopped talking and they stood there for a while after passing the cow sheds and the young orchards.

"You see the orchards in front of you? They're mine and they're young. We have to make sure they aren't diseased and that they get enough water. Come on, I'll show you where you'll sleep," said Kishler, beginning to walk towards his house.

They came to the chicken house, Kishler opened the door and passed through the cages, where chickens clucked loudly. At the end of the row of cages, in a corner of the chicken house, was a bed and a small closet.

"See, this is where you will sleep," said Kishler, handing Joseph the bag he'd brought. "In the bag are work clothes I hope will fit you. Arrange your things here and come to my house for supper. It will be dark soon and you'll need your sleep. Don't worry, the chickens are quiet once it's dark. Tomorrow morning, we'll get up early and start work." Kishler instructed him and left the chicken house.

Joseph sat down on the bed. He wasn't sure coming there to work was the right decision. There was a small space around his sleeping quarters, so it wasn't crowded there. The roof was made of asbestos and Joseph wondered if rain would come into his corner of the chicken house, which was open on both sides to the wind and rain. The walls there weren't sealed, but netted with iron mesh. He arranged his things inside the little closet – two pairs of pants and two shirts, one good set and one for daily wear, two pairs of underwear and socks, and a small towel. Joseph also arranged the pants, shirt and work shoes Kishler had given him. When he was done and went outside to Kishler's house, he noticed the water tap next to the front door.

Kishler ushered Joseph inside, directing him to a little kitchen where there was a table and four chairs. On one chair sat a young man, Zalman, Kishler's son, and standing at the sink was his wife, Zelda.

"This is Joseph," Kishler said to his son and wife. They stared at the visitor and Kishler added: "Sit here, we'll bless the bread and eat."

Hesitantly, Joseph sat down at the table.

Kishler handed him a yarmulke, saying: "Keep the yarmulke, and try to wear it all the time, particularly when you come into the house."

Kishler made the blessing and they began to eat. Occasionally, they glanced at Joseph, examining him. During the meal, Kishler and Zelda talked about him in Yiddish. Joseph understood some of what was said, for he'd learned a little Yiddish from the children at the orphanage. He understood that Zelda wasn't happy about the dark-skinned boy who'd come to their home, and Kishler hushed her, saying that it was all right, he wasn't living in the house with them, he would only come inside to eat. When they finished supper, they made the blessing after the meal and Joseph left the house.

Kishler called after him: "Sleep well because I'll wake you at four in the morning; there's a lot of work to be done."

It was evening and the sky was growing dark. Joseph hurried to the chicken house, took his towel and went to the tap at the entrance. He washed and toweled himself dry and hurried to bed. There was no light in the house and Joseph didn't want to walk about in the dark. He lay musing in bed. Tomorrow, I will ask Kishler for soap, candles and some jute sheeting. He thought he'd fix the sheeting to the mesh in his corner to protect him from the wind and rain.

Joseph woke to the sound of Kishler's voice: "Good morning, get up, there's work to be done."

It was still dark and Joseph could barely open his eyes. He felt so tired.

"Get up, Joseph, no time to waste and there's a lot of work we have to finish before dawn."

"I'm up."

Joseph rose with difficulty, ran to the tap with his towel, washed his face and put on the work clothes Kishler had left him the day before. The old clothes were a little too big for him but the shabby shoes fit him. When he was done dressing, he went to Kishler's house for breakfast. Then they went to the chicken house with Zalman and collected eggs, placing them in trays and setting them outside the house door. From there they went to the milking shed and Zalman began to milk the cows over a bucket, which they poured into iron containers with lids. Kishler gave Joseph a rake and a wheel barrow and ordered him to clean out the cow sheds. Work in the cow sheds continued until ten in the morning. During this time, Kishler met the driver and gave him the eggs and milk, then went to check on the pregnant cows. From there, they went to the orchard. Kishler announced a break and they ate sandwiches they'd brought from the house and drank water. When they were done, Kishler gave Joseph a rake and explained to him how to check the beds around each tree and fix the corners so that, when they were watered, the water wouldn't run out of the beds. Joseph worked from one bed to another with the rake, after which Zalman watered the beds with a hose pipe. Occasionally, Joseph was scratched by the thorns of the grapefruit trees, but continued working on the beds. After the lunch break, they continued working, fixing leaky pipes and irrigating. When it began to grow dark, they put the tools away in the shed and each of them went to wash and prepare for the evening meal.

Joseph entered the house to find the Kishler family seated at the kitchen table. He sat down in his place. On the table there was fresh bread, cut-up cucumbers, cheese, water, plates and forks. Zelda prepared omelets with farm eggs. She served Kishler and Zalman and gave Joseph a small portion of eggs.

Kishler looked at her, at Joseph's plate, then said in Yiddish: "That's no way to behave. Joseph needs to be strong, and we must give him the same amount of food as Zalman, no more and no less."

Joseph understood but was silent. Chastened, Zelda added more of the omelet to Joseph's plate and sat down. Joseph asked Kishler for soap, candles and jute sheeting.

Kishler replied: "I'll get you soap, you don't need candles. The jute you'll get in the autumn."

Joseph finished his meal and left Kishler's house slightly depressed.

The days and nights passed swiftly. Joseph got up every morning before dawn and worked all day until dark. In the evening, he slept in the chicken house – as Kishler said, the chickens were quiet at night. Kishler was satisfied with Joseph's work and, every Friday, paid him one lira for a week's work, which was barely enough to travel to the orphanage. Occasionally, on a Friday, Joseph would visit the orphanage and was always welcomed with open arms. The orphanage and its occupants were still his home and the only family he had.

On one of his visits to the orphanage, Scheinzon noticed that Joseph arrived in shabby clothes. Joseph explained to Scheinzon that these were the only work clothes Kishler had given him and that his earnings weren't enough to buy clothes. Scheinzon decided to buy him new work clothes. Happy and light-hearted, Joseph returned to Kishler's farm at Kfar HaRoeh. Kishler noticed the new clothes and asked Joseph how he'd got them, knowing that he didn't pay him enough to buy clothes. Joseph explained to him, but Kishler wasn't convinced. He thought Joseph had come by the clothing dishonestly, and even said what he thought. Joseph was very insulted by Kishler's accusation. He was as angry with Kishler as he was with Zelda for how she treated him. However, he didn't say a word.

One Friday when Joseph didn't go to the orphanage, Kishler sent him to the store to buy some things for the house. It was the first time he'd gone to the store. Until then, he'd only stayed at the farm or gone to the bus stop at the intersection. The little store was built on a hill at the edge of the moshav, which was reached by a dirt track. Joseph walked along the sandy path and began to climb the hill. Near the door to the store sat an elderly Yemenite shoemaker. He was surrounded by tools but he wasn't busy at the time, just watched as Joseph approached the store.

When he arrived, the old man addressed him: "I see your shoes need mending."

"They're fine," replied Joseph.

He knew he couldn't pay to have his shoes mended.

"Come closer," said the old man in Yemenite, and Joseph didn't quite understand what he said but did step closer.

"Don't you understand Yemenite?" asked the old man in Hebrew, "you're a Yemenite, aren't you?"

"Yes, I'm Yemenite, but I can barely remember the language."

"Come to me," continued the old man, "a little closer." Josef stepped towards him until he was standing beside him. "Let me see your face."

Joseph leaned over the old man, looked into his face and immediately looked down. The man before him evoked old memories, a faint sense of home, of family.

"Look at me," said the old man, taking Joseph's chin in his hand and turning his face upward so he could see him better.

"Are you Yichyieh Edvy's son?" he asked heavily and Joseph, surprised, was struck dumb. "Answer me," requested the old man, but Joseph remained silent.

He was very excited and, finally, murmured: "Yes, I think so."

"You have two older brothers who came to this country, and a sister who remained with your mother in Yemen, right?"

"Yes," replied Joseph, his eyes filling with tears.

It was the first time that anyone had referred to his immediate family, and those who had remained in Yemen. He couldn't remember his mother and had forgotten that he had a sister.

"You're Yichyieh's son, continued the old man, "Yichyieh Edvy's son, may he rest in peace. I knew your father. He was a good man and a great Torah scholar. What are you doing here in this country?"

"I was sent here."

"Where are your signs?"

"They were cut off... I haven't regrown them since then."

They sat there in silence for some time, and Joseph told him a little about his hard work. The old man asked questions, told him something about his own life in the community, and where some of the families were living. He invited Joseph to come for Friday night dinner and, perhaps, spend the Sabbath with them.

"Take off your shoes and I'll mend them for you. Don't worry, I'll mend them in honor or your father, and won't take payment for it."

Joseph took off his shoes and thanked the old man for his help. When he returned to Kishler's house with the shopping, Kishler looked at the mended, cleaned shoes and asked:

"Now what, how come you have new shoes?"

"There was an old Yemenite man at the store. He knew my father in Yemen, and he mended the shoes and shone them too. They look new." said Joseph with a satisfied smile.

Kishler looked at him and blurted out in Yiddish: "That's impossible, that story can't be true, it's a lie."

"I'm not a liar," replied Joseph in Hebrew.

"Did you understand what I said?" asked Kishler in surprise.

"Yes, I understood," replied Joseph.

Kishler was angry with himself and with Joseph for understanding what he and his wife had been saying and not letting on. He was angry with Joseph for coming back with a fictional story and new shoes, in addition to the story about Scheinzon buying him new clothes.

He grasped Joseph's ear, held it tightly and said: "Come with me right now to the store. I don't believe you. We will go there right now together and check with the shoemaker."

They walked all the way back to the store, Kishler leading Joseph painfully by the ear.

"Is that the old man?" Kishler asked Joseph, when they reached the store.

"Yes," muttered Joseph.

Humiliated and in pain, he looked at the old Yemenite who was still sitting there with no work.

"Do you know him?" Kishler addressed the old man.

"And who are you? Why are you holding the boy by the ear?" scolded the old man.

"Do you know him?" asked Kishler again.

"I knew his father in Yemen and today I met the boy. Why are you still hurting him? What has he done?"

Kishler let go of Joseph's ear, and asked: "Joseph told me that you mended his shoes, is that true?"

"It is," answered the old man.

"And you didn't ask for payment?"

"I did not, I mended his shoes out of respect for his father, who was a great Torah scholar."

Kishler stood there, embarrassed, and looked at the old man, at Joseph, back at the old man and again at Joseph. He realized he'd made a big mistake.

"Thank you, and I apologize," said Kishler to the old man and, taking some money from his pocket, he held it out and said: "A reward for a mitzvah – a good deed."

Turning around, he began to make his way back to the house, his head bowed. Joseph followed, at a distance. He knew there was nothing for him at Kishler's farm – working from morning till night was very hard, Zelda didn't particularly like him, making him feel that he wasn't wanted, and Zalman was a strange young man; Kishler didn't trust or believe him, speaking to and treating him as if he were one of the animals on his farm. Joseph remembered Kishler's last words to the old man: "A reward for a mitzvah – a good deed," and thought to himself: you would have performed a very great mitzvah, if you'd only mended my torn shoes. That's it, I've made up my mind – I'm leaving. I'm leaving that house and the hard labor, and I'll find something else, something better.

When they got back to the house, Joseph went to the chicken house and put his things in a bag. He took his work clothes too, and also packed his work shoes. They no longer belonged to Kishler, they were his. He went to Kishler's house, informed him that he was leaving and asked for the payment owed him for the days he'd worked. After receiving what he was owed, he said goodbye and set off into the settlement. Joseph went from farm to farm looking for work and asking about work conditions. All the farmers, who were religious, gave him the same answer – the work was similar to what he'd done for Kishler, and the conditions were all the same, one lira a week, working from morning till night, and the same living conditions in the chicken house. Joseph realized he had to stop looking for work in the way he'd been doing. He realized that the farmers couldn't care for their farms alone and needed farm hands, and it was hard to find good workers who would do the work quickly and efficiently. He started going around the farms again, offering them contract work – some of the work had to be done within a certain time frame and fast, like planting trees, sowing potatoes in large areas and picking them, etc. Fortunately, he met a farmer with twenty five dunams who needed help with his potatoes and who had no workers. The farmer suggested that Joseph take full responsibility for managing the twenty five dunams and grow potatoes in return for two hundred lira. Joseph calculated and discovered that it took two to three months to sow and pick potatoes, and immediately agreed.

But then he farmer added: "I need more workers. If you want the work, you will have to find the workers," said the farmer, "and I will pay them."

Joseph agreed and they shook hands. It was October and the sowing time was short – it had to be done by mid-November, when the rainy season was at its peak. Over the coming days, Joseph found workers. He worked from morning till night and slept in the farmer's chicken house until he finished the sowing. The farmer was satisfied and paid Joseph one hundred lira.

"I'll pay you the other hundred lira," he said, "after the potatoes are harvested."

Joseph was satisfied and proud of himself. It was his first agricultural job and he'd succeeded. He had to wait two-three months, and pray for rain to do its job, so the potatoes would be large and good to eat. While he waited, Joseph decided to visit his brother Aharon for the first time since coming to the Holy Land. He bought vegetables, fruit and eggs for a nominal price, put them in a large suitcase and went to visit his brother. He knew he'd be fined if he was caught; after all, it was forbidden to trade large quantities of vegetables. The farmers had to sell their produce to legal organizations who would then resell to venders in the city. Joseph knew that Aharon barely made a living, and that he had a wife and two little girls, so it was important that he arrive with a full suitcase, despite the risk. He reached the Mahane Yosef neighborhood where his brother Aharon lived, and found the house without difficulty. Excited, Joseph stood hesitantly at the large wooden door. Beyond that door lived the family who had not come to visit him all those years since he'd come to the Holy Land. Beyond that door was his elder brother, whom he hadn't seen for all those years he'd been alone, longing for a supportive family. He knocked loudly on the door, the door opened and, in front of him, stood two girls of about thirteen, staring at him.

"Hello," they said.

"Hello," responded Joseph, "is this the Edvy family?" he asked.

"Yes."

"Are your mother and father home?"

"Father," called the girls, "someone's looking for you."

"Coming," a man's voice was heard.

A man came heavily to the door.

"Yes, girls."

Aharon stood behind his girls and looked at the young man before him.

"How can I help you?" he asked, examining Joseph from head to toe.

"Are you Aharon?" Joseph couldn't remember his brother's face.

"Yes," responded Aharon, still examining him, "how can I help you?"

Joseph looked intently into his brother's face and tried to find some familiar feature, but failed.

"Aharon, I'm your little brother, Joseph."

Aharon gazed intently at Joseph, at his shy, smiling face.

"You're my brother, Joseph?" he asked, a tremor in his voice.

He'd recognized Joseph, but stood there motionless.

"Yes, I'm Joseph, yours and Menachem's brother."

"Come in, come in, let me hug you, let me kiss you."

Joseph approached him and Aharon pulled him into a hug and

kissed him three times, pushed him away, gazed into his face, and passed his hands over Joseph's head and face.

"Let's go inside… Esther, Mazal, come inside," he instructed his girls who were standing there wordless.

Going into the little kitchen, they sat down at the table. Aharon held Joseph and, with tear-filled eyes, told him he wasn't very well, and that his wife was very ill and could barely function. Joseph opened up the suitcase, took out the produce, and Esther and Mazal helped him put it all away. Despite his anger, he didn't ask Aharon why he hadn't come to visit him. He felt his questions were unnecessary. He looked around, and saw that his brother lived in poverty. He could barely take care of himself, his wife and his girls. He didn't remember Aharon, and felt almost nothing for his brother. At that moment, he decided to end the meeting as soon as possible. He didn't know if it was his anger at his brother for abandoning him, the fact that he didn't know him at all or, perhaps, a sense of profound shyness that made him get up so fast.

"I have to go now," he said.

"I understand," said Aharon, "promise me you'll come and visit us," he added.

"I promise." Joseph went to Aharon and hugged him, then he also hugged Esther and Mazal, "I promise I'll come and visit again," he said and left the house.

Joseph kept his promise and, in the course of the months he spent waiting for the harvesting season, he visited his brother twice, laden with produce. Aharon was glad to receive the produce – some of which he kept and some he sold in the market. The following visits strengthened the connection between Joseph and his brother and his anger towards him subsided. He understood what Aharon had gone through and why he hadn't come to visit him. He got to know his brother again, his daughters Esther and Mazal, and his wife.

When the time came, Joseph began potato picking. Fortunately for him, they were large and good. Again, he began to work from morning till evening, finding workers, and he had to make the deadline, for the potatoes would go rotten if they weren't picked on time. He finished the harvest within a month and, finally, the last sacks of potatoes were tossed onto the truck. The farmer paid him one hundred lira and added twenty as a bonus. He was very satisfied with Joseph's work and suggested he take over the management of a peanut crop in an empty field.

Joseph felt he'd finished his time at Kfar HaRoeh village. He had no friends there and he had reservations about how the farmers treated their workers. He refused the offer and decided to return to Tel Aviv, to Aharon. He was sixteen by then and felt he had learned how to cope with the outside world, to earn well and be self-sufficient. He could be a help to his brother, while making his own decisions. He had money in his pocket and he was sure he could manage in Tel Aviv.

Chapter Eleven

The money he had saved at Kfar HaRoeh had quickly run out and Joseph he realized he couldn't go on living at his brother's little house – the room and a half was already too small to accommodate Aharon, his wife and his daughters. However, the salary he received from the carpentry shop wasn't enough to rent a room for himself. Together with Aharon, Joseph applied for assistance from the Youth Immigration Department who sent him to work for a farmer at Ben Shemen Village. Having no other reasonable options, Joseph went to work in agriculture on the moshav of a religious farmer. When he arrived at Aharonowitz's farm in Ben Shemen, he was emotionally prepared to receive the same attitude he'd suffered from Kishler at Kfar HaRoeh. It was clear to him that this was just a stepping stone to something greater, and that he'd spend as little time at Ben Shemen as he could.

The farmer's house was large and had two stories, which greatly impressed Joseph. He stood at the entrance and knocked on the door.

An elderly woman opened the door and said: "Hello, welcome, who are you?'

"I'm Joseph, the Youth Immigration Department sent me."

"Please come inside, don't stand out there in the cold."

"Thank you," he replied.

The woman asked him to sit down and wait in the spacious living room. A few minutes later, an elderly man entered the living room and introduced himself.

"My name is Aharonowitz. I was told you'd be coming to work for us. How are you? How was the journey?'

"Very well, thank you."

"First you'll have a rest, eat dinner with us, and tomorrow morning we'll show you how we work, what we do and when," explained Aharonowitz with a smile, "please come with me."

Aharonowitz took Joseph around the house, showing him the kitchen, where two youngsters were sitting. From there he showed him the toilets on the ground floor, where they took off their work clothes and where they left their dirty clothes. They went upstairs to the second floor where Aharonowitz showed him the toilets and bathrooms.

He approached a door, opened it and announced: "This is your room."

"Are you sure?" blurted out Joseph in surprise, "*my* room?"

"Yes," answered Aharonowitz, "I know that there are places where farmhands are treated as outsiders, but we like to have Youth Immigration workers stay with us in the house."

"Thank you."

"Well, Joseph, settle in, have a shower, and come down to eat with us. We'll sit down to eat in about an hour," said Aharonowitz and left Joseph alone in the room.

The entire room was made of wood, the walls as well as the floor. The large bed in the corner near the window beckoned to Joseph and he sat down, feeling how comfortable it was. The sheets, white, fragrant, and clean, were stretched tightly over the mattress. Next to the bed was a table on which were several sheets of paper and a pencil. Opposite the bed was a large closet. He got up and went to the open window, put his head out and looked at the view in front of him. He saw several houses similar to Aharonowitz's and, behind them, were cultivated plots of land.

Beyond the houses and farmland was a dirt track, and beyond that – groups of adjacent buildings.

Joseph arranged his clothes in the closet and left the room, where he met Aharonowitz's wife, Ruth.

"Have you had time to shower?" she asked.

"No."

She took a towel from a nearby closet and directed him to the shower.

"Do you have underwear and a change of clothing? See, this is the laundry basket."

Joseph was embarrassed to say that he had very few clothes and underwear, and entered the bathroom. When he was finished, he went down to the ground floor where he was introduced to the whole family – Aharonowitz's parents, his wife Ruth, his son Aharonchik and his daughter Mira'leh, the two youngsters he'd seen in the kitchen, and little Yitzhak, Mira'leh's son.

Without any inhibition, Yitzhak asked: "What's your name?"

"Joseph," he responded with a shy smile.

Everyone sat around at the table, blessed the food, and began to eat. When they were done, they all went up to bed.

The next day, Aharonowitz, Aharonchik and Joseph rose before dawn, and went straight out to the yard. Aharonchik called Joseph to go with him and Aharonowitz went off toward the village buildings.

"You see, Joseph, there are four cow sheds for milking here, and another shed for pregnant cows. We have a large warehouse with a tractor and plough and many other tools in the shed. If you look further," he pointed out into the distance, "you'll see fields. We have a hundred and five dunams of farm land where we grow wheat, barley and clover for seeds. In the winter, we grow cabbage and cauliflower, as well as food for the cows. In the summer we grow corn. Beyond our land is the Ben Shemen Youth Village, a children's boarding school."

Aharonchik stopped talking and looked at Joseph.

"There is a lot of work here, and it's never done," he said.

Joseph nodded understandingly. He wasn't afraid of hard work, but he was skeptical about the kindness he'd received. His experience at Kfar HaRoeh hadn't been a good one, the pay was minimal and the farmers were condescending, alienating and treated their workers shamefully. It was hard for him to believe that it would be any different with Aharonowitz, and he planned to leave if they treated him anything like he'd been treated at Kfar HaRoeh.

"Hey, Joseph, are you dreaming?" Aharonchik interrupted Joseph's thoughts, "let's have breakfast and then we'll go to work. My father has already gone home."

The rest of the family was already seated and waiting for them when the two young men entered the large dining area. The inviting table was laid with home-made bread, cheese, vegetables, butter, milk, hard-boiled eggs, and even omelets. But it was the butter that caught Joseph's eye, and he took a slice of bread and sparingly spread a little butter. Aharonchik looked at him, asked him to pass him a slice and, taking his knife and cutting off a good piece of butter, he spread it thickly on the bread.

He said smilingly: "This is how we eat bread and butter here."

Ruth watched the scene and added: "Joseph, we want you to feel comfortable here and eat as much as you heart desires. We work hard because we have to make a living. You'll be working hard, too, and will need to keep up your strength, so eat, my boy, and please don't be shy."

When Aharonowitz finished his meal, he urged Aharonchik and Joseph to eat up and go to work.

Over the following days they worked from morning till evening – milking, cleaning the cow sheds, ploughing and sowing, harvesting and gathering, irrigating and fixing pipes. In the evenings after work, Joseph would have supper and immediately go to bed. On Friday evenings he would usually stay up later, as it was comfortable and pleasant there and the family accepted him as one of their own. Often, he didn't go to pray and they didn't scold him about it, but they did ask him to wear a yarmulke for meals. At first they paid him two lira for a week's work but, once he'd proven himself as a good and honest worker, they raised his pay every week until they were paying him twelve lira a week. Joseph was satisfied with his pay and with how they treated him. On a Friday or Saturday, he'd sometimes go over to the Ben Shemen Boarding School and spend time with boys his own age. There, he met Abraham Barzilai, who told him his parents lived in Holon, and they'd sent him to Ben Shemen to get an education.

"Most of the students are orphans from Europe," Abraham told him, "and only a few have parents living in the Holy Land."

Abraham was the son of a traditional Jewish Yemenite family; he didn't wear sidelocks or fringes. Their friendship grew stronger. Occasionally Abraham would come to visit Joseph and stay at the Aharonowitz's house, and Joseph would stay with Abraham at the boarding school.

The time had come to harvest the ten dunams of corn, and Joseph and Aharonchik reaped and collected the corn in sacks. Whenever a sack was full, they tied it and left it for Aharonowitz to come and load onto a cart. When the cart was full, he'd drive it to the warehouse, where he arranged the sacks, then returned with an empty cart to the field. Aharonchik taught Joseph how to reap, watching him from time to time to make sure he was doing it properly.

Suddenly, while Aharonowitz was back at the warehouse, Aharonchik addressed Joseph impatiently: "You aren't reaping properly, that's not how I taught you."

"I'm reaping just like you," replied Joseph.

Aharonchik approached Joseph.

"You aren't doing it properly," he said with an anger that surprised Joseph, who had never seen him get angry.

Joseph just stood there looking at Aharonchik as he continued coming towards him, ripping out an entire sheaf of corn and shaking it.

"I am reaping properly," said Joseph, somewhat hesitantly this time.

"No, you aren't," responded Aharonchik, waving the sheaf at Joseph.

Joseph didn't move; he was stunned by Aharonchik's behavior.

Aharonchik waved the sheaf above his head and brought it down hard, striking the side of Joseph's body. Joseph turned slightly, raising his arms to protect his face. Aharonchik continued beating Joseph on his back while shouting at him.

"That's not how to reap! How many times have I taught you, and you don't learn!"

The pain in Joseph's back became more severe and he felt humiliated. He hurriedly escaped in the direction of the house, without looking back. At the house, he met the grandfather and told him vehemently and with alarm what had happened. The grandfather tried to comfort him and apologized for Aharonchik, but Joseph was still upset.

The grandfather tried to explain to Joseph: "You see, Mira'leh is pregnant again. Aharonchik is stressed, because she isn't married. Unwedded pregnancy is frowned upon in the village and it means another stain on the family name; we're already raising one child outside of marriage. Aharonchik doesn't know what he's doing and he's taking his frustration out on you."

Joseph didn't stay, despite the grandfather's pleading. He went up to his room at once, gathered his belongings and ran down to the ground floor. Even before Aharonchik and Aharonowitz came home, Joseph swiftly made his way out of the village without talking to anyone; all he wanted was to get out of there. Memories of the beatings from his first orphanages and, later, the humiliations at Kfar HaRoeh, were flooding back.

As he ran, he looked upward and shouted in fury: "Where are you, God in heaven? Where?"

He had experienced quite a lot in his sixteen years and knew how to control himself. However, tears flowed unrestrainedly down his cheeks. He wept out of bitterness and frustration until he reached the road to Tel Aviv. When Joseph arrived at Aharon's house, he told him what had happened.

Aharon encouraged him: "You did the right thing coming straight to me," he said. "Things are still not good here. I make a meager living, but we'll all manage in this small house."

Aharon slept with his wife and little son in the bedroom. The two girls, who were already thirteen, slept on one side of the family room, and Joseph slept in the little kitchen. All the money he'd earned from his work at Ben Shemen went to maintaining the home, and he couldn't find a permanent job. Joseph grew thinner. Occasionally he'd find temporary work for very little pay, which he'd use to buy food for his brother's family. He didn't visit Scheinzon at the orphanage; he wanted to, but he was ashamed to tell him of his situation. There were times when he would approach the orphanage, look at it from a distance, and then turn back to his brother's house.

A few months later, Aharonchik arrived at Aharon's house and asked to speak to Joseph. Joseph was reluctant to speak to him.

"Aharonchik regrets what happened," Aharon told Joseph, "and he's apologized for what he did. I believe him, please talk to him."

"Joseph," Aharonchik addressed him. Joseph looked silently down at the floor. "I was wrong Joseph, I want you to know that. I should never have done such a thing, it was unforgivable."

Joseph was silent.

"Joseph," Aharon said to him, "tell Aharonchik how you feel. Don't keep it inside, it's not good. He's come to ask your forgiveness."

"I forgive him, I have forgiven him!" said Joseph, leaving it at that.

"Joseph, please forgive me," Aharonchik said gently, "forgive me... I didn't know what I was doing..."

"I have forgiven you," Joseph interrupted him.

"You see, my sister got pregnant again... and I was sure it was you who was responsible," groaned Aharonchik. "In the end, it turned out to be the father of her first child, and not you... I'm sorry."

Again, Joseph interrupted him: "I said I've forgiven you, it's all right... it's all forgotten."

Aharonchik looked at Joseph, who had grown very thin since leaving Ben Shemen, and said, "You don't look well. I know the situation in your brother's house isn't good, and that it's hard to make a living. Everyone in the family misses you, they really do."

Joseph stayed silent and Aharonchik continued: "My father was very angry with me for how I treated you. It wasn't easy for me to come here to ask your forgiveness, to apologize for my behavior. I'm asking you now to forgive me and come back to us, if only for a short while. Work and earn a little money to help Aharon. Only then will I really believe that you have forgiven me. I promise I will never raise a hand to you again, no matter what. For us, you are family, and family forgives."

Joseph examined Aharonchik's face. He saw sadness, pain, regret, and expectation for how he'd respond.

"I do forgive you, Aharonchik," Joseph relented.

Aharonchik approached and hugged Joseph and, that very day, the two returned to Ben Shemen. Before they left, Aharonchik took twenty lira out of his pocket and gave it to Aharon.

He explained to Joseph: "That's the sum owed to you on the day you left."

At Ben Shemen, the entire family received Joseph with love, and everyone, including Joseph, went on with their routine as if nothing had happened. On the first Saturday after his return, Joseph went to visit his friend Abraham at the boarding school. He explained to him what had happened over the past two months and why he hadn't been in touch with him. He added: "I really missed you and our conversations."

"I've really missed you too," said Abraham, "I thought something happened to you. When I asked the Aharonowitz family where you were, they said you'd decided to leave and they didn't know where you'd gone."

"The Aharonowitz family couldn't tell you what really happened, they were probably too ashamed." Abraham and Joseph sat talking for hours – about Abraham's studies, about Joseph's work, about future plans, about the Haganah[14], Etzel[15], and Lehi[16], about the war and the Jews in Europe, about girls in the village and at the boarding school, and how Abraham was in love with one of them.

"You know, Joseph," he shared a secret, "you can enlist in the Haganah here at the boarding school."

Joseph looked at his friend in surprise.

"You enlisted and didn't tell me?" he said.

"I'm not allowed to tell anyone."

Until that moment, Joseph hadn't given any thought to the organizations and they'd never discussed it.

"You haven't answered me, did you enlist? You know I won't tell anyone."

"Yes, I enlisted a few months ago, just before you left. But you can't tell anyone."

"What's it like?" asked Joseph.

"Look, Joseph, you're like a brother to me. I'm not allowed

---

14. The Haganah – (The Defense) was the main Zionist paramilitary organization that operated for the Yishuv in the British Mandate for Eretz Israel (Wikipedia).
15. The Irgun (Etzel) was a Jewish underground organization, founded in 1931 by a group of Haganah commanders who left the Haganah in protest against its defense charter (Jewish Virtual Library).
16. Lehi Lohamei Herut Israel – Lehi, "Fighters for the Freedom of Israel," was a paramilitary militant organization in Mandatory Palestine. Its avowed aim was to evict the British authorities from The Holy Land by use of violence, allowing unrestricted immigration of Jews and the formation of a Jewish state (Wikipedia).

to tell... I haven't even told my family. I shouldn't have told you; I can't tell you anything else and it's important that I not say more... try and understand please."

"Oh... I'm your friend and you can't tell me... it must be important."

Joseph's expression seemed so astonished that Abraham looked at him and asked: "Do you want to enlist? I'm sure you'd like it. The Haganah acts for the good of the Holy Land, for the good of the Jews, and they talk about establishing a state where all the Jews in the world can come live in safety, a state that will belong to us... what do you say?"

Abraham looked searchingly at Joseph.

"Sure... I'd like to," he answered without a second's thought.

"Joseph, don't forget, you cannot tell anyone anything, not even about this conversation."

After that Saturday with Abraham, Joseph returned to the Aharonowitz home and continued his daily routine as if nothing had happened. He kept the Haganah secret to himself. At the end of the following week, he spent the weekend with Abraham, who introduced him to the young man who had recruited him to the Haganah. That very Saturday evening, Joseph reported to the recruiters, who asked him a lot of questions and listened to Abraham's recommendation. They immediately decided to enlist Joseph and he swore an oath of loyalty to the Haganah. From that day onward, and every weekend, Joseph would meet Abraham in his room and the two would go out on field drills in the vicinity of the boarding school together with about twenty other recruits. Before every drill, they were given wooden rifles to practice with. They the patrolled the fields at night and, during the day, they trained on various obstacle courses and in military discipline. Their commanders gave them lessons in civics and history, explained about the Jewish army that was being established in the Holy Land, about the various underground organizations, and the differences between them. The British Government wasn't allowed to know about the Haganah, so he hid his activities, as did the others, and behaved like an ordinary adolescent boy. Joseph continued to work on the farm and in the cow sheds five days a week, from morning till evening. On Fridays, he worked a half day and went straight to Abraham at the boarding school. Although Abraham no longer visited the Aharonowitz home and Joseph spent every weekend with him, the family asked no questions. They understood that Joseph preferred to spend time with his friend there, and accepted it. They knew nothing about Joseph's clandestine activities.

The corn harvesting season came to an end and Joseph felt it was time to leave Ben Shemen and return to his brother. The school year at the boarding school was also coming to an end. He and Abraham spent hours discussing plans for their future. They were both seventeen, members of the Haganah, though they hadn't yet seen any real action, only the training. They decided to return to the center, to work and rent a flat together in Holon. They informed their commander that they were leaving the area and he gave them the name of the man in charge of the Haganah in Holon. Abraham told the Head of the boarding school that he was leaving and Joseph informed the Aharonowitz family. The family equipped him with food and extra clothing, gave him a bonus and said their farewells.

Joseph headed for Aharon's house and Abraham went to his parents. They'd planned to wait a few days before meeting up again. On his way to his brother, Joseph went to see Scheinzon at the orphanage, who was very glad to see him. He noticed Joseph's maturity, his self-confidence, which had grown along with his articulate speech. Joseph told Scheinzon about his plans and said that he wanted to donate one hundred lira to the orphanage. Despite Scheinzon's refusal, Joseph insisted he accept his donation.

"I want to give back to the orphanage, even if it's only a fraction of what I was given here," he explained.

Scheinzon finally relented, smiled at Joseph and wished him success.

"You know that there will always be a home for you here," he said when they parted.

When Joseph reached his brother's house, he told him that he planned to move to Holon and rent a place with his friend. Aharon was glad to hear that his little brother had found a good friend and that he had plans. He, too, noticed the change in Joseph – the quiet, reserved boy had become a confident man. It was a relief to him that Joseph wasn't going to live in his little house. Joseph bought new bed linen for his brother and some kitchen utensils he needed, and gave him some money. With one hundred lira left in his pocket, he set out for Holon and Abraham.

Thanks to the many stories that Abraham had told his family about their friendship before Joseph's arrival, he was received with open arms and immediately became one of the family. He realized that this family, too, lived frugally in a small home, and it was clear to both of them that they had to find an apartment as soon as possible. With this purpose in mind, they started walking through the streets of Holon and Tel Aviv searching for well-paid work. They also contacted the local commander of the Haganah who already knew their names and was waiting to meet them. He told them the days and times of the drills and the night patrols that they were expected to carry out as part of their Haganah activities in Holon. They didn't yet have real weapons, and patrolled empty-handed.

After several days of looking for work, they met someone who told them: "I know a building site where they're looking for workers. The pay is good but they work very hard, from morning till three-four in the afternoon."

The two went to the building site and met the construction manager, who was glad to take on extra hands and put them to work at once. From that day on, Joseph and Abraham worked every day from morning until the afternoon and, some nights, they practiced in the Haganah and carried out night patrols.

Not long after, Joseph decided to study at night to become a construction manager and get his license. He realized that this meant progress and better wages. However, Abraham didn't join him. After working and saving for a few weeks, they found an apartment. Joyfully, they moved in and arranged the place how they liked. They bought an old motor bike, although they didn't have a license but, now that they were mobile, they could travel to the building sites in Holon and Tel Aviv more easily. Their employers quickly realized that the two young men understood the work and did it quickly and efficiently, and they sent them to other sites. On one occasion, when Joseph was traveling from one site to another in Tel Aviv, a British policeman tried to stop him. Joseph was alarmed because he didn't have a license and drove off. Driving quickly from one street to another, he arrived at a small bar on HaYarkon Street, where he hid the motor bike and went inside and sat in a dark corner. A few minutes later, the British policeman came in and surveyed all those present. He passed among the tables and chairs until he reached the corner where Joseph was sitting.

"I saw where you hid the bike," he said in English, and sat down opposite Joseph.

Joseph wondered what to do, should he run away or stay where he was? He was afraid the policeman would fine him and confiscate the bike.

"Do you have a license?" asked the policeman.

"I have a license for the bike," replied Joseph in English, still thinking of how to escape.

"I was asking if you have a driver's license."

"I don't, but I..."

The policeman stopped Joseph.

"No, no, don't tell me you're a good driver. I know that, but..."

"Would you like a beer?" Joseph interrupted the policeman's fluent speech.

Joseph was betting on the man's love of beer and knew that British policemen didn't earn much. In his pocket he had enough money to stand him a few beers.

"Sure," replied the policeman, to Joseph's surprise, and he ordered him a beer.

Cold beers were placed on their table and the two sat and sipped them.

"Why don't you take out a license?" asked the policeman between sips.

"Don't know, haven't had time for it," replied Joseph.

"Would you like to take out a license?" asked the policeman.

"Yes, of course," responded Joseph enthusiastically.

"Let me think about it," answered the policeman and, after examining Joseph, he said: "It will cost you five lira."

Joseph took five lira out of his pocket and gave it to the policeman.

"There you are."

"Be here tomorrow at ten o'clock in the morning with a photograph and identification papers and I will take care of the license."

Joseph had no intention of missing this opportunity and asked the policeman to wait. He went out via the barman, gave him two lira and told him to keep the beers coming. Half an hour later, Joseph was back with the pictures and the documents. He was afraid that the policeman had left the bar, but found him there still drinking his beer. This time it was the policeman who asked Joseph to wait. An hour later he returned and handed Joseph a driving license, said 'goodbye' and turned on his heel. Joseph went outside the bar, looked in the light at the license, and discovered that it was a truck driving license. This meant that he had a permit to drive a motorcycle, a car and a truck, even though he'd never driven a car and certainly not a truck. He joyfully returned to the building site and laughingly told Abraham about the British policeman, about his escape and being caught, and about the new driver's license he'd received.

Joseph and Abraham decided to stop working for a daily wage and become independent contractors. They would determine a fee with the building contractors, hired more laborers and oversee that the job was done quickly and efficiently. The work paid well and Joseph could help his brother who, in the meantime, had moved from Tel Aviv to Holon to a larger house. The general contractors greatly respected their work and they became well-known in Tel Aviv and Holon. It didn't take long for orders to come in. They had to postpone work and even raise their prices. Joseph continued to help his brother and contribute to the orphanage, at least twice a year, on Passover and New Year. Joseph and Abraham enjoyed buying new things for the apartment, especially a radio. They learned from the transmissions that the war in Europe had ended, that the Germans had been defeated, that thousands of people had died, and that the Germans had annihilated most of the Jews in Europe; the world was talking about establishing a Jewish state in the Holy Land, however, the Arabs were determined not to let this happen, even at the price of a war against the Jews.

One night, Aharon arrived at Joseph and Abraham's apartment, bringing Menachem with him.

"Hello Joseph" said Aharon, and introduced Menachem: "This is your brother Menachem. He came to see me and I thought you two should meet; after all, you haven't seen each other since we were in hiding in Aden."

Greatly moved, Joseph inspected Menachem. He didn't recognize the disheveled man standing in front of him: he was unshaven, his hair was rather long and loose, his clothes were shabby and his shoes were worn.

With glassy eyes and looking a bit strange, Menachem said, "Hello, little brother." He approached him, hugged and kissed him three times, and asked, 'how are you?' not seeming at all excited by the meeting.

"Well, Menachem, my brother, well," responded Joseph, still overjoyed.

He tried but failed to remember his brother's image from childhood.

"I have to go," Menachem suddenly said, and turned to leave the apartment, "I live in Jaffa and want to get home."

Aharon and Joseph followed him.

"Stay with us a while... you can go home later," said Aharon.

"No, no... I have to get back," he said to them and went on his way.

The two watched the scruffy figure as he walked away from them and Joseph didn't understand what had just happened. Suddenly, Menachem turned and came back to them.

He addressed Joseph: "I need a cart to sell cactus pears in Jaffa. Aharon told me that you can make me a cart."

"I'll make one for you," replied Joseph.

"I'll come and fetch it tomorrow evening," said Menachem and turned around again, quickly walking away and disappearing into the night.

Aharon explained to Joseph that something had happened to Menachem, but he didn't know what. Aharon felt sorry that he couldn't help him.

"Menachem became a loner and moved to Jaffa. He cut off all contact with me," he said.

The next day, when he reached the building site, Joseph made a strong cart and took it back to his apartment. That evening he waited for Menachem but, when he arrived, he didn't say much; he again kissed Joseph three times, took the cart, said 'thank you' and immediately left Joseph's home, muttering: "I have to get back to Jaffa."

Joseph wondered how Menachem was living – and where he lived. Why hadn't he stayed a while? Aharon was right – something terrible must have happened to Menachem, to cause him behave so strangely. That night, like the previous night, Joseph had a hard time falling asleep.

Chapter Twelve

All the neighbors gathered in Joseph and Abrahams's apartment to listen to the live transmission from the UN – would they vote to establish a Jewish State in the Holy Land or not? Joseph, like everyone else listening, knew that the Arab states would never agree to the establishment of a Jewish State there, and tensions ran high. Joseph, Abraham and other members of the Haganah had been instructed to be on alert. They had already carried out secret firing range drills and knew how to use a rifle. They knew exactly where to go if they were called up. The Arabs in and outside of the Holy Land had announced that, if the State of Israel was established in the Holy Land, they would go to war against the Jews and expel them.

The joy of the listeners knew no bounds – thirty-three states voted in favor of ending British rule in the Holy Land and the establishment of a Jewish State and an Arab State. Only thirteen states objected. The decision to establish a Jewish State was accepted. They all began to dance in the apartment and then moved out into the streets, drinking anything they could get their hands on. Joseph took out two bottles of cognac and gave one to Abraham. They opened them and began to drink directly from the bottle, roaring "Long Live the State of Israel!" They were swept into the flow of celebration, dancing and drinking for hours, until they were exhausted.

The next day, still joyful, they listened to the radio which again transmitted the tallying of the vote, as well as the shouts of joy from the whole country. The British were still in power and there was no decision yet as to when they'd leave the country. "Until they leave, there won't be a 'State of Israel,'" explained the reporter, "until then, life goes on as usual." Joseph and Abraham went on working, although the Haganah had given orders to all its members to be ready. The two had to spend more and more time training, patrolling and guarding the border of the Arab neighborhoods, for fear they'd harm the nearby Jewish residents. There were the occasional incidents between Arabs and Jews, and the British army arrived to restore order, although it seemed to Joseph that the British army tended to support the Arabs. It was still forbidden to own a gun and all drills took place in secret, far from the watchful eyes of the British.

The time came for the British to leave the Holy Land and Ben Gurion declared the establishment of the State of Israel, even before the last of the British had left the country. Ben Gurion also declared that, from then on, there would be no underground, but one army, the Israel Defense Force. All members of the underground were required to return any weapons to the IDF and enlist in the army. Joseph and Abraham had no weapons, but they went to the meeting point, where they enlisted in the IDF and were sent to the Givati Brigade. They and other soldiers were sent to the sand dunes of Tel Arish, to guard the border between Holon and the Arab Tel Arish neighborhood. They were told that Arabs were firing on Jewish homes in Holon. Joseph and Abraham took turns guarding for six hours and going home for six hours. They heard about several incidents in the country, about lethal attacks in Tel Aviv, Arab revolts against the Jews, and speeches by the leaders of neighboring Arab countries who called for a war of attrition against the newly established State of Israel. On one of their forays home, Joseph went to ask after Aharon. He found his brother sitting in the yard under a canopy where a luffa bush was growing. Aharon seemed pensive and sad.

"How are you Aharon? What's wrong?" asked Joseph.

"This mess has gotten to us too," replied Aharon.

"Has something happened to the children, your wife?"

"No, nothing has happened to them, but Menachem, our brother, something has happened to him."

"What happened" Where is he?"

"Sit down, Joseph, sit down here beside me," said Aharon.

Joseph sat down and looked worriedly at Aharon.

"You know that Menachem has been living among the Arabs in Jaffa..." said Aharon chokingly, "I was called by Hadassah Medical Center in Tel Aviv to come in, but they didn't say why. I got there and I was asked to identify a body. They took me into a room with refrigerators... opened one of them and showed me..."

Aharon paused, then continued, in a trembling voice: "They... they opened the refrigerator and showed me Menachem's head. Menachem is dead... they killed him."

Aharon couldn't speak. He was choked with tears. Joseph hurried into the house and brought his brother a glass of water and hugged him. He too was distressed, but didn't react, continuing to hold Aharon until he'd calmed down.

"They killed him. He never did anything to anyone... never harmed a soul..." continued Aharon, quivering, "they slaughtered him. They dismembered his body... I was told they found his dismembered body in a sack... the sack with his body washed up on shore. The murderers threw his body into the sea in a sack... and that's how they found it. I saw the pieces of his body in the refrigerator, they actually dismembered it... they actually murdered him. Why did they murder him? Why?" Aharon was grief-stricken.

Joseph held his hand and listened to him, heartbroken.

"We buried him in the cemetery yesterday..." continued Aharon. "You were in the army and I couldn't find you... we had to bury Menachem... I buried him and prayed for him and said

Kaddish[17] in your name too... said goodbye to him... and went home to mourn him. Why? Why would the Arabs in Jaffa kill him? Why?" asked Aharon, looking up at the sky.

Joseph also looked up at the sky. They sat in silence, staring at some vague point above them. Finally, Joseph rose.

"Aharon, I have to get back to the army for my shift, they're waiting for me."

He kissed Aharon and hurried away.

At the sand dunes opposite Tel Arish, Joseph told Abraham about his brother Menachem's murder and Aharon's grief. The two promised to look after each other and make sure they'd both return home, safe and sound. As they were talking, the Arabs from Tel Arish began to approach the border of Holon and the dune they were guarding. Together with the rest of the platoon, they spread out and took up positions before dozens of Arabs who were screaming *Itbah al Yahud* – slaughter the Jews, as they approached, shooting at them. Joseph began to shoot back at them, followed by the rest of the platoon. The moment some of the attackers were injured, they began to retreat, and the platoon was ordered to charge in a counter-attack. Their targets were three tall buildings from which snipers were shooting at houses in Holon. Joseph, with Abraham at his side, came out from the dunes and the rest of the platoon came out on either side. Firing, they ran forwards. They didn't have time to run far before they heard, from behind, the voice of one of their commanders calling them to retreat immediately to the dunes. During the retreat, one of the soldiers, Jacob Katz, was wounded and fell. Joseph and Abraham dragged him back to the dunes. They arrived panting, looked at each other and at Jacob Katz lying between them. He'd been shot in the head and it was clear to them that he'd been killed. His body was taken to the rear and the platoon remained in the dunes in anticipation of what would come next.

---

17. Kaddish – Jewish prayer for the dead.

That evening, the commander gathered the platoon and announced: "Some of you will remain in the dunes. Three soldiers will join Commander Moshe Cohen at the outskirts of the village of Tel Arish. They will blow up the three buildings that are a threat to Holon."

Joseph, Abraham and another soldier were selected to go with Moshe. At midnight, the four set out, laden with explosives. The commander went first, then Joseph, another soldier, with Abraham bringing up the rear. They moved silently down the path and from there toward the buildings, going from one to the other and setting the explosives. Nobody saw them and, a few minutes later, they were done and backtracked. They pulled the cable connecting the explosives to the generator. When they reached a safe place, they activated the generator and the three buildings exploded and collapsed. Within moments, firing came from the direction of the Arab settlement in Holon and the four raced back to the dunes. As they ran, Moshe fell and was unable to continue. Bullets whistled from all directions. Joseph called to everyone to take shelter while he crawled towards his commander. As he crawled, he got a bullet to the leg. He glanced at his bleeding leg and thought the wound wouldn't prevent him from saving his commander. But Moshe was afraid; he froze and resisted, and Joseph couldn't persuade him to get up. The wounded Joseph realized that they were all in danger, so he called Abraham to crawl to him and, together, they pulled Moshe to a safer place. They waited a few minutes for a pause in the fighting. When they felt the firing die down, they picked the commander up, Abraham pulling him from the front and Joseph, limping, pushing him from behind. The other soldier led them along the path to the dunes. When they arrived, the medic removed the bullet from Joseph's leg, bandaged it and informed him that he'd be fine.

The next morning Joseph was called to the rear, to a building that served as the IDF Headquarters. Together with the commander of his platoon, he was taken into a room where the regional commander was sitting. The platoon commander told him about Joseph's acts of heroism during the course of the previous day and night.

He said, "He should be promoted. I want him to be my squad commander."

"Joseph, your commander tells me you showed courage and leadership, even though you were wounded."

Joseph shyly replied: "The whole squad did what had to be done, and the injury is very slight."

"I think you should be made squad commander, we don't have enough good men like you to lead." responded the platoon commander.

The regional commander agreed, "I think he's right."

"I would like to remain an ordinary soldier… I don't wish to command," replied Joseph, to everyone's surprise.

He didn't want to be responsible for soldiers, didn't want to give them orders, put them at risk or get them killed. It was bad enough his brother had been killed, as well as the soldier who'd been killed right next to him. He also remembered his squad commander, Moshe, who had been immobilized by fear as they retreated from the dunes, and worried it might happen to him.

"I don't understand," responded the regional commander.

"I don't want to be responsible for other soldiers," insisted Joseph.

The regional commander looked at Joseph and wondered what to do with the rebel in front of him. On one hand, he'd heard about his actions and saw Joseph's potential and, on the other, Joseph was refusing an order, and he was in desperate need of commanders.

"Go back to your platoon, I'll figure out what to do with you": he said in frustration.

With a slight limp, Joseph left the room.

Joseph and Abraham spent the following days doing shifts on the dune. They were busy fortifying the dune with sand bags and preparing sniper positions, while examining the Arab houses opposite and guarding against sudden attacks by Arab rioters. They were told that neighboring Arab countries were assembling their armies in preparation to vanquish the fledgling Jewish country. It was clear to them by what was being broadcasted on the radio that their relatively calm days were over, and days of confrontation awaited them.

About a week after Joseph's conversation with the regional commander, the platoon commander came to him and told him that he'd been transferred to the transportation unit.

"You have a driving license for a truck and unit needs drivers," he said.

"I do have a license," said Joseph, "but I've never driven a truck."

The platoon commander refused to accept his explanation and instructed him to go to the address he gave him. Joseph didn't resist. He parted from Abraham and they agreed that, whenever one of them got back to the apartment, he would leave notes for the other about what was happening.

Joseph entered the Tzrifin military base near Rishon Lezion that had been captured from the Arab Legion a few days earlier and where there were still prisoners. He found the Transportation Headquarters and was received by a mustached man who immediately asked him questions about his driving experience and license.

Joseph replied, "I don't know how to drive a truck, although I do have a license."

Without hesitation, he told Joseph to get into a truck and took him on a drive, all the while explaining how to operate it. He did that several times every day until he sensed that Joseph was ready to take the reins. Toward evening, he instructed Joseph to drive the truck to a control post near Negba[18], load explosives from an

---

18. Negba – A kibbutz in southern Israel.

Egyptian storehouse that had been captured by the Givati Brigade, and return to base.

"The first truck that was sent on this mission went over a mine. It was damaged and the driver can't drive," he said.

Fearfully and without confidence, Joseph took the truck for his first solo trip. He drove slowly and cautiously, fearing mines and ambushes. He traveled for hours, following the directions he was given, until he reached the control post. There, Shimon, the saboteur sergeant was waiting for him and told him that he'd checked the mines and they'd all been neutralized. They immediately loaded all the boxes of mines onto the truck, Shimon jumped into the passenger seat and they set out for the return trip. The whole way, Shimon urged Joseph to drive faster. His driving seemed too slow to him and he was worried about ambushes. Joseph ignored his pleas

and drove slowly and cautiously because it was an off-road, unpaved track. He looked in front of him, examining the road for mines. There were also mines on the truck, which were very sensitive to being bumped on the way. A short while before reaching Tzrifin, when they were already driving along an asphalt road, Joseph accelerated. Shimon mocked him, saying he was a 'crazy driver.' Joseph smiled. He parked the truck where Shimon told him to and, immediately, other explosive aficionados came over and began to unload the truck.

The local sabotage officer asked Shimon: "Did you check that the mines were neutralized?"

"Yes," replied Shimon.

"I see that the boxes are sealed and not opened, so how did you check?"

"I didn't open the sealed boxes."

"You have to open every single box and check; let's open the sealed boxes. The officer and Shimon opened one of the boxes on the floor and found that the explosives were already hooked up to the mines.

"Everybody, move away!" roared the officer, and everyone scattered. "Shimon, you made a mistake that could have cost you and the rest of us our lives… you should have examined this before loading them! You know that one good bump in the road and the truck would have exploded with you and the driver inside… do you get that?"

"Yes, sir," answered the embarrassed Shimon, "sorry."

He looked at the officer, then at Joseph, 'the crazy driver,' and nodded his appreciation. He then understood that part of his good luck was thanks to Joseph's slow and careful driving.

"Okay, nothing happened, everything is alright," responded the officer. "Let's unpack all the explosives, slowly and carefully… everyone else, move away from here – now."

When they finished unloading, Shimon addressed Joseph.

"Where are you stationed?"

Together they approached the mustached officer, who informed Shimon: "From now on, Joseph belongs to the fifty-first Givati Brigade. He'll return with me to the post at Negba."

The two argued until the mustached officer gave in. Joseph was glad to return to the Givati Brigade, to which he'd been sent when he enlisted. Joseph and Shimon set out for the post and, this time, Joseph drove an armored vehicle they'd been given at Tzrifin. Again, he drove slowly and carefully, this time without comment from Shimon.

On the way, Shimon told him about the brigade's operations, about the Egyptian army facing them, and the occupation of the hills overlooking the 'monster' – the 'Iraq Suwaydan Police Station – and about the plans to capture this fortress.

"The entire Givati Brigade is supposed to capture 'Iraq Suwaydan. If we take the police station, we know that the Egyptian army will return to Egypt. There are a lot of Egyptian soldiers there and a lot of ammunition and weapons. It will be hard to capture the police station… in the meantime, we're managing to take the surrounding hills."

Joseph continued his cautious driving while listening to Shimon. And then a thought went through his mind: maybe Abraham is there, he's also in Givati. They arrived at Post 113, near Negba, and heard firing in the background. Shimon directed Joseph to hide the truck right next to an ammunition store that was relatively protected.

"Joseph, stay close to me. I have to make sure all the battalions on the hills have ammunition."

Shimon made sure ammunition was loaded onto the truck and sent Joseph to deliver it to the various units. Thus, in the course of the coming days and nights, Joseph drove among the units, delivering ammunition and weapons. Machine gun bullets occasionally whistled past him, but he wasn't hit. Several mortar shells exploded nearby, but he continued, understanding the importance of his mission. In the distance, he saw the 'Iraq Suwaydan Police Station, and it really was a fortress, truly a 'monster.' Everywhere he went, he asked if Abraham Barzilai was there, but didn't find him.

One evening, after traveling among the units for a month, they were all called back, except for the guards who remained at their posts. Joseph ran with all the other soldiers to the gathering point, where the Major General made announcement:

"The Brigade is going to capture the 'monster.' Our brigade will lead the force."

All the soldiers began to talk excitedly and anxiously among themselves. The brigade had attempted five times to capture the 'monster' and failed each time; however, the brigade hadn't actively participate, but covered the soldiers who did.

"It will be a huge operation, a complex one, with many casualties," continued the Major General, "primarily due to the numerous fences, mines and strong wall fortifying the police station. In the past five failed efforts to capture the place, many of our soldiers were killed... but this time it is our mission, our brigade. We will carry it out successfully. Our intention is to start the attack at dawn, one hour before sunrise. The first stage – a platoon will advance under cover of darkness toward the fences, cut them quietly and create an open entry path; second stage – our artillery will fire as many shells as possible at the police station; third stage – we will send in an armored vehicle loaded with explosives that will explode against the wall. While moving in towards the location of the explosion, the entire force will take up their positions as close as possible to the location of the armored vehicle's explosion; fourth stage – immediately after the explosion, the entire force will advance toward the opening and capture the 'monster.'

The Major General added that this operation had been planned for some time, and "every Unit Commanders and every brigade knows its role and what is to happen at any given moment."

Joseph's mind started to wander and he lost his train of thought. He didn't precisely understand what was going on, but it was clear to him that, at dawn the following day, chaos would ensue.

He went up to Shimon and asked: "What is my role?"

"I don't know yet," responded Shimon, "but I don't believe anything has changed and you'll continue to deliver ammunition to brigade units in preparation for the attack. In the meantime, we have to find out which units are in need of ammunition."

"I need a driver and an explosives expert to volunteer," echoed the Major General's voice. Driving the armored vehicle to the fence is dangerous, and there's little chance of coming out unscathed," he explained, "I need volunteers to drive the armored vehicle loaded with explosives... by a show of hands – who volunteers?"

Not a soul moved an inch.

"Who is willing to volunteer?" the Major General asked again.

"I'm willing," called out Joseph.

"Who said that?" The Major General couldn't see Joseph.

"I'm willing to volunteer," Joseph called out loudly, and took a step forward toward the Major General.

Shimon, surprised by Joseph, followed him.

"Joseph, Joseph Edvy, is that you?" a shout was heard from a group of soldiers. "It's Abraham, Abraham Barzilai…"

Joseph stood still and tried to see where the shout was coming from.

"Abraham, where are you?" Joseph called out.

"Here… wait there, I'm coming to you."

In front of everyone, Joseph and Abraham hugged and kissed each other with great emotion.

"What is going on over there?" asked the Major General. "Come here, soldier. I have some questions for you."

Joseph continued to approach the Major General with Abraham's arm around his shoulders and Shimon close by.

When he reached the Major General, he asked Joseph, "And who are you?"

"My name is Joseph, I'm one of the truck drivers who delivers ammunition to the units."

"Are you married?"

"No."

"Do you think you're up for this? Reaching the location with the explosives in the armored truck is of supreme importance."

"I'm sure that Joseph is up for it," recommended Shimon, "I'm his saboteur sergeant… I'm the one who sends him to supply the units with ammunition and weapons." Shimon looked at the Major General and then at Joseph. "I'm volunteering to be the saboteur who helps Joseph to reach the point of the explosion," he added decisively, putting his hand on Joseph's shoulder, "we'll both carry out this mission."

Thus, the three of them – Joseph, Abraham and Shimon – faced the Major General, their faces a mixture of worry and fear at what was to come.

"Okay, soldiers… I'm glad we have volunteers. Everyone – back to your units, where you'll receive detailed instructions from your direct commanders. And the two of you…" the Major General addressed Joseph and Shimon, "come with me to receive a full briefing."

Joseph and Abraham hugged again and parted. Abraham knew that the mission Joseph had taken on himself was dangerous, and Joseph knew that Abraham would be among those attacking the fortress, many of whom would be wounded.

"Look after yourself," said Joseph to Abraham.

"You, too. Remember that we promised to look after on another... and that we'd both return to the apartment safe and sound."

Joseph and Shimon didn't sleep that night. They checked their weapons, their military belt, and the armored car, already loaded with explosives. They started the engine and checked that all systems were working. They were ready. They talked very little, mainly going over the route they were supposed to take. The hours passed slowly and Joseph was tense, but managed to suppress his fears.

"It's time," they called him, and he and Shimon got into the armored car and drove in darkness, without lights, to the starting point, where they waited. The commotion began. They heard the firing of shells, the noise of the explosions and then they were given the signal to set out. Joseph began to drive the armored car along the path he'd learned by heart, advancing towards the 'monster.' He drove slowly and meticulously while, next to him, Shimon looked out through the slit in the armored car. Illumination bombs were fired from the Police Station, lighting up the area near the wall. A mortar shell was fired at them and exploded nearby. About three hundred meters from the wall, they were stopped by a unit of soldiers, some of whom were wounded, asking them to retreat because they'd only been able to cut through two of the five fences. Joseph maneuvered along the narrow path and successfully returned the armored car to the starting point. This attack also failed. They were all ordered to return to their units.

Joseph and Shimon felt relieved but were frustrated that they were part of the failed attack. Dawn broke and, that morning, it was decided that the next day before dawn they would again carry out their plans and attack again. Everyone hoped that this time the unit would succeed in breaking through all the fences, enabling the armored car to reach the wall, where it would explode. When Joseph returned to the unit, the Major General called him aside to speak to him alone.

"Joseph, I've just received tragic news." Joseph straightened and looked at the Major General. "I've been informed that your brother, Aharon, has died."

"What happened?" asked Joseph, "and what about his family?"

"As far as I know, the family has not been harmed," replied the Major General, "according to what I've been told, Arabs from Tel Arish surrounded his neighborhood in Holon and Aharon was besieged. It took the rescuers time to reach his house and, when they did, they found him dead."

The Major General put his hand on Joseph's shoulder.

"Joseph, I understand that you had two brothers. Menachem, who was murdered by Arabs in Jaffa when the State of Israel was declared, and Aharon, who has now died under siege... I also understand that you have no other family in Israel, apart from your brother's children."

Joseph nodded, trying to absorb the painful news, and again straightened up.

I'll understand and accept your decision if you choose not to drive the armored car," added the Major General.

"I'm going out in the armored car tonight," said Joseph decisively.

"Are you sure?"

"I'm sure. I'm the driver of the armored car and I will carry out the mission," and he added, "am I dismissed?"

"Yes," responded the Major General.

Joseph turned and went back to the armored car. He thought about Menachem and Aharon, about the mission he had to carry out. He was swept up in a whirlwind of emotions. He felt sadness, fear, anger, tension, mourning and revenge. Yes, revenge, he thought to himself, this is my chance to avenge the deaths of my two brothers. I will drive and get the armored car up to the wall and make sure it explodes there. Nothing will stop me. He sat in the driver's seat of the armored car, resolute and tense.

Before dawn, focused and determined, Joseph again drove the armored car with its ton of explosives to the starting point, where he waited for the order to go.

"What's wrong, Shimon?" asked Joseph.

He'd noticed Shimon's discomfort.

"I can't do it again. I have a wife and children at home... I can't," muttered Shimon, and he got out of the car and walked away.

Joseph didn't say a word. He decided then and there that, even if he didn't have a saboteur, he'd drive the armored car to the wall by himself. He, too, had been trained to explode the armored car in the event that the saboteur was wounded and couldn't carry out his mission. He remained in the driver's seat and waited for the command. A minute or two later, the door opened and a soldier Joseph didn't know got in and sat in the seat beside him.

"I'm your saboteur now," he said.

The seventh attack on the fortress began. Again the artillery shelled the Police Station, again illumination bombs were fired in the air, and again explosions were directed in the area opposite the Police Station and at the police.

The two were tense and ready. They received their command and Joseph began his slow journey along the path that was supposed to be open and without fences. The nearer he got to the wall, the more shots were fired at the armored car. The bullets hit the metal but did no damage. Shells exploded around them, and Joseph continued his slow journey, maneuvering between them and the barbed wire, remaining on the path and hoping the wire wouldn't tangle in the chains of the armored car, forcing him to stop. He also maneuvered around pit holes made from exploding shells on the path and completely ignored what was happening around him. He could already see the wall – it was about a hundred meters in front of him, and he continued his slow journey. He wasn't tempted to slow down, although he was visible to everybody. Illumination bombs lit up the armored car and its surroundings, and the firing at him increased. Anti-tank shells were exploding all around him when, about thirty meters away, he noticed a fence that had not been cut away. He checked to see how he could circumvent the barbed wire fence – it was too late to turn back, he had to advance and find a breach in that fence. Just before he reached the fence, the armored car was hit by a burst of shots and then by an anti-tank shell that hit the right door of the armored car; the saboteur was flown from the vehicle. Joseph sensed he'd been hit in both legs, but continued to drive. He was right at the fence, maneuvering to find a break in order to continue up to the wall. The fire was very heavy. Another shell hit the armored car, which set it on fire and, in an instance, Joseph decided to open the door and pulled his legs out. Then another shell hit the vehicle, throwing Joseph completely out. His legs were hit by more shrapnel. He got up in terrible pain, pulling at his legs and trying to move away from the armored car. Two bullets hit his left leg and he fell to the ground. Then the armored car exploded with a terrible noise, catapulting Joseph straight into a ditch at the side of the road. Hit again by shrapnel, he lay there dazed and wounded, his leg in horrible pain. In a moment of delirium, he thought he saw Abraham in front of him, telling him that everything would be all right and that they'd return to their shared apartment. Then he lost consciousness.

Chapter Thirteen

He was surrounded by doctors and nurses. Joseph could barely see them but he could hear them perfectly, and see a blur of white coats around him. They were moving him on a bed with wheels, talking amongst themselves about the severity of his injury. He noticed that they were progressing along a corridor, and then stopped once they were inside a room. Joseph had lost a lot of blood and he could feel it. The four doctors around him lifted him with the sheet and transferred him to another bed. Above him floated small lights that made it even more difficult for him to focus. He heard the doctors beside him consulting with each other regarding which surgery to perform. He felt dizzy. A nurse approached him, jabbed his arm with a needle, and connect him to various machines, some of which began to beep. She stroked his head and asked him how he felt. He tried and failed to lift his head to see what was happening in the area of his legs, which he hadn't felt for some time.

With great difficulty he answered the nurse, "Alright."

Somewhere in the background, he could hear the doctors talking and managed to understand that they were debating what to do about his legs. He made a greater effort to make out their words.

"I don't know what's best…" said one doctor.

"Let's first stabilize him and get some blood into him… he's lost a lot. With regard to the legs, we'll remove the shrapnel and see how he responds..." said another doctor.

"I think it would be safer to amputate both legs... he'll recover more quickly that way and we won't be taking a risk."

"Look, about the amputation, we have to explain it to the soldier so he can decide..."

"Can't you see he's dazed and can't speak?"

Joseph wanted to shout to them not to amputate, but couldn't. He couldn't bear the thought of his life without legs. Without both his legs, he'd be a broken man. He didn't have anyone to help him financially, and he wasn't ready to accept charity. He again tried to say something, but nothing came out. His upper body moved with the effort to speak, and he managed to move his head. The dizziness was like a blow. The nurse noticed that he was trying to speak and called the doctors. Dismissively, they replied that they were in consultation and would soon begin surgery.

The nurse bent down to Joseph, took his hand, and asked: "Is everything all right?" He pressed her hand. "Do you want something?" she asked.

Again, he pressed her hand and tried to speak.

"Okay... what do you want? You're going to surgery in a moment and I have to anaesthetize you."

He pressed her hand as hard as he could, slightly raised his head and, out of nowhere, blurted out a shout: "Don't... don't... amputate... my... legs..."

That final effort took all of his last strength and left him completely dazed. He felt he was about to lose consciousness when he heard the nurse tell the doctors: "Now you know what has to be done."

And then, the ceiling of the room with all its lights began to spin above his head. Everything became completely blurred and he felt he was falling, being enveloped into an abyss. He was trying so hard to hear the doctors but couldn't. He felt he was being sucked into a deep ravine and lost consciousness.

For two days Joseph lay there, in and out of consciousness, exhausted. He awoke every few hours, sighed, and immediately fell asleep again. Finally, he awoke and managed to open his eyes. At first, his sight was hazy and he couldn't see anything. He felt as if he'd been run over by an ammunition truck. As hard as he tried to open his eyes and look around, he couldn't and closed them again. A few hours later, he began to wake again. This time he managed to open his eyes and saw a white ceiling, a simple light hanging from an electric cable and a stain next to it. He felt pain in his legs. He still didn't understand where he was, but he couldn't lift his head to look around. He saw several beds with people lying in them. He tried to speak, but failed, and the pain in his legs increased. He was still trying to understand where he was; he didn't remember how he got there, stuck to a bed. Closing his eyes, he tried to think: What happened? Where am I? Why are my legs hurting? Where are my friends? And then the realization hit him. He eyes opened wide, and out came an incomprehensible scream, of anguish, uncontrollable pain, a scream of suffering and shock.

"Where is everybody? Where…"

And then he fell silent, He tried to understand why he'd screamed. His eyes darted from one side to the other, searching for the missing information. He head felt dizzy and heavy.

From a distance, he heard someone calling, "Nurse… nurse… come and see what's happening in that bed over there. He's screaming and it's hard to understand him…"

Joseph saw a woman in a white coat approach him.

"What's wrong?" she asked, but he was silent, trying and failing to understand who she was. "Are you in pain?" she asked, and he nodded. "Here, this will make you feel better…" she answered.

Skillfully, she injected something into his arm. He looked up at her, trying to identify her. His eyes began to close of their own accord. He fought it, trying to keep them open to understand what was going on around him, but failed. He fell asleep. It was many hours before he woke again. His head was still dizzy and the pain in his legs struck again and again. He opened his eyes and, again, noticed the stain next to the suspended light. A woman in white came to his bed and he managed to raise his head a little and look at her.

She smiled at him and asked, "How are you feeling?"

"I'm in pain," he replied, "where am I?" he asked heavily.

"In hospital. You were wounded and brought in here..." she said, and began to examine him.

"How did I get here?"

He searched his memory and couldn't connect the hospital and his last memory. He remembered being in the armored vehicle next to the saboteur as they advanced to the place where they had to explode the armored vehicle with all the explosives inside it. He remembered the darkness, the stars and the illumination bombs that helped him see at night, the saboteur beside him, the terrible tension, the gunfire and explosions coming from all sides, and his promise to reach the wall and blow up the vehicle. More than that, he couldn't remember. He replayed the events over and over in his mind, trying desperately to remember, but always came back to the last memory of the journey towards that wall, and there the memories stopped. He looked dreamily at the room and then at the nurse, who smiled at him again.

"You know, the doctors didn't know what to do with you and they took a risk... are you hungry? Thirsty? You haven't had anything to eat or drink for a few days now. You know what, I'll go and get you something to drink," she said and left him.

Joseph realized that he'd been wounded, but still didn't remember how. He began to examine himself: he tried to move his arms and succeeded; slowly, he raised his hands in front of his face and saw they were whole. He tried to move his aching legs, but it hurt too much and he stopped. His legs had been injured, that much he understood. The nurse's sentence, 'the doctors didn't know what to do' sounded familiar. He dimly remembered the doctors' standing around him in conversation, something about his legs, remembered their deliberations about whether or not to amputate and his anxiety that they would, and his desire to speak out and tell them he didn't agree to that, that he'd do anything to stand on his legs again.

The nurse returned with a glass of water and tried to help him sit up, but his head spun and flopped back down on the pillow. The nurse then supported his head, raising it a little and brought the glass to his lips. He drank a little and stopped.

"It's all right... drink slowly..." she said, offering him the glass again.

He took another sip and said, "thank you."

She smiled again. "The doctor will be here soon to examine you and talk to you. In the meantime, tell me... how much pain are you feeling?"

"Nurse, I feel pain in my legs, but I can't move them. You didn't amputate my legs, did you?" he asked, his eyes full of dread.

"No, no, but talk to the doctor about your legs... it's not a simple situation," she said, stroking his hand. "You must understand that your situation is not an easy one, and you will need a lot of strength."

Stopping her, he asked, "Will I be able to walk?"

The nurse was silent. She tried to answer him, gazing into his large, piercing eyes, then saw the doctor approaching and sighed with relief.

"Here's the doctor," she said.

The doctor stood by the side of the bed and addressed him, "Hello, Joseph, how are you feeling?"

"Will I be able to walk on two legs again?" Joseph ignored the doctor's question, "I have to walk... and I will. Just tell me I'll walk on my own two legs again."

The doctor considered his question and started to answer, "Listen... I think..."

Joseph stopped him and said determinedly, as if establishing a fact, "I will walk again. My legs hurt a lot... like someone's poking me with needles; I can't move them – they refuse to respond… but I will walk again."

The nurse looked at him and then the doctor. She remembered what the doctors had said about Joseph, and knew they weren't confident his legs would ever recover.

She took Joseph's hand, stroked it, and said to the doctor, "Talk to Joseph… explain it to him; he deserves to know."

The doctor came up to the head of the bed and began in a low voice: "Joseph, let me explain what is happening. You arrived severely injured…" Joseph looked into the doctor's eyes with his large eyes, listening to him, and the doctor continued: "You were injured from the pelvis to the soles of your feet. Your legs were covered in blood. Yes, you lost a lot of blood and they gave you many blood transfusions. Your legs were full of shrapnel, some large and a lot of small fragments. We had to consult quickly – we didn't want to lose you. And then we heard you shouting, 'Don't amputate.' Although most of the doctors thought it was best to amputate both legs, they didn't in the end. We operated and took out all the large pieces of shrapnel and some of the smaller ones. We removed all the dangerous shrapnel."

The doctor paused and took a deep breath. Joseph was silent and continued to look at the doctor.

"You've been sedated for several days so that you won't be in too much pain. You must understand that we did all we could to save your legs. But I'm not sure you will be able to walk again. I don't know if it's possible as your legs are severely injured. We will be examining you every day, with the hope that we won't have to amputate them in order to save your life."

Joseph put out his hands, trying to feel his legs, and said, "I will walk on these legs again. I will leave the hospital on these two legs."

"Listen to me, Joseph," the doctor interrupted, "we will do everything we can so you can walk out of here on your legs… but it isn't a simple matter. All we can do is pray…"

"Pray?" replied Joseph, and groaned with the pain that had accompanied him since he'd woken up, "you have no idea how often I've prayed... and the worst always happened. You do your job, and I will make sure I walk again. You won't come anywhere near them with a saw... do you understand that?"

"We will do everything we can," said the doctor. "In the meantime, what is important is that you recover from the surgery and start eating and drinking."

Then he turned to the nurse, "Make sure he eats and drinks... I want to remove the intravenous line as soon as possible."

The doctor turned back to Joseph. "You do your job, and we'll take care of your health. Now I must get to the other patients. Rest and regain your strength, we have a lot of work before us."

The doctor turned and went off on his rounds.

The nurse stroked Joseph's arm and said: "It will be all right, Joseph, it will be all right."

She too, turned to go, and followed the doctor out. Joseph was left lying there, gazing at the ceiling. His mind was busy with worrying thoughts about his legs. Almost every movement caused him unbearable pain.

The next morning he felt better. The same doctor came to him and told him they couldn't operate to remove the small pieces of shrapnel, as his body wouldn't survive the anesthetic and further surgeries.

Joseph replied, "If the shrapnel has to come out, then do it. Without an anesthetic... so what if it hurts? Do what you must do."

The doctor looked at him in disbelief. "Are you suggesting we operate on you without an anesthetic?"

"Yes, yes... if you say I won't survive the anesthetic, maybe I'll survive the pain."

The doctor looked at him in astonishment. "Look, I'll have to consult..." he turned and left.

A few moments later he returned with another doctor.

"I want the Head of the Ward to hear this. Tell him what you told me."

Joseph repeated his request, "If the shrapnel has to come out, take it out... without an anesthetic, if necessary."

The Head of the Ward looked at Joseph in disbelief. "Do you realize that the pain will be excruciating?"

"Do you understand that I am walking out of here on my own two legs?" replied Joseph. "So I'll scream with pain... so it will hurt. But, in the end, my legs will recover."

Joseph's face was contorted with pain as he declared that he intended to fight for his legs until he stood on them. Both doctors looked at each other, perplexed, murmuring together in consultation.

"Listen Joseph," began the Head of the Ward, "we could... attempt it today. I'm not promising anything... we'll look for the pieces of shrapnel, mark the locations of those that must come out... and we'll see how it goes."

They went away, leaving Joseph exhausted from the effort of talking to them. Now that the doctors clearly understood him, he could breathe more easily, despite the pain. He closed his eyes and allowed his contracted muscles to relax.

Joseph awoke to the sound of voices around him. He'd managed to sleep for several hours until the discussion between the nurse and Head of the Ward woke him. His sleep was intermittent and interrupted by nightmares and memories he couldn't remember when he awoke. Flashes of an intense and deafening explosion and terrible pain in his body were part of the nightmares. He opened his eyes and looked at the nurse bending over him:

"We're taking you to the operating theater," she said, covering him, "the doctor who will do the surgery is here."

She began to wheel the bed towards the ward exit. A few minutes later, she rolled him into the operating theater, where two other doctors were waiting. They transferred him to the surgery table, and injected something into his legs.

"We are injecting a local anesthetic, not a full anesthetic, but the pain will be considerably less..." said the doctor, and Joseph didn't respond. "We have to make sure there is no gangrene... we'll begin now, Joseph."

The doctor drew back the sheet covering Joseph's legs and began to remove the bandages. Joseph didn't look at the doctors or at his legs. He fixed his eyes on the ceiling, looking for a point on which to focus.

"We're starting..." said the doctor, and Joseph felt a terrible stab where the doctor set his scalpel. He groaned in pain, but didn't scream or move. Occasionally, he felt he was about to faint or lose consciousness, but managed to stay awake. He heard the doctors whispering that another piece of shrapnel had been removed from his body. He also heard them say they couldn't' remove all the pieces, and that some would have to remain. At a certain point, the pain was intolerable and Joseph lost consciousness.

It was almost evening when Joseph awoke, his hands over his ears, and a terrible noise. He looked at the familiar stain on the ceiling near the light and realized he was back in the ward and had woken from another nightmare. The pain in his legs was unwavering.

"Nurse..." he called out.

A nurse who was nearby approached him.

"Yes, Joseph?'

"I'm so thirsty."

"I'll pour you a glass of water and help you to drink."

She gave him the glass and supported his head. With her help, he took a few sips, said, 'thank you,' and lay back against the pillow. Joseph's stay in the ward lasted several days. Every day brought the ritual visits from doctors and nurses, together with another round of extracting shrapnel in the operating theater. With every passing day, he woke in the ward after the procedure feeling even weaker, but he took heart from the knowledge that he had to continue the effort and withstand the pain, or they'd amputate his legs.

A week later, the Head of the Ward and the nurse came to Joseph.

"Listen, Joseph, we've extracted as much shrapnel as we could. I hope we haven't missed any potentially dangerous fragments... however, you do have remaining shards that we'd prefer not to touch if we don't have to, and hope that they won't lead to any negative consequences."

"You won't amputate my legs?"

"That depends on how your body recuperates," said the doctor, "and it depends on you. I hope you manage to get through it safely... we will examine your legs every day to see how they are, and we'll watch for gangrene. Our fight is against bacterial infection developing... do you understand?"

"I will do everything I have to," replied Joseph, and the doctor continued to explain about the leg, arteries, veins and the development of gangrene. Joseph no longer understood what the doctor was telling him and closed his eyes. The nurse tugged at the doctor's arm, pointed at Joseph and indicating to him that Joseph had fallen asleep.

"Okay, get some sleep, build up your strength... you have a long way to go," said the doctor and left.

The days passed, one week ended and another began. Joseph began to move his legs. At first he would stop as soon as it became too painful. But soon the pain became tolerable and he managed to move his legs a bit. The rest of the time he stared at the familiar stain on the ceiling, his thoughts straying to the friends he missed. Visitors occasionally came into the ward, but not to see him. Relatives would come to the ward especially on Fridays to spend time with their family members, bringing them candies and food. Nobody came to visit Joseph. The wounded in the bed next to him would come and go, soon replaced by others who would recover and leave the hospital. Some left within days, others took weeks. Unable to stand on his feet, Joseph remained lying there. He barely spoke to the others and the stain next to the light on the ceiling became his only friend, one that never left him, faithfully remaining in the same spot. Every day, Joseph would try to move his legs, and the effort became less painful. He felt he was recovering and that his legs were responding more and more, even if he couldn't yet get out of bed. One Friday afternoon, two months later, an old woman approached his bed and stood facing him. He stopped his exercises and looked at her. He didn't know her and she didn't seem to know him. Maybe she thinks I know her, he thought.

She stared at him and then asked, "what's your name?'

"Joseph..." he responded weakly, waiting for her to speak.

"Joseph, my name is Sonya. Does anyone visit you?" she asked.

"Who are you?" asked Joseph shyly.

"I'm just an old woman asking you if anyone visits you," she answered, with a motherly smile, "you know, now that we're at war, a lot of people are alone," she added.

"I'm not alone... I have friends, but they're very busy."

"I know... they're at the front and can't come," she said, taking his hand, "where were you wounded?"

Joseph looked at her. She was a complete stranger, but he found something comforting in her tone of voice.

"Mainly in my legs," he replied.

"How are you feeling?"

"A bit better every day... I feel stronger every day."

"I understand that you were badly wounded and that you did battle with the doctors."

Joseph looked at her in wonder.

"What do you mean, I did battle with the doctors?"

Again she stroked his hand.

"You know, I may just be an old lady asking how you are... but I'm also the mother of a son who fought and was wounded, and lay in the ward adjacent to yours. It was before you got here; I came almost every day to see him. On Fridays, when I left my son's room, I'd pass your door and peep in. That's what I did every Friday afternoon..."

She stopped and sighed. Joseph was silent, listening without interruption. He suddenly realized how he missed conversing with another person, how long it was since anyone had spoken to him about anything except his wounds, treatment possibilities or recovery. Continuing to look at her, he waited.

She asked, "Would you like something sweet?"

"No, thank you... they give me everything I need here."

She continued: "So this old lady called Sonya would peep into your ward almost every Friday. And then I noticed that you never moved from your bed. I wasn't sure it was always the same person, so one day I came in when you were sleeping and saw your face. For some reason I was curious and asked the nurse about you. She told me... she told me you battled with the doctors to prevent them from amputating your legs. She also told me you have no visitors."

Joseph looked deeply into her eyes, trying to see why she would take an interest in him. Had someone sent her to find out how he was?

"How is your son?" he asked.

"He's been released and is back at the front," she replied worriedly.

"I wish I could get back to the front," said Joseph.

"You have to focus on your recovery," she replied as if protecting him. "I have to be getting home now. Here is the candy you don't want," she said with a smile, and held out a slab of chocolate. "It's the best chocolate I've ever tasted... remember my words, it's the tastiest chocolate, bitter chocolate."

She waved goodbye and he watched her as she left the ward. He didn't know who she was or who had sent her, nor did he know if he'd see her again. She'd asked the nurse about him and, perhaps, the doctors. You don't go to doctors just like that to find out about some wounded soldier, he thought. He was convinced that someone had sent her to check on him. After she'd left, all his questions remained unanswered. He began to peel off the chocolate wrapping, thinking about Sonya and the candy, which he'd seldom ever tasted. Actually, he thought, he could count on one hand how many times he'd tasted bitter chocolate. He broke off a small piece of the chocolate and put it in his mouth. It tasted like paradise, sweet with a light tang of bitterness that remained on his tongue for a long time. Sonya was right, mused Joseph, it really was the best bitter chocolate he'd ever tasted.

Over the coming days, Joseph was in better spirits. The taste of the chocolate, which he ate a little at a time, together with the motherly talk with Sonya, improved his mood, and he tried harder to move his legs but still couldn't get off the bed and stand on them. The doctors continued to examine him every day, primarily concerned that infection or gangrene might develop. They even warned him not to overdo things, as not all the lacerations had healed.

The doctors' skepticism didn't prevent him from trying to move his legs, although he did so cautiously.

Friday came again, and Joseph lay in bed watching the door, hoping that Sonya would pay another visit. Although he didn't know who she was or why she'd visited him, he hoped she'd come again. It had been a long time since he'd looked forward to someone's company, someone to talk to him and care about him. Afternoon came and Joseph continued to look toward the door to the ward. To his joy, Sonya finally arrived, her black bag slung over her shoulder. Smiling, she walked slowly towards his bed.

"Hello, Joseph."

"Hello, Sonya," he said, a contented smile on his face.

"How was your week?" she asked, sitting down on a chair next to his bed.

"It was one of my best weeks."

"Really? What happened this week?"

"You were right," said Joseph, taking out the last remaining piece of chocolate, "it really is the best tasting chocolate there is."

"Nu... I told you," she said with a smile.

"Would you like the last piece?" he asked.

"No, it's for you… and I brought you another slab of chocolate," she said, taking out a packet of bitter chocolate from her bag.

Her smile, too, was contented.

"Sonya… why are you still coming to the hospital?" asked Joseph.

"You know, my son was laid up here for a month and I visited him almost every day…" Sonya stopped and looked at him, "and when he was released back to the front, I didn't know what to do with myself. Almost everyone was sent to fight, while we elderly sit and wait…"

"We're waiting to live here in peace and quiet… without being persecuted," replied Joseph.

"Yes, yes… without being persecuted," reiterated Sonya.

She seemed reflective and somewhat disheartened.

"Is something wrong?" he asked.

"No, no… everything's fine. I was remembering my only son who is at the front… remembering the family I left in Poland, whom I will never see again because, like you said, we are being persecuted. Just because we are Jews… I have to be getting home now."

Sonya rose, waved goodbye and walked towards the exit. Joseph watched her go.

From day to day, Joseph's condition improved. Months passed along with daily examinations by doctors, attempts to move his legs and Fridays with Sonya, which he anticipated with impatience. The short conversations with her, together with the delicious bitter chocolate she made sure to bring with her every time, were a comfort to him. He didn't know much about her. Her Friday visits were so brief – she'd ask how he was, how the family he didn't have was doing, and said almost nothing about herself and her own family. From the little she did share, he understood that she was born and raised in Poland, where she married and had children. At a certain point, she'd emigrated to the Holy Land with one child, who was in the army. She didn't say more than that, and he sensed it was hard for her to talk about it. Every word related to her family and what she'd gone through evoked a shift in her mood and impending sadness. He didn't want to bring her spirits down, so he didn't ask her any questions. The brief visits usually ended with, 'I have to be getting home now,' raising curiosity about Sonya's personal life and past, and her unwillingness to tell him about herself. It was clear to him that she'd endured tragedy. He also realized that the hardships he had endured were nowhere near as tragic as what had happened to Sonya. It was the taste of bitter chocolate that constantly reminded him of her and the insights he had, thanks to her, despite his pain; despite waking from nightmares; and despite the fact that walking solidly on his own two legs was still a long way off.

Chapter Fourteen

Joseph was standing at the threshold of the room that had been his home for the last year, with Abraham beside him. He looked at the bed, the little cabinet, the window, the ceiling with its stain next to the light – everything he'd gazed at for hours on end in his room, every corner of which he knew so well. He stood there on both legs, aided by a walking stick held in his right hand. Dozens of tiny fragments of shrapnel were still stuck inside his legs, which the doctors had decided to leave. He remembered the fateful conversation with his doctors during his first days in the hospital, when they attempted to persuade him to let them amputate his legs, and how he'd vigorously resisted and promised them, and particularly himself, that he would walk out of the hospital on his own two feet. He was indeed standing upright and was on his way out into the big world. He'd been shut up in that hospital for an entire year; an entire year on his own between these four walls, and now he was free to go. He turned around and began to walk down the corridor. He'd already parted from the doctors, the nurses, from Sonya and his room. As he walked, he surveyed the department and the building, as if saying goodbye forever; then, looking ahead and with Abraham at his side, he limped toward the exit gate.

On their way to Holon to their new apartment, Abraham told him that he'd prepared the apartment and cleaned it, and that it was ready for Joseph's return. He proudly informed him that they already had several work offers and that some of the contractors had returned to work almost full-time.

"Wow," said Joseph when they entered the apartment.

"So, what do you say, my friend?" asked Abraham.

"Wow."

"Right, wow! This is the living room, I brought the radio and your record player... we'll be celebrating here, you'll see," replied Abraham, showing Joseph old furniture he'd managed to get hold of. "Here, on the left, is our kitchen, it's small but more than enough for us. And these two doors here, this one leads to your room and the other to mine... so we don't disturb each other... have a little privacy."

Joseph smiled and limped into his room. It was small, just enough space for a bed and a small closet for his clothes, with enough room to get from the door to the bed and from the bed to the closet. He put the few clothes he had in the closet and lay down on the bed. After a few moments, Joseph was fast asleep. The way there and the excitement at this new beginning had tired him.

The following morning, the two friends sat and drank coffee in the kitchen.

"You realize that I'm disabled," said Joseph.

"I know, but everything will be all right."

"Look, I have a disability allowance from the IDF, so I shouldn't have a problem with income right now."

"I know that too," replied Abraham, "which means you don't have to be under pressure. We'll get organized, take a look at the jobs we have lined up... what we can, we'll do and what we can't, we won't. There is a lot of work."

"All right."

"Joseph, I owe you an apology."

"For what?" asked Joseph, surprised.

"For not finding the time to visit you at first, when you were lying alone in hospital."

"Never mind that," interrupted Joseph, "you were fighting in the war and I was safe... I know you wanted to be there and I know you are my friend, like a brother... you don't have to apologize or explain. Everything is alright, especially now."

"At least I managed to come towards the end of your hospital stay," said Abraham with a smile.

"You didn't miss much, and it was great that you finally could come."

"And now to work," replied Abraham, "I'm going out to a contractor who wants us to construct the skeleton frame of a building, and you'll examine these two work proposals I received... what do you say?"

"You're not giving me a second to acclimatize."

"Of course not! Here are the two proposals. I'm off, bye," said Abraham and left the apartment.

Joseph remained alone in the apartment on his first morning outside the hospital. He wondered where his legs would take him. Taking his cup of coffee in one hand and his walking stick in the other, he wandered through the bedrooms, the living room and the little kitchen. He glanced into every corner, at the walls, the ceiling, the windows, the record player and the radio. He opened the little cabinet underneath the record player and found the records in there; he switched it on and played a new Louis Armstrong album. He left the music on and went outside, leaving the entrance door open. Sitting on the stoop, he looked out at the street facing him and stared at the traffic. He sat like that for hours, watching passersby and the few cars driving past. Occasionally, he made himself a cup of coffee and went back to sit on the steps. Towards evening, Abraham came back from work and found him still sitting there.

"What's up?" he asked.

"Everything is fine," answered Joseph, "I sat down here for a breath of fresh air. Looked at the street."

"Nu... and have you looked over the orders?"

"No."

"Have you had anything to eat?"

"No, only coffee."

Abraham realized that he had to give Joseph some time.

"I'm making something to eat... you want some?" he said as he entered the house.

"No, not now... don't feel like it. I'm fine just where I am."

"More coffee?"

"Good idea."

A few moments later, Abraham brought over two cups of coffee and sat down next to Joseph. Abraham was puzzled by Joseph, who continued to stare out at the street. He recalled the first days, when the fighting was over and he came home. He particularly recalled the nights, when he'd lie awake and go over in his mind what had happened to him and his friends in recent years.

"Joseph," he said, putting a hand on his friend's shoulder, "the coffee's good, ah?"

"Mmmm... it is."

"Take your time, Joseph, don't hurry... I know that I shouldn't make you rush into things."

"Believe me, I don't know anything right now."

"I understand."

"All I feel is weakness, helplessness. Sometimes memories come up, particularly at night."

"I know," replied Abraham, "the doctors told me it would take time for you to recover."

Joseph didn't respond. They stopped talking and continued to sit on the steps in silence, sipping the coffee that had grown cold, and looking out at the street opposite, at the sky, then back at the street. Only towards midnight did they get up and go into the apartment, each to their own room. This became a ritual. Every morning, Abraham went out to work and Joseph remained at home, made coffee, sat on the steps and observed the street. Towards evening, Abraham came home, sat beside him with two cups of coffee, a little conversation, quiet, and then, close to midnight, they would go to bed.

After about two weeks, Joseph sat down opposite Abraham at the kitchen table and ate breakfast with him.

"I want to go to work with you today," he said, and Abraham nodded.

They finished eating and went together to the construction site. From then on, Joseph began to examine the work orders and occasionally went with Abraham to help him as best he could. His limp and the walking stick hampered him. At first, he went out for a few hours in the morning, going home in the afternoon to sit on the steps with a cup of coffee. Then he would check the calculations and plans for the work proposals they were supposed to submit. There were times he didn't go out with Abraham but stayed on the steps, and there were days he was out from morning till evening. There were days when Abraham felt he should stay home with Joseph, and he did. When they both stayed home, they didn't talk much, except about work. Abraham knew Joseph well enough not to pressure him or ask embarrassing questions. In the meantime, Abraham accompanied Joseph on his regular visits to the orphanage where he saw Joseph handing Scheinzon a box of money, and on his visits to Aharon's wife and two daughters, to whom he brought vegetables and fruit as well as some money. From month to month, Joseph's mood improved. His physical state also improved until, one day, he decided he'd had enough of the walking stick.

Joseph and Abraham worked from morning till night and arrived home exhausted. The physical labor benefited Joseph. Managing the employees, climbing scaffolding and ladders, lifting cement sacks and the various construction jobs he carried out improved the condition of his legs and strengthened him considerably. The nightmares lessened, though they didn't completely vanish. Joseph realized that, the busier he was, the more distant his troubling memories became. He couldn't understand that they were part of him, part of his life, and a part of who he was, and would continue to accompany him. He wasn't able to internalize that he had to deal with the pain and suffering, not bury or try to forget it. Constant work and keeping busy was his way of dealing with the occasional nightmares and memories. Even when he got home, he kept himself busy in the little garden and with fixing things in the house. He spent less time sitting on the steps with a cup of coffee. He tried to keep busy until he was completely exhausted and all he wanted was to sleep. During these months, Abraham noticed Joseph's behavior and his impatience with the workers.

Abraham decided it would be good for both of them to spice up their lives a little with some socializing – going out to events, parties, organizing evenings of entertainment with acquaintances and friends at their house as well – they were living in a bachelor's apartment, and the time had come for their apartment to be happy and cheerful, just like their previous one-room apartment before the war. From the moment Abraham decided that they had to change the atmosphere, he began to play records at home, mainly tango and jazz. Sitting on the steps in the evenings was replaced by sitting in the living room with a glass of cognac. The music that filled the apartment, particularly over the weekend, brought acquaintances and friends to their home and, if it was a weekend – they'd arrive with a bottle of Arak or cognac, nuts and fruit. And very soon there was dancing in the small living room. Occasionally Abraham convinced Joseph to go out to a café in Tel Aviv, where they'd sit with a drink, listen to music, and talk. These enjoyable activities had a positive effect on Joseph and his old smile appeared more frequently. Abraham felt that happiness and optimism were returning to his friend's life, which filled Abraham with a sense of satisfaction and joy. The bachelor apartment became a joyous place and Joseph began to return to himself, to the old mischievous, playful, happy, smiling, dancing, singing Joseph, who was content most of the time.

One cheerful Saturday night in their apartment, a tango was playing on the record player. Joseph and Abraham were sitting and talking to the people who had come to their apartment; they didn't know all of them. Joseph caught sight of a group of three girls giggling in a corner. He was especially drawn to the girl sitting in the middle.

Joseph pointed her out to Abraham and asked, "What do you say?"

"They look nice," replied Abraham.

"I see only one of them," responded Joseph, continuing to gaze at the girl, "look at the one in the middle, she looks nice."

"You find her attractive, my friend?"

"Come on... don't exaggerate," said Joseph.

He sat gazing at her, at her long, wavy hair reaching just below her shoulders, at her gentle face, kind eyes, and a smile that captivated him.

"Look in the mirror, my friend! Wow, are you in love?"

"You're an idiot," replied Joseph and went to the bathroom.

He found himself thinking about the girl, her melting smile. He had to get to know her. When he came out of the bathroom, he went right over to the group of girls and invited the one in the middle to dance. She declined. The girls on either side of her encouraged her to get up and dance with Joseph but, remaining firm, she refused. Embarrassed, Joseph went back to his seat beside Abraham.

"Doesn't she want to dance?"

"No."

"And you're just going to give up?"

"Idiot. What do you want me to do... force her?"

"No need to force her, but... when you want something, you go get it."

He sat gazing at the girl, and noticed that she was looking back at him. The moment she saw him looking at her, she looked away. Joseph turned to Abraham.

"Tell me, Abraham, is she looking at me?"

"No, she's talking to her friends."

"Look again, and tell me," requested Joseph.

"Well, she's looking in our direction. Maybe she likes you?" he asked, and without waiting for an answer, "and you're still sitting here, my friend?" Abraham encouraged Joseph, giving him a smack on the back.

Getting up rather hesitantly, Joseph went over to the girl and again asked her to dance. This time she agreed.

"My name is Joseph, what's yours?"

"Malka[19]," she answered with a shy smile.

"Queen Malka," he replied, his confidence returning to him, "where do you live?"

"In the Yemenite Quarter, in Tel Aviv."

"Yes, I know the neighborhood. I've been there..."

"What were you doing there?"

"Well... I was in the Haganah and then in the army. We patrolled there too."

"I served in Etzel and in the army," she replied.

"Etzel? Beautiful *and* tough!"

"Yes... and if I were you, I'd be careful," she said with a laugh.

"What did you do in the army?"

"I was in the air force, I've only just been discharged."

The dance ended and Malka turned to go back to her friends.

"Malka," Joseph stopped her, "can I see you again?" he asked, his heart beating hard.

"Yes," she replied.

She went back and sat down with her friends. Joseph was overjoyed and, with a smile from ear to ear, sat down with Abraham.

"You're in love, my friend!" Abraham declared excitedly, "I've never seen you like this. What happened?"

"She said yes!"

---

19. Malka – the Hebrew word for queen.

"Yes to what? Getting married?"

"No... no..." responded Joseph with a smile, "I asked her if I could see her again, and she said yes. Oops... what a fool I am. We didn't arrange anything."

Abraham laughed.

"In love, and a fool as well. Certainly confused... well, go over and arrange it. Joseph went over and they agreed to meet the following evening at five o'clock at the square next to the sausage vendor, opposite the Mograbi Cinema in downtown Tel Aviv.

The next day Joseph arrived at the square and waited for Malka. On the spur of the moment, he mischievously hid behind the corner near the sausage vendor. At two minutes to five, he saw her walking from the other direction and looking for him. He didn't emerge from his hiding place but continued to watch her. She arrived at the meeting point they'd agreed on, stopped, and surveyed the square. She did so several times, waited five more minutes, again surveyed the square, and began to retrace her steps.

Joseph, realizing she had no intention of waiting any longer, chased after her, calling: "Malka, Malka."

She stopped and turned to him.

"Where are you going? I was waiting for you and you didn't show up." he said slyly.

"I did come, I waited, didn't see you and decided to go back home," she said innocently. "Maybe we were right next to each other and didn't notice."

"Maybe," said Joseph with a smile, "let's sit down somewhere and have a drink."

They sat at a nearby café and talked for hours. Joseph told her about what had happened to him and she took great interest, asking a lot of questions. Joseph felt comfortable confiding in her. She told him about her life and he was captivated, staring at her and absorbing every word she spoke. Time passed quickly and darkness began to fall.

"I have to go home," said Malka, and Joseph accompanied her.

They parted, but not before deciding to meet the following day, at the same time and place. They met again and again at the same place, sometimes every day and sometimes twice a week. On one date, Joseph told her that friends of his were getting married, and he invited her to go with him to the wedding celebration.

"The party will be held at noon in Holon," he said.

"I'll let you know next time we meet, I have to check with my mother," she replied.

At their next date, she told him she'd come with him to the party on condition he came to her home to fetch her and would bring her back before the start of the Sabbath. Joseph at once agreed. On the Friday of the wedding, right on time, Joseph came to Malka's house in a taxi. She was standing coifed and looking lovely at the entrance, wearing a white dress that reached her knees. Joseph looked at her, got out of the taxi and opened the door for her.

She couldn't help but say,   "How handsome you are."

"Thank you," he said, getting into the taxi.

It was an hour before the start of the Sabbath and the party wasn't over yet. Joseph asked Abraham if he'd take Malka home on the motor bike. Abraham started the engine, Joseph helped her get on and said goodbye. Before he had time to go back to the party, he heard the motor bike return. He turned around at once.

"What happened, Abraham? Where's Malka?" he asked.

Still seated on the motor bike, Abraham said, "I started riding, when I saw a taxi on the other side of the street. I asked him to stop and take Malka home."

"What?" asked Joseph, "You sent her home alone?"

"What's wrong with that?" asked Abraham.

"Don't switch off the motor bike," said Joseph, sitting behind Abraham. "Now, move fast until you find that taxi... you'd better find it if you know what's good for you," he ordered.

Abraham put the bike in first gear and pressed on the gas. He reached the place where the taxi had picked up Malka, but couldn't see her. He drove at high speed along the route he thought the taxi would take to the Yemenite Quarter. Within a few minutes, he saw her and signaled to the driver to stop. Joseph jumped off the bike, opened the door and sat down beside the astonished Malka.

"I didn't want you to go home alone," he said, feeling upset and guilty.

Malka was silent. Joseph asked the driver to go on to the Yemenite Quarter. Malka looked at him, then put her hand in his. He felt butterflies in his belly. He felt her warm, slightly trembling hand in his. He placed his other hand on the back of hers and looked at her. At that moment, Joseph realized that he was completely in love; that was the instant he decided to marry her. Leaning over, he kissed her lightly on the lips and she put her head on his shoulder.

"Come inside," said Malka when they reached the house.

The entrance path to the house led into a large open courtyard. On the left was the toilet and shower, adjacent to a small room. On the right were two larger rooms. Stairs led up to the roof and, opposite the staircase, was a large sink with a tap. At the end of the courtyard was a small kitchen. Above the door to the kitchen hung braided heads of garlic and, underneath the stairs leading up to the roof was a long counter on which were utensils, a copper mortar and pestle, a stone, and a grinder. The long table was set for the Friday night meal. Seated around it were Malka's parents, both of whom were Yemenite. Her mother's skin was lighter and she dressed the traditional galabiyah; her father, dark-skinned, wearing in a suit and tie and a yarmulke on his head, radiated dignity. Malka introduced Joseph to her parents and they asked him to join them at the table.

"Joseph, it's late already and you won't get home before the start of the Sabbath," said Malka, looking at her parents.

"You know I don't keep the Sabbath," he replied.

"You may not keep the Sabbath," replied the father, "but if we don't invite you to spend the Sabbath with us, then we won't be keeping the Sabbath either. If we send you home, and the Sabbath starts before you get there, then we will have caused you to violate the Sabbath," argued the father. "Thus, it is both my right and obligation to invite you to spend the Sabbath with us."

Both parents scrutinized Joseph and awaited his response.

"And, aside from that, Joseph," intervened her mother, "Malka has been going out with you for some time and we want to get to know you."

Joseph looked at Malka, who smiled at him. He turned to her parents and agreed.

"Joseph, I'm going to the synagogue in a while and I'd be glad if you'd come along," said her father, and Joseph agreed again, although he hadn't taken any interest in religion, or prayed, for years. Malka pulled him away, gave him a towel and sent him to shower. When Joseph came out, he found that she'd prepared some clean clothes belonging to her brother, hoping they'd fit him. Malka handed him a yarmulke, which he put on his head. Her father and Joseph, accompanied by Malka's three brothers, left for the synagogue. Joseph didn't think he'd remember the prayers and certainly not the Yemenite pronunciation but, quite quickly, most of it came back to him. Sometimes he'd make the odd mistake – either with the words or pronunciation.

When the prayers ended, father and sons walked home, singing the liturgy: *"Peace upon you, ministering angels, messengers of the Most High, sent by the King, King of Kings, the Holy One, Blessed be He..."*

Joseph sung along with them, which evoked vague and distant memories.

They continued: *"Come in peace, messengers of peace, messengers of the Most High, sent by the King, King of Kings, the Holy One, Blessed be He..."*

When they arrived home, they sat down at the table and immediately began singing the prayer that he remembered Zachariah singing to his wife, Shimei.

"Who can find a woman of valor? For her worth is far above rubies.

The heart of her husband safely trusts her; so he will have no lack of gain. She does him good and not evil all the days of her life..." (Proverbs 31:10-12 New King James Version).

Malka, her mother and two sisters took their seat at the table and the men continued.

"Favor is deceitful, and beauty is vain: but a woman that feareth the Lord, she shall be praised." (Proverbs 31:30. New King James Version).

When they'd completed the liturgy, her father rose, a glass of wine in his hand, followed by Joseph and the boys.

"Thus the heavens and the earth were finished, and all the host of them..." blessed the father. *'Blessed are you, O God, our Lord, King of the Universe, creator of the fruit of the vine."* (Jewish blessing over the wine).

Everyone chorused, "Amen."

"Blessed be Sabbath Temple."

Again, they all chorused "Amen."

The father sipped and passed the glass to the mother. She sipped and passed it to Joseph, who passed it to Malka, the eldest; one by one, they all sipped from the glass of wine in order of their ages, from the eldest to the youngest. The father made the blessing over the challah, tore off a piece for each one, and they sat down to eat.

The next morning, Malka's father woke him and her brothers and, together, they went to the synagogue. During the prayer, her father asked Joseph to go up to the Torah to read. Joseph hesitated. He hadn't read the Torah with the Yemenite pronunciation since his bar mitzvah.

"I'll come up with you," her father encouraged him, "and, if you make a mistake, it doesn't matter, I'll be with you and I'll help you."

Joseph agreed, and went up to read from the Torah with her father. At first, her father corrected him several times but, as he progressed with the reading, he made fewer mistakes. When he finished, her father said encouragingly, "may your strength persist," and the two sat down. After prayers, they went home and sat down to eat Kubana[20], Jachnun[21], hard boiled eggs and fenugreek. After the meal, her father lay down to rest. Joseph and Malka went for a walk through the streets of the Yemenite Quarter, holding hands and talking.

"My father liked you, you know?"

"I hope so," replied Joseph and stopped, "I want you to be my wife," he said without a second's thought, "I want to marry you. I love you... will you be my wife?"

Joseph looked at Malka, waiting for a response.

"Yes," she said, without hesitation, "I want to marry you and be your wife."

Joseph pulled her to him and tenderly kissed her on the forehead, and then on her lips. Gently, she pushed him away.

"Not here, not in the street," she chided, adding: "you know you have ask for my parents' consent..."

"Yes, yes, I know... I'll talk to them at the first opportunity," he replied, trying to think how and when he'd do that.

That afternoon, her father came out of his room, took out some Ja'ala[22], cognac, and the Diwan[23], placed them on the table in the courtyard and called to Joseph to join him. Her mother brought out glasses and small plates. A few minutes later, friends of Malka's father came in and sat down at the table and began discussing the weekly portion. They sipped the cognac and continued the conversation. Occasionally, they'd burst into Yemenite song from the Diwan, which Joseph didn't know. Her father looked at him, pushed the book towards him and pointed to the words of the poems. Joseph drank with them and tried to sing, drank and tried again. He didn't really succeed, although the pleasure and some of

---

20. Kubana: a round and airy challah-like pastry, rich in melted butter and made with yeast dough.
21. Jachnun: a Jewish Yemenite pastry traditionally served on the Sabbath.
22. Ja'ala: a mixture of nuts and grains.
23. Diwan: A book of Yemenite poetry, most of which was written by Rabbi Shalom Shabazi.

the words brought back the same dim memories of his early years, when he used prayed or read from the bible. The cognac took effect and Joseph asked to go and rest.

He woke to the sound of the father's liturgy in the courtyard and went outside. It was already evening and the father again stood at the table with a glass of wine in hand and recited the blessing for the end of the Sabbath. Beside him stood Malka. Her father hadn't woken Joseph for the prayer.

When he saw that Joseph was awake, he gestured for him to come and sit beside him, and continued to make the blessing.

When he finished, he asked him, "How are you feeling?"

"I'm all right," replied Joseph.

"The cognac affected you... just as well you slept a while," he said understandingly.

At the end of the meal, Joseph asked to speak to Malka's parents, in her presence. They sat down, as usual, at the table in the courtyard. Joseph sat facing them and Malka stood next to her parents.

"You know that I've been seeing Malka for some time."

"We know," replied her father, while her mother nodded.

Joseph paused, took a deep breath and said, "I would like to marry Malka and I respectfully ask for your permission and blessing."

Her parents looked at Malka, who nodded her consent.

"I understand that Malka has agreed to marry you," said her father.

"Yes, yes, I agree," intervened Malka and her mother hushed her.

Her father looked at her lovingly.

"Do you understand that, from the day of your marriage, you will be responsible for Malka? Responsible for making a living, for keeping a roof over your heads, for her health."

"I understand," replied Joseph.

"If so," her father looked at her mother, who nodded assent, "we agree. Congratulations."

Her father rose and fetched the cognac again with two glasses, putting them on the table. He poured one glass for Joseph and the other for himself.

"To Malka and Joseph and a happy life. May your marriage be a blessing to you and to us, may you be happy and bring many children into the world, Amen."

They all chorused, "Amen," as her father and Joseph drank the cognac.

Joseph spent the following Sabbath at her parents' home, at their invitation. Her father asked Joseph to come early, before the start of the Sabbath. When he arrived, he asked Joseph to wait for him at the table in the courtyard. A few moments later, he came out of his room, sat down facing Joseph and asked his wife to make them tea.

"How are you?" asked her father.

"I'm fine," answered Joseph.

"And how are things at work?"

"Work is flourishing, my legs are getting better all the time, it's easier for me, and we finish jobs more quickly... a lot of contractors want to work with us."

"I'm glad. I want the marriage to take place as soon as possible... for once you've decided to marry, you should do so! There's no point in waiting."

"I thought we'd marry after I build the house in Holon... I've bought a plot and want to build a house there for me and Malka."

"No, no... look, as you have no parents with whom I can consult or come upon an agreement, I'm talking to you. If your parents were here, they'd understand me. Don't wait, get married," said her father. "Moreover," he added, "after the wedding, you will move in with us. I'll give you both a room here, and you can stay until your house is ready."

Joseph looked at Malka's father and realized that, if he didn't agree to his suggestion, he would be insulted. Joseph didn't know how to respond and felt he should agree. In any case, when he finished building the house, they'd move into it, so why not live temporarily with her parents?

"Very well, we'll stay here until we have a place of our own," he said.

"Good," said the father contentedly. "The wedding will take place here. There's plenty of space in the courtyard, the rooms and, if necessary – we'll put tables in the street." Her father looked at Joseph and continued, "and now we must set the date for the wedding."

"Very well, when do you think would be a good time?" Joseph allowed her father to make the decision.

"I think the wedding should be in two months' time."

"Very well," he replied.

In the following days and weeks, between his work and other responsibilities, Malka and Joseph were preoccupied with preparations for the wedding. They had to order a bridal dress, clothes for the groom, hire tables and chairs, take care of the food, a cake, buy rings and more.

One evening, about a month before the wedding, two military personnel arrived at his apartment in Holon. At first, Joseph thought they'd come on military business, but he was a disabled veteran and he was mystified as to the purpose of their visit.

"Don't stay outside, come in," he said.

"Are you Joseph Edvy?" asked the senior of the two.

"Yes, and who are you?"

"I'm a staff officer in Holon, and this is a staff psychologist."

"Psychologist?" wondered Joseph, "I know I have an issue with anxiety, what you call 'shell shock,' but I'm usually fine. Why are you here?"

"We're here to give you some news."

"What news could the army have for me? Usually, it's only

when something bad happens that you come to a civilian's house! And I'm a civilian now..."

"We have something rather important to discuss with you," intervened the officer. "Is your mother's name Leah Dahari, also known as Luluah, and whose first husband's surname was Edvy?" asked the officer.

"What?" asked Joseph completely taken aback.

He tried to understand what the officer was asking him. The psychologist rose and sat beside Joseph. He put his hand on his shoulder.

"Look Joseph, we need to know if this is your mother. Take your time... relax..."

"What are you talking about? I don't remember anything about my family. Nothing. Not my mother or my father. I barely remember my brother, Menachem, who was murdered... I only remember my brother Aharon."

Getting up, he went into the kitchen, followed by the psychologist.

"What do you want from me?" he asked, pouring himself a glass of water.

He drank quickly. The psychologist put his hand on Joseph's shoulder again.

"We want to tell you that, if she is your mother, then she's here in Israel, safe and sound and with a large family... come, let's sit down again."

They sat down.

"Look, Joseph, we completely understand that, if she is indeed your mother, then this is a shock for you."

"How can I know if she's my mother?" he asked, "I haven't seen her since I was very young," he said angrily, "she abandoned me... left me when I was a baby. A mother doesn't abandon her children..."

The psychologist tried to calm him.

"We have no idea why it was that you came here without your

mother. No idea… you know, almost everywhere in the world, Jews who were persecuted smuggled their children out… they didn't abandon them, they saved them. Maybe this is what happened to you… if this is your mother, you will have to talk to her to know what happened…"

The psychologist's sentences pounded on Joseph's head like a five-kilo hammer. Was it possible that his mother had not abandoned him after all? It could be. Nobody had ever talked to him about it, not Aharon nor anyone else. No one had ever spoken to him about his mother. Could it be that she had no choice?

"It's important we know if she's your mother," the psychologist interrupted Joseph's thoughts.

"How did you find me?"

"HaMahane HaOlim[24] in Afula contacted us. They have a community of emigrants from Yemen and they told us a story we felt we had to investigate. We approached the family and understood from the mother that, long before the declaration of the state, she had sent a small boy through various places in Yemen to Israel. She knows he reached Israel, was in the army and was killed in battle. She kept insisting on knowing the location of his grave. At first, the management of HaMahane HaOlim ignored her request, but she didn't give up… she didn't stop talking about how she wanted to go to her son's grave. Her stubbornness and persistence found us."

The psychologist stopped his flow of speech. Joseph was intent, fascinated by the story.

"And what happened?"

"As I told you, we approached the family. She didn't have a photograph, only a memory. We tried to get more accurate details from her, such as a date of birth or date of emigration, but we didn't succeed. What we did manage to do was get your name from her – Joseph Edvy, her name – Leah or Luluah, and the information that he'd been in the army, had fought in the war and been killed.

---

24. HaMahane HaOlim – A camp for emigrants.

We asked her how she knew he'd been killed, and she told us that the army had informed her. We examined military documents and saw that no such information had been given her, but we did find the name Joseph Edvy, so we got out your file and located you.

She is now known as Leah Dahari and she is married with several children. We returned to her and asked who had informed her, and she still insisted that it was a soldier from the army. We asked her children, the neighbors... it took us a long time to find the soldier who had told her. Once we caught up with him, it turned out that this Yemenite soldier had served in the Givati Brigade, but not with you. He didn't know you, but knew your name. He told us that on one of his visits to his family at HaMahane HaOlim, he heard the story of a mother looking for her son, Joseph Edvy, and went to see her. After making enquiries, he thought she'd verified the name and approximate age of her son who, as far as he knew, had died in battle. He told her that, although he didn't know you, someone called Joseph Edvy had been in the battle at the 'Iraq Suwaydan Police Station, and the car in which he'd been traveling had exploded and he was killed. He also told her that someone from the army would come and tell them when his burial would take place. When we asked him why he'd assumed this responsibility, he answered that, to the best of his understanding, he was right in giving the information. After all, how many Joseph Edvy's were there in the army? What's more, none of the institutions or administrations bothered to check her claim that she had a son of that name in Israel, and she was asking for help to find him..."

"What's her name? Tell me again, please," said Joseph, still upset, but no longer angry.

"Leah or Luluah Dahari, and she says that her first husband's surname was Edvy."

"Look, I really have no memory of her or her name, but it appears that I really am her son... I hope you understand that my entire world has been turned upside-down. I need some time to absorb this," he said.

Joseph was trying to work out what to do with this revelation. Once the psychologist was convinced that Joseph was in a reasonable state of mind, they agreed to meet and talk again the next day and decide how to proceed. That very evening, Joseph went to see Malka. He recounted what had happened and asked her advice. Malka didn't think twice, called her mother, and asked Joseph to tell her the story and share his deliberations with her. Joseph told the story again.

"You and she will know instantly if you are mother and son… believe me," began Malka's mother, "if she has gone to all this effort to find her son or his grave, she deserves to have you make every effort to find her. If it's a mistake, the price of a mistake is nothing compared to the price that this mother has paid, is still paying and will continue to pay."

Looking at Joseph, she stroked his head.

"You must go and see her," she told him, "and you must go with him," she told Malka.

Chapter Fifteen

Malka, Joseph, the officer and the psychologist traveled together in a military vehicle. They were already half-way to the emigrant camp in Afula. Before the trip, the officer and the psychologist visited the woman and told her they may have found her son and would bring him to her. The excitement and tension were at a peak. Malka held Joseph's hand all the way there.

They drove into the emigrants' camp. Rows and rows of tents had been put up and all around them were children and adults. They drove slowly and cautiously along a dirt track between the tents. The children excitedly ran alongside the moving vehicle.

"Who have you come to see?" asked one of the children.

They traveled on slowly. When they reached the tent, they all got out of the car.

"You're going to Luluah... it's Luluah's son!" shouted the children, pointing at Joseph.

Joseph felt his legs were about to betray him, in addition to the fact that he still limped. With Malka supporting him on his left and the psychologist on his right, they entered Luluah's tent. As soon as they were inside, Joseph sat down. Facing him was an elderly Yemenite woman dressed in traditional clothing, gazing at him. One of the elders asked him to kiss her hands and Joseph refused. He had never kissed anyone's hands.

He heard the elderly woman say in Yemenite, "Leave him alone... Nobody taught him that I'm his mother!"

Joseph was astounded that he understood, for he barely knew the language. He also realized that the elderly woman facing him was protecting him. He approached and embraced her and she returned the embrace, murmuring, "You are my son."

They continued to examine each other. He noticed the resemblance between them, but felt nothing.

"You are my son," she repeated, continuing to speak Yemenite.

This time Joseph didn't understand a word of what she was saying and looked to Malka for help.

"I don't understand either," she said.

Joseph looked around the people in the tent with a plea for help.

A girl approached and said, "I understand, I can translate."

The psychologist asked everyone to exit the tent and leave Joseph, the translator and the elderly woman alone. Joseph held onto Malka's hand and announced that she was staying with him. All the others left the tent. In an instant, Joseph decided to call her 'mother.' He was convinced the woman in front of him was his mother – they were so alike, and she constantly repeated 'You are my son.' No woman would just sit there saying to someone, 'You are my son,' if he wasn't. From the moment he decided to call her 'mother,' she began to talk at top speed and the translator tried her best to slow her down so she could translate her words for Joseph. Slowly, Luluah slowed the pace of her speech. She realized that translation was needed if she wanted them to understand each other.

"Do you remember Salma, Joseph my son, my eldest?" asked Luluah.

"No, mother," replied Joseph shyly, "who is Salma?"

His reply saddened her.

"Salma is your sister."

"No, mamma, no."

"Your sister Salma who used to play with you."
"Joseph thought hard but didn't remember.
"No, mother, I don't remember."
"You loved her more that anyone, my eldest son."

Joseph continued to rake through his memories, but couldn't remember his sister.

"My son… Salma was six and a half when you were born. She was beside you from the moment you opened your eyes. You looked for her all the time… she was your little mother…" Luluah continued, "you left us when you were four, and Salma was ten and a half… she missed you so much. She wept for nights on end and I couldn't comfort her…"

Joseph looked at his mother, sensed her pain and considered telling her that he vaguely remembered Salma.

"Help me, mother, help me to remember…" he said at last.

"My eldest son… you are my first son. Oh, Salma…"

"Mamma, help me. Tell me about her and about me… tell me."

Luluah's eyes filled with tears and she took Joseph's hand and stroked it. She tried to remember something that had happened between Salma and Joseph that would help him to remember her. Suddenly her eyes opened wide.

"Samma," she whispered to Joseph, trying to imitate his voice when he was a little boy, "Samma," she repeated, "Samma… that's what you called her."

She looked at Joseph to see his response.

"She was always asking you 'what's my name?' and you would answer "Samma."

The name sounded familiar to Joseph and he was overwhelmed with feelings of affection and love at the sound of the name 'Samma.' He looked into his mother's tear-filled eyes and memories began to flow back to him. At first, he remembered running among chickens and a little girl running with him. This memory was distant and blurred. Then he remembered the girl's rolling laughter and, finally, he remembered the name 'Salma.' Yes, he remembered his sister. Vaguely, but he did remember calling her 'Samma,' the running and her special rolling laughter.

"Mamma, now I remember… I remember her, I remember Samma. I remember running with her among chickens… and I remember her unforgettable rolling laugh…"

His mother was still stroking his hand and smiling with contentment.

"You must remember …" she continued stroking his hand.

"Where is Samma?" he asked, "Isn't she here?"

"Oh, my son, Salma stayed in Yemen." Her eyes filled with tears again.

"Why didn't you bring her with you?" asked Joseph gently; he realized something had happened.

"Oh, my son…"

She told him and he listened attentively. She told him about the death of his father when he was four years old, about the fear of the authorities taking him to an orphanage and converting him to Islam; about the decision to bury his father without a name, to smuggle the boys out of Yemen, and about the time between their escape and her arrival in Israel. She told him she'd been left on her own and had returned to her parents' home with Salma. She had to gain time so the boys could escape from Yemen without being caught.

One month later, the authorities came to Na'ama's house and asked Luluah what had happened to Yichyieh and the boys. She told them that they had gone to visit relatives in Sanaa and hadn't yet returned. The authorities didn't believe her and said that if Yichyieh didn't return soon, they would come back and do their duty. At that point, they couldn't smuggle Salma out of Yemen. A week later, the authorities returned and took Salma with them. They informed Luluah that they'd issued a warrant for the arrest of Yichyieh, Aharon, Menachem and Joseph. The rumors that reached the village were that Joseph had remained in Sanaa, whereas Menachem and Aharon, together with their friend, Shimon, were on their way to Aden. Later rumors were heard that Salma had been converted to Islam and was being raised in a Muslim orphanage on the far side of Sanaa.

Three months after the boys were smuggled out, Uncle Yehuda returned alone to the village and told them he'd left the ailing Joseph with Reuma and Ya'akov in Sanaa, and continued to Aden with Shimon, Menachem and Aharon. He told her that, with Zachariah's help, they'd found a ship that was sailing to the Holy Land and decided that Shimon would join Menachem and Aharon on the voyage, whereas he, Uncle Yehuda would return to Sanaa to fetch Joseph. When Uncle Yehuda arrived in Sanaa, he found that Joseph had already been sent to Zachariah in Aden. Uncle Yehuda went on to say that, after talking to Reuma, he decided to return to the village.

"I didn't know what to do… I didn't know what was happening to you, my boy. I didn't know what happened to Menachem and Aharon. I didn't know what fate awaited Salma… my husband was dead, I didn't know what to do. Oh, my boy, there were so many rumors and it was hard to know what to believe. I couldn't do anything except pray. I prayed a lot…" she told Joseph.

She continued her story.

After Yehuda returned to the village, Luluah collapsed and didn't leave her mother's house for many long months. She didn't want to live. What kept her alive was her desire to know what had happened to Joseph, her eldest son, and the hope that one day she'd meet him again. Six months later, Dahari approached her parents and asked for her hand in marriage. He told her parents that he knew what she'd been through and wanted her to be his wife and the mother of his children. Dahari was older than she, had never married, and was anxious to have children. He promised to take care of all her needs and help her find her children again. He also promised to try and restore Salma to her. After talking to her and getting her consent, Luluah's parents decided it would be the right thing to do and agreed to a marriage between their daughter and Dahari.

"Joseph, my son, it was the right thing to do. I was still a young woman and I was alone... Dahari wanted me, my parents had aged a great deal... I had to marry him. I always prayed I'd see you again, always..."

"What happened to Salma?" he asked again.

After the wedding, she took care of Dahari and immediately fell pregnant, giving birth to her first daughter. After the first daughter, she fell pregnant every year and gave birth to sons and daughters. In time, she and Dahari tried to get Salma back, but the authorities refused. At a certain point they lost contact with her. Rumor had it that Shimon, Aharon, Menachem and Joseph did reach the Holy Land. They knew nothing more. Later on, they heard that the Holy Land had become Israel, a new Jewish state. Then came the war between the Arabs and the Jews in the Holy Land. The rumors were apparently true, because the Muslims in Yemen began to harass the Jews and occasionally even murder them. The Jews didn't feel safe in Yemen, and began to think about escaping to Israel. They lived in constant terror of being harassed. They were afraid to try and escape from Yemen, as the Muslims announced that anyone attempting to escape would be punished. Yehuda, his wife and children tried to escape. Since he knew the way, he thought he could escape without being caught. Unfortunately, he was caught and jailed, and his wife and children were returned to the village. Yehuda was severely tortured. A few months later, he was released and also returned to the village. He was a broken man and died soon after he and his family finally reached Israel. They didn't see Shimon again and lost trace of him. When the news came that the Jews had beaten the Arabs and the State of Israel had been established for the Jews, the authorities changed their policy and allowed the Jews to leave Yemen for Israel.

"We lost no time," said Luluah, "we were afraid the Muslims would change their minds and refuse to let us leave Yemen. We were even more afraid they'd hurt us. So we were glad when they informed us that the Israeli authorities were sending planes to take us to Israel."

"And what happened to Salma? Why didn't you bring her with you?" asked Joseph.

"Oh, my boy, once we began to think of escaping from Yemen, before they informed us that there were planes coming, we looked for her and found her address… she was married to a Muslim in Sanaa. I went to speak to her… she said she was staying with her husband and children…"

"Why didn't you bring her, Mamma, why didn't you persuade her? She's a Jew, not a Muslim, she should be here… with us…"

"Oh, my son, we went to see her again. When they told us planes were coming to take us, I went to talk to her. I said, 'my daughter, we are leaving for the Jewish Land, for Israel. The Muslims here are allowing us to leave… come with us. You are Jewish and should come with us… you're Jewish.' And she…" Luluah stopped her flow of speech, coughed and continued, "and she said…" again Luluah was choked with tears. "Oh, my son… she said she knew she was Jewish, but she was now the mother of Muslim children. She was the wife of a Muslim, and she wouldn't leave her children in Yemen to go to Israel. Salma, Salma, she had to choose between her children and being a Jew in Israel. She had no other choice… she chose to remain with her children. My poor girl…"

Luluah and Joseph were silent; both had tears in their eyes.

"My son, I'm sorry I couldn't…" Luluah tried to continue, but Joseph stopped her, stroked her hand and kissed her.

"Mamma, you aren't to blame. You tried to bring her here. And neither is Salma to blame… that's what happened, lots of things happen, Menachem and Aharon have also passed away."

"Yes, my son, I know that both your brothers are dead."

After a short pause, Luluah continued, telling him that they quickly got ready and took everything they could and flew to Israel. She and Dahari came to Israel with ten sons and daughters, and she was pregnant again. They disembarked from the plane and were sent to tents in Afula until a decision was made about where to house them. She tried to find out where Joseph was and nobody helped her. She tried to ask those in charge of the camp, but nobody could help her. Nonetheless, she persisted and continued to ask anyone and everyone about her son. Almost the entire camp knew that she was looking for her son. And then Luluah got the terrible news.

"My son, an Israeli soldier came to see me and told me that you'd been wounded in the war. I asked where you were, I wanted to come to you... I was so happy that you were alive and that I'd see you again... and then the soldier told me that you were badly wounded and had died. I wanted to die, my boy, I wept... I was angry with them. Angry with all of them...even with G-d. And yet here you are... you're here, with me..."

She kissed him again and again, then continued, "He said you'd been killed in an explosion in a vehicle, and someone from the army would come to tell us where you were buried. It was hard to accept. We sat Shiva for you, my son, we sat Shiva... we mourned and wept. Everyone, everyone wept... everyone was waiting to see you. I told your siblings so much about you..."

She took a deep breath and continued, "And then our son was born and we knew we'd call him Joseph. Oh my son, we called him after his brother who'd been killed... after you. Joseph, my eldest, we called him after you..."

Joseph was moved to the depths of his soul. Luluah called over her daughter, Naomi, who was holding a six month old baby in her lap.

"Come and meet your brother, little Joseph..." Luluah said to him.

Joseph looked at his namesake and smiled at him.

"Hello Joseph, I'm Joseph... and I'm your big brother," he said lightheartedly.

Luluah laughed and said, "You're both called Joseph. You're

big Joseph and he's little Joseph... we'll call little Joseph 'Yossi' and we'll call you Joseph..." She added with a smile: "In Israel, they shorten names... Aharon is called Arik and Yehuda, Yuda, so we'll call little Joseph 'Yossi'..."

Her husband, Dahari, and all their ten children crowded into the tent. They brought food which they laid out on the table in the middle of the tent.

"And now we'll sit down to eat," Luluah told them all.

When they'd finished eating, the officer hinted to Joseph that they had to leave. After parting from Luluah and her family, and Joseph and Malka, the officer and the psychologist left the tent, got into the car and began the drive back to Tel Aviv. Joseph was still excited by the reunion with his mother and the family he didn't know.

"You know, Malka, she is my mother. I'm almost positive. It hurt to hear everything she's gone through, it really hurt... I have a fragment of a memory of Salma, but not of Mamma. And it's like a dream... I don't know what to feel. Yes, I was very upset and my stomach is still churning. I have to take it in... I have to think about it."

Stroking Joseph's hand, Malka was silent the whole time. The officer and the psychologist didn't respond, leaving Joseph to his thoughts. Malka asked them to drop her at home in the Yemenite Quarter. When they arrived, she told Joseph:

"Tonight, you're sleeping in my parents' house."

She didn't want him to be alone in the apartment. Both her parents were waiting for them in the courtyard. When they came in, her mother went to Joseph and embraced him.

"You did the right thing," she said, adding: "sit down with us, I'll make tea."

They sat down and drank.

"She is my mother... I'm her son, but I don't feel as if she's my mother. I don't feel as if I'm her son... even she understands that. She even said, 'nobody taught him that I'm his mother!' I feel as if something's wrong with me, that I'm not feeling what I ought to feel..." mused Joseph aloud.

"Oh my boy," said Malka's mother, "you need time to digest it all. It's complicated... remember, she had no choice... remember that if she hadn't broken away from you, you might not be here with us, a Jew in Israel. They might have taken you by force, converted you to Islam, and you'd have remained in Yemen, like Salma. You need time, and you have your whole life ahead of you to understand what your mother went through. As I see it, she did the right thing and you have done the right thing too... I promise you it will all come right in the end.

"Mother is right," said Malka, holding Joseph's hand, "it's only a matter of time."

Epilog

Malka and Joseph stood side by side on the courtyard steps of her parents' home, their backs to the courtyard which was full to capacity. Both of the large bedrooms were prepared for the event and were also crowded with people. Tables were arranged right up to the street in front of the house and were laden with dishes of food, sweet desserts and drinks. Joseph's mother sat with Malka's parents, opposite Joseph and Malka. Scheinzon and Abraham sat beside them.

The rabbi stood above them on the steps and looked out at the guests. The whole crowd craned their necks to see the marriage of Malka and Joseph. The rabbi began to bless Joseph and Malka, who were visibly moved by the ceremony. Joseph placed the wedding ring on Malka's finger.

"If I forget Jerusalem, I'll forget my right hand," said Joseph, and stamped on the glass wrapped in a thin towel[25].

"Congratulations… congratulations!" cries of joy were heard from the guests.

Joseph and Malka approached their parents and hugged and kissed them. Joseph also hugged Scheinzon and Abraham. The

---

25. Breaking the glass at a Jewish wedding symbolizes the fragility of a relationship and reminds the couple to treat their relationship with care. It also symbolizes the destruction of the Second Temple in Jerusalem.

guests made space in the middle of the courtyard where Malka and Joseph stood to dance together, their beloved tango playing in the background to the sound of the guests clapping. As they danced, Joseph looked at Malka and, kissing her tenderly, his eyes filled with tears.

He said, "I've done it… we've done it. We are building a family here in the State of Israel."

"Yes," she said.

"Look at my mother. Yes," his eyes brimming over, "my mother, how happy she is. Look at your parents smiling, look at Abraham, my friend, my brother, to whom I owe so much. Look at my teacher and parent, Scheinzon, who has aged. Sonya is missing…"

Malka put her finger on his lips to hush him, saying, "Look at the tables. There is bitter chocolate on every table, ours as well… it reminds us that Sonya is also here with us, sharing our joy, demonstrating how life is a balance of joy and sadness, hope and disappointment. Now, right now, it all tastes of sweet chocolate… doesn't it?"

Acknowledgements

It's been four long years since I first sat down in front of the computer and began to write. The journey was like a crazy flight, taking off to unfamiliar heights then banking sharply, turns no one prepared me for, nights like sleepless air pockets and hard landings that shook my whole being. Throughout this flight, my partner, Lilia, held my hand so I wouldn't fear the turbulence; nonetheless, my heart often lost a beat. There were also interim landings in the form of breaks for months on end, when I felt I'd had enough, I'd exhausted my strength, wanted to rest, feel the ground beneath my feet. I felt I couldn't fly again. It was at these times that my nephew, Didi Koby, who spent months at my home fighting a severe illness with courage and determination, inspired and empowered me; my brother, Aharon, would often come to encourage me to continue writing; my daughters, Ariela and Hadar, would also give me a push onward; Addie Tovy was insistent that there was no way I wasn't going to finish writing the book. Later on, my sisters, Osnat and Varda, buoyed me and reinforced my efforts. Before me were the images of my parents, may they rest in peace, who inspired me with their spirit, filled me with strength, courage and purpose, to keep writing, keep flying, in spite of the stormy, bumpy ride – and to land safely and complete the book.

Printed in Great Britain
by Amazon